Smoky Mountain Murder

Foggy Mountain Intrigue

Book One

Ashley A Quinn

TCA Publishing LLC

Smoky Mountain Murder

Copyright © 2019 by Ashley A Quinn

ISBN is 979-8-9853441-7-2
Library of Congress Control Number: 2022916363

ONE

Trowel in hand, Gemma Mabley sat back and surveyed her handiwork. Pops of color shone brightly in the now filled flower beds surrounding the house she shared with her brother, Tristan, just outside of Foggy Mountain, North Carolina. The late-May sun beat down on her, making her sweat. She swiped at the beads of perspiration trickling down the side of her face, leaving behind a trail of dirt. Her shoulders and arms ached from all the planting, but the satisfaction from the result dulled the pain. Hot out or not, she was happy to feel the warm sun on her skin and see the brilliant shades of red, yellow, pink, and purple lining the front of her house. The winter had been brutal, and she'd done a happy dance the first day the temperatures rose above freezing and stayed there. She'd waited no longer than necessary to usher away the last dregs of the cooler weather by planting a plethora of flowers.

She had other reasons, though, for deciding today was the day to plant flowers. Her brother knew no boundaries. Three hours ago, in an attempt to use mindless action to calm herself, she returned from the local garden center with a trunk load of flowers. After donning her gardening clothes, she attacked the flowerbeds with a vengeance befitting Genghis Khan, imagining her brother's face with every stab to the dirt.

Gemma loved the man dearly, but she'd had it with his overprotectiveness. At twenty-eight years old, she did *not* need her older brother continually butting into her love life. In the past year, he'd sabotaged four different relationships. Every time she got remotely close to a man, Tristan stepped in and intimidated the guy to the point he would rather cut and run than be subjected to the "I'm a badass" stare her brother perfected over the years in the military and as a cop.

And, if the stare wasn't enough, the questions certainly were. One of her dates compared his questioning tactics to the German Gestapo.

Tristan claimed it wasn't him who was the problem. It was the men she dated. He insisted that when she found the man worthy of her, he wouldn't scare away. Gemma kept insisting that if he didn't even give anyone a chance to try to get to know her first, none would ever bother to try. She couldn't fathom there was a man on the planet who would willingly subject himself to that kind of treatment for a woman he didn't even know. Every time a new relationship crashed and burned before it ever left the ground, she and Tristan had the same argument. It had grown beyond tiresome.

Gemma sighed as she started on the final row of flowers. Last night's fiasco was the last straw and the reason she was out here imagining her brother's face in the dirt. She'd kept her relationship with David Masterson a secret for two months before she finally let him pressure her into telling her brother about them and arranging a meeting.

She'd had such high hopes for David. Gemma had gotten to know him better than any other man since college, and he'd been fully briefed on how difficult Tristan could be. David reassured her repeatedly he could handle whatever Tristan dished out. She foolishly thought their relationship had a footing strong enough to withstand Tristan's probing.

Gemma scoffed as she scooped more dirt and plunked a small flower plant in the hole she created. One look at Tristan's scowling face, his six-foot-two-inch frame packed with muscle, and the gun and badge attached to his belt, and David started to quake in his fancy Armani loafers. He stood strong through most of Tristan's interrogation—he was an attorney, after all —but Tristan could scare the paint off a barn.

And Tristan was smart. And ruthless when it came to his baby sister. She saw the gleam enter his eyes when he noticed David shrink back from the sheer weight of his presence. The blasted man pressed his advantage until David's normally warm skin tone was pasty white. He all but fled from the house once Gemma convinced Tristan he should save some of the questions for another time—she wouldn't want him to come up short, should he get a second chance to peel away the flesh from her date.

Her evening with David was a slide downhill to disaster after that. They ate a very stoic dinner that settled like lead in her stomach. David's normally engaging and friendly demeanor turned polite and reserved, and she once again felt like a piece of spun glass that was to be admired only from afar. After dinner, David drove her home and deposited her on her doorstep with a pat on the shoulder.

Dirt flew as she dug the final hole, muttering to herself. She still couldn't believe he'd patted her like a child. On their last date, he had his hand up her blouse, for crap's sake!

The front door slammed. Gemma looked up to see the object of her ire hurry outside, gun and badge clipped to his belt, truck keys in his hand.

Alarmed, she stood up. Today was Saturday and Tristan's day off. If he'd been called in, something terrible must have happened.

"Gotta go, Sis." Tristan cleared all the porch steps in a single leap and flew past her to the large gray truck parked beside her SUV in the driveway.

"What's going on?" she called after him.

"Dead body in Pisgah National Forest. Up near Hot Springs," he said over his shoulder. "I'll call you later."

Gemma felt her anger at him die as he roared out of the drive. She could never stay angry with him when he was going off and putting himself in the line of fire. She learned that early on after he joined the Army and headed off to Afghanistan. He might drive her nuts, but she knew it was because he cared, and she would be lost without her big brother around.

She sighed the tired sigh of long-suffering little sisters everywhere and bent down to tuck the last bit of soil around the last plant. Giving the dirt one last pat, she gathered up her tools, praying all the while that Tristan would be safe.

The warm sun beat down on Special Agent Ben Davidson's back even through the tree canopy as he stood near the trailhead, talking to the local sheriff, John Raymond. Parked next to them, the medical examiner, Dr. Cullen Tate, rummaged around in the back of his van, gathering supplies to assess the body in the field.

A headache brewed between Ben's eyes as he thought about what awaited him in the woods. If this was the work of the serial killer he'd been tracking, it promised to be gruesome. He just hoped this woman's body yielded more clues than the last four. This killer was rather adept at leaving a clean crime scene. As a result, Ben had very little to go on after over a year of investigating and four murders.

Getting a bit impatient, he resisted the urge to tap his foot as they waited for Raymond's detective to arrive. On the off-chance this wasn't his case, Ben had agreed to wait to have a local detective join them. Even if it was the work of the killer he was after, he would still work closely with local law enforcement until he exhausted all leads or the killer was caught. He didn't want to burn any bridges or step on anyone's toes by charging full steam ahead, leaving people out of the loop. His life was much easier if the locals cooperated.

"Major Davidson?"

Startled at the title he hadn't heard in years, he turned to see a chestnut-haired man looking at him in surprise. Sunglasses covered his eyes, but Ben knew that if he took them off, they would be a brilliant blue. "Captain Mabley?"

"It's Detective Mabley, now." Tristan extended his hand, smiling, as the two men took stock of each other.

A lifetime ago, Ben had been the commanding officer of their Ranger unit. Tristan Mabley was his second-in-command. The younger man left the service before Ben's last deployment, and they lost contact. The back of beyond in North Carolina was the last place he ever expected to see him again.

"Sir, it's good to see you. I heard you retired after your last tour went sideways. How's the leg?"

Lifting his left foot, Ben's mouth tilted slightly. "It works, but not as well as it used to." He'd taken shrapnel to his leg, shattering the bones and tearing up the soft tissue. It was a testament to the dedication and talent of the Army doctors that he still had a leg to walk on, let alone one that functioned as well as it did.

"So, what brings you out to my neck of the woods?" Tristan gestured around them. "Literally."

Ben held up his badge. "You aren't the only one with a new title. Seems my case may have landed on your doorstep."

"FBI, huh?" Tristan frowned. "The DB in the woods is yours?"

Ben nodded. "I think so. I've been tracking a serial killer in the region for a little over a year now. We've got a flag in the system to alert us to bodies found in wooded areas. As soon as the location of this one hit the airwaves, I got a call. I was on my way back north to Richmond when it came in, so I detoured here. From the cursory description we've gotten from the people who found her, it sounds like she may be related to my other victims."

"Great. A serial killer is just what we need roaming the hills. There are so many places to hide in the Smokies."

Ben agreed. It made tracking someone difficult.

"How many victims have you attributed to the guy?"

"This one, if she is in fact connected, will make five we know of. This case landed in my lap when he crossed state lines from Tennessee to Virginia. He's left two in Virginia, two in Tennessee, and now this one."

Sheriff Raymond, who'd been silently listening to the exchange, motioned toward the trees. "Well, let's get on with it before we're finding victim number two around here."

Dr. Tate stepped down from the van just then, a large bag slung across his chest. His assistant, a young man in his twenties, stepped out of the van as well, a camera around his neck and a hard case in his hand.

Silently, the men filed into the woods behind the park ranger, who answered the initial call from the hikers who stumbled across the body.

The stench of death assaulted Ben's nose about the same time the yellow police tape came into view. It didn't matter where or when a murder occurred, Ben could always count on the smell to point him to the body. Even the recently deceased had a smell. It hung in the air like smog on a hot day, and it was unavoidable.

He bent beneath the crime scene tape and got his first glimpse of the body as he passed through the trees. Taking in the grim scene with a detached eye, he assessed it for similarities to his other victims. The woman swayed in the slight breeze, where she hung by her neck beneath the branches of a large oak. Completely naked, evidence of torture was apparent on her bloodied body. Deep gashes marred the skin of her torso. Purple bruises colored her legs, and her fingers looked like gnarled willow branches. Where blood had once flowed freely, it was now dried on her fingertips. Ben felt a sinking sensation in his gut. At just a quick glance, she was identical to the other four victims. He suspected when the M.E. did the autopsy, he would find she'd been raped, that both her legs were broken in several places—crushed by a hammer or pipe—and that she died from a broken neck or asphyxiation from hanging.

"Jesus."

He spared a glance at the sheriff, who stopped beside him. The man's face was devoid of all color, and Ben could see him fight to keep the contents of his stomach where they belonged. Ben was far past being affected by grisly sights. He'd been cured of that after his first tour in Afghanistan. Now, nearly two decades later, he examined scenes like this one with a calculated eye, looking for clues to help him bring down the monster responsible. He sincerely hoped this woman yielded more answers than the previous four victims.

The M.E. stepped forward to look at the body as his assistant snapped pictures in quick succession.

"She hasn't been here long," Dr. Tate remarked. "There's not much decomp yet, and she's still in full rigor." He glanced back at Ben and the other investigators. "Once we get her down, and I get a liver temp on her, I can give you a more accurate time of death. But just based on looking at her, I'd say she died sometime late last night or very early this morning."

Ben felt a surge of hope. None of the other four victims were found so soon after death. In every other case, nature had a chance to wash away vital evidence. It hadn't rained last night, so they might very well find clues on or around her.

Tristan seemed to be on the same wavelength. The doctor's proclamation galvanized the man into action. Ben watched as he made a beeline for where the rope was tied, eyes trained on the ground.

"There are fresh prints here. Definitely male, probably a size ten or eleven." Tate's assistant came over and started snapping pictures of the indentations. "We might get a weight on the depth of the tracks," Tristan remarked, reminding Ben how astute the younger man was. He was damn glad to have the man working this case with him.

The team worked diligently for several hours, processing the scene. Even with the freshness of it, there wasn't much forensic evidence. They found tire tracks to an ATV in addition to the boot prints, but little else. The rope was a generic nylon sold in many sporting goods and hardware stores. Unless the killer slipped up this time, there wouldn't be any DNA evidence on the body. With the lack of clothing and other belongings, they likely wouldn't find any fingerprint or fiber evidence, either.

Frustration gnawed at Ben. He just wanted a break in this case. It haunted him on dark nights that he couldn't figure it out. He hated unfinished business.

"So, what's the plan?" Sheriff Raymond asked as they gathered in the parking lot after Dr. Tate drove away with their victim.

Ben glanced around at the crime scene techs packing up their equipment and at the spectators the police presence had drawn. "All my files on this case are in Richmond. I'll call my office and have someone drive down with them tomorrow. In the meantime, make sure we get statements from the hikers who found her and interview the park rangers who work this area. Find out if any of them have noticed anything unusual."

He looked down at the older man. "Sheriff, this is your territory and the people know you, so why don't you handle crowd and media control? I'd like to take Detective Mabley and head to the station to run down the woman's identity."

Sheriff Raymond gave a short nod and walked off to delegate interviews and handle the inevitable press that came with a case like this.

Ben turned to Tristan and swirled his finger in the universal "saddle up" gesture. "You lead, Mabley."

Two

Gemma glanced up as the front door opened and two sets of heavy footsteps made their way across the hardwood floors. They thudded down the hall toward her in the kitchen, where she was busy putting the finishing touches on dinner. Tristan called several hours earlier to tell her the feds were involved in his case and he was bringing the lead agent home tonight. Knowing that after a day spent canvassing for and cataloging evidence the two men would be ravenous, she immediately rummaged through the freezer to pull out the enormous steaks Tristan insisted they always keep on hand.

She heaped vegetables onto plates next to the cooked steaks and slid them onto the table just as the men walked into the kitchen.

"Smells great, Sis," Tristan said, reaching out to ruffle her hair in greeting.

She swatted his hand away and glared at him.

He grinned at her, then looked at the other man. "Major, this is my sister, Gemma. Gemma, this is Special Agent Ben Davidson, my former commanding officer."

Gemma felt her heart hiccup in her chest as she smiled at

the newcomer. A movie star-handsome man was not what she expected when she thought of a federal agent. Eyes the color of turquoise sea glass studied her from a ruggedly handsome, tanned face. Silver streaked his dark hair at his temples and laugh lines bracketed his eyes and sculpted lips. He was a tall man—at least a couple inches taller than her brother—and built just as solidly.

Agent Davidson returned her smile. "Ma'am. It's nice to finally meet you. Tristan used to talk about you a lot when we were overseas. Thank you for the hospitality. It's nice not to have to find a hotel room in the area after the day I've had."

Gemma felt her face flame. *Good lord, the things the man had probably heard about her!* She had a colorful childhood and adolescence. The phrases "accident prone" and "disaster magnet" came to mind.

She cleared her throat and forced her smile to stay in place. "Yes, well, we're happy to have you, and I'm hoping everything he said about me was good. But I know my brother, and I hope you won't let his stories cloud your judgement of me."

Agent Davidson laughed. "It wasn't all bad, I assure you."

"Good." She motioned to the table. "Won't you please sit down?" She gestured to her brother. "You too, Tris."

She offered both men a beer, grabbed the basket of fresh biscuits off the counter, and sat down. Both men immediately attacked their food. They ate like it was their first meal in days. Within minutes, their steaks were half gone, while she only managed a few bites of her much smaller filet. Once they all appeased their initial hunger, Gemma asked them about their case.

"I take it from the fact the feds are involved this is more than a simple case of a hiker wandering off the trail and falling prey to Mother Nature?" she asked.

"Yeah," Tristan answered. She could tell from the way his face shut down it had been a grisly scene.

"Do you know what happened?"

"We're still piecing it together," Agent Davidson replied. "We don't even know who she is yet."

Gemma shook her head. That was so sad. No one deserved to die the way she suspected that woman did. Then to be unidentified and left to the elements—Gemma could hardly fathom it.

"We're hopeful, though, Gems. She was found pretty quickly." Tristan glanced at Agent Davidson. "Quicker than what we think the killer intended, and that may help us catch him."

Gemma certainly hoped so. The prospect of a killer roaming their quiet hills was disconcerting. She spent a lot of time both hiking and riding the trails in the area. She would think twice now about going out unarmed until the killer was caught.

~

Ben glanced up from the file he perused later that night as his hostess shuffled into the kitchen. Clad in pink pajama pants and an oversize purple t-shirt that hinted at the curves beneath, Gemma was the picture of a beautiful, sleepy woman. The urge to wrap his arms around her and feel that warm softness for himself smacked into him, taking him by surprise.

He shifted his eyes from her pajama-clad form to her long, chestnut-colored hair. She'd removed it from its earlier ponytail and it now spilled down over her shoulders and back in silky waves. Ben was disconcerted to find he wanted to see if the tresses felt as soft as they looked.

Unaware of the effect she was having on him, she looked at him through slightly sleepy eyes and offered him a soft smile.

He cleared his throat and thrust his lustful thoughts into a lockbox in his brain. "Did I wake you?"

"Yes. But don't worry about it," she hastened to reassure him. "I'm not used to any kind of noise in the middle of the night, so the slightest sound will wake me up. Tristan sleeps like the dead, and it's a rare occasion he gets called out this late."

"Still, I'm sorry. I didn't mean to chase you from your bed." Ben groaned inwardly the moment the words left his mouth. Images of her in bed *without* the oversize t-shirt flooded his mind. He never would have guessed he'd have this kind of reaction to Tristan's sister. When the man suggested Ben stay with them, he hadn't given saying yes a second thought. Tristan's stories led him to think of Gemma as a twiggy adolescent with braces and not a lot of grace.

What confronted him when he walked into the kitchen had been the absolute opposite. Whatever Gemma Mabley was as a teenager, she had outgrown it to become a stunningly gorgeous woman. He felt like he'd been poleaxed when he saw her standing there next to the table, a hesitant but welcoming smile on her pretty face.

And she is entirely too young for you and clearly not the type of woman who does casual relationships, his conscience screamed. Ben steered clear of women like her. He didn't do permanent.

Ben shoved thoughts of Gemma's curves and bright smile into that special box in his brain, only to have her shove the door right back open again as she stretched into a cupboard to pull down a glass. Her shirt pulled taut against her curves, making it abundantly clear she didn't sleep in a bra. He glanced away and willed his suddenly raging hormones under control. Sexy or not, she was off limits.

Glass in hand, Gemma waved off his concerns about

waking her. She stepped behind him to get to the sink. "I was thirsty, anyway."

She never made it past his chair. Her gaze landed on the file in front of him. It was open to a closeup image of the victim's face after she was pulled down from the tree. Ben watched Gemma's face turn ashen. The glass she held slipped through her fingers to crash to the floor, shattering into hundreds of tiny shards.

"Gemma?" Ben stood, intending to block her view of the file spread out on the table. He never meant for her to see those grisly images.

She had other ideas, though, and reached around him to pick up the photograph with a shaky hand. "Is this the woman whose death you're investigating?" Her voice was a frail whisper.

Ben nodded, frowning. Her knees wobbled. His hands shot out to grasp her arms to keep her upright. *Christ.* She looked like she'd seen a ghost.

She stared at the picture several moments longer before her gaze connected with his. "I know her."

Shock rendered Ben momentarily speechless. Then, only one question entered his mind. "How?"

His sharp tone seemed to snap her out of the fog she was in. She drew in a shaky breath and broke his hold to lay the picture back on the stack of papers before focusing on him again.

"Her son, Caleb, is one of my patients. Her name is Diana Lowell, and she lives in Asheville with him and her mother, Marcie Trent." She sank into his vacated chair and covered her face with her hands. "Oh my God. I can't believe this."

Ben squatted in front of her and pulled her hands away from her face so he could look her in the eye. He tucked her chilly fingers between his own. "What do you mean, one of your patients?"

She drew in a shaky breath. "I'm an equestrian therapist. Her son is a high-functioning autistic, and she's been bringing him in twice a week for nearly three years. The riding allows him to work on his social skills by helping him tune in to another's being's emotions. Oh, he's got to be devastated that she's missing."

Ben agreed. It was always bad when there were kids involved.

Brain in overdrive, he mentally went over the list of missing persons he and Tristan had compiled earlier. "Gemma, are you sure this is her? She isn't on our missing persons list." He reached up to cup the side of her face to bring her gaze back to his from where she stared at their clasped hands.

She nodded. "It's her." Her eyes grew wide. "And she wouldn't be yet. She's supposed to be out of town. I just remembered. I saw her Thursday morning when she brought Caleb in for his session. She's a nurse at a hospital in Asheville, and she said she was getting ready to head to Atlanta for a nursing conference. She and Caleb live with her mother. If she dropped him off at home after his session, then left for Atlanta as planned, Marcie wouldn't know anything was wrong. She wasn't supposed to be back until Monday morning." She jerked her hands out of his to cover her mouth as she choked on a sob. "Oh God! They don't even know she's missing, let alone dead!"

Ben gathered her close as she fought for control. He couldn't help but think there was one thing about Gemma that hadn't changed from Tristan's stories. She was still as compassionate as ever. The woman felt everything for everyone.

~

Gemma gently pulled back in Ben's arms. He loosened his hold, but didn't let her go completely. She wiped her eyes on her t-shirt and sniffed. She felt like she was in the middle of a nightmare. It just didn't seem possible that Diana was dead. Especially not this way. Diana was a sweet woman who was doing her best to help her son have every advantage he could to live in a world that, to him, was overwhelming.

And poor Caleb! She closed her eyes tight, fighting back the tears threatening to spill over again. His mother and grandmother were his world. Without Diana, Gemma feared Caleb would sink further inside himself, to a point where Marcie wouldn't be able to reach him.

Awareness of where she was crept back in, and the muscular arms around her registered. Gemma opened her eyes to find herself at eye level with Agent Davidson's strong neck. She followed the solid line of his jaw up to his remarkable eyes. Through her haze of grief, she marveled at how clear they were. The color was nearly solid, with no flecks of brown or gold marring their clear blue-green surface.

He reached one hand around to brush her hair away from her face.

"Are you all right?" he asked, his voice soft.

Gemma let the smooth whiskey tones of his voice wash over her and push away some of the grief. It helped her to pull herself together and focus. She needed to help Caleb, and the best way she could do that right now was to help Ben and Tristan find his mother's killer.

She nodded and pushed him back enough that she could stand. She needed to move if she was going to keep the restless energy that now filled her at bay. "I'll be okay." She lifted a foot to step around him, but she never got the chance to set it down. Instead, she found herself whisked off the ground by the same powerful arms that were wrapped around her just seconds ago.

"Agent Davidson!" Gemma clasped her arms around his neck on instinct. "Put me down!"

"There's glass all over the floor. And my name is Ben." His boots crunched over the broken glass as he carried her out of the kitchen to the living room, where he deposited her on the couch.

"Where's your broom?"

"Let me grab some slippers." She started to rise, but he gently pushed her back down.

"Sit. I'll get it. Now, where's the broom?"

Gemma took one look at the hard cast to his face and decided not to argue. They must teach them that look at basic training. She'd seen the same one on Tristan numerous times in the last decade. "There's a mudroom off the back of the kitchen. It's in the closet in there."

He pointed a finger at her. "Don't move. We need to talk about your friend."

Gemma nodded and sank into the cushions.

When he returned a few minutes later, he had the file, a bottle of whiskey, and two tumblers with him. Wordlessly, he laid the file on the coffee table and handed her a tumbler. Gemma gratefully accepted the amber liquid he poured into it. She needed the fortification and took a hearty gulp.

Ben took a sip of his own whiskey before settling back against the couch cushions. He looked tense, even though he'd obviously tried to relax some earlier. His black oxford shirt was unbuttoned and pulled free of his jeans, revealing the gray t-shirt underneath. His short hair was ruffled as well, like he had run his fingers through it multiple times.

"Was there anyone she mentioned lately? Someone new in her life or that made an impression—bad or good? Or anyone from her past who resurfaced?" he asked, jumping right in.

Gemma took a deep breath and thought back. "She did

mention a man she'd met. She said they made plans to go out for dinner after she got back from her conference."

Ben frowned. "Tell me about him. Did you ever meet him or see a picture? Did she tell you his name?"

"She didn't say much about him, but that's not unusual for her. She didn't date much because of Caleb and was rather private. She said that dinner date was going to be their first real date. As far as his name, she only gave me a first name—Andrew. I never saw a picture, but I did ask her what he looked like. It could be any man, though. Light brown hair, average height, average build, white. That's all I know." God, she wished she could help more. Diana was so secretive, but she had reason to be. Her ex-husband was a real piece of work.

"Do you know how she met Andrew?"

Gemma sucked her lower lip between her teeth, looking away as she replayed their conversation. "Yes." She met Ben's gaze. "She said she met him in the hospital cafeteria. He was there visiting a sick relative."

"Did she say when?"

"Just that it was a few weeks ago. She said they went for coffee a few times before she agreed to dinner."

"Is there anyone from her past who would have a reason to hurt her?"

Gemma shook her head. "Just her ex-husband, but I don't think it was him. She hasn't heard from him in years. She put him in jail for domestic violence several years ago, but he's been out a while and doesn't have any contact with them, good or bad." Gemma's mind whirled. She could only imagine how Diana's mother, Marcie, would to react to her daughter's death. When Diana left her abusive ex-husband, Marcie hadn't hesitated to take in her daughter and grandson. Diana was Marcie's only child, and they had always been close. Gemma didn't think it ever crossed either of their minds for Diana and

Caleb to find a place of their own since they moved in with Marcie.

Ben rolled his glass between his fingers as he considered her words. "Do you know if she went anywhere new lately?"

Gemma shook her head. "Probably not. Diana was a creature of habit. Between her job and her son, she really didn't have time to vary her routine much."

"Was there anything else out of the ordinary that she mentioned?"

Gemma chewed on her lip and thought hard. "No. Not that she talked about with me. Her mother might be able to think of something. I'm sorry, Ben. I wish I could be of more help."

He reached out to grab her hand. The strong fingers helped anchor her emotions. "You've helped plenty. We know who she is now, which we might not have until her mother noticed she hadn't returned from her conference. Don't blame yourself. I'm just glad you saw the picture."

"So where do we go from here?" Gemma turned her hand to grip his.

"We pick Diana's life apart. The answers are there. We just have to find them."

THREE

Ben woke to bright light and the feel of something warm and soft draped over him. He opened his eyes slowly against the assault of sunshine pouring in from the windows. It took him a moment to remember where he was.

North Carolina. Serial murder case.

The identity of the warm weight on his chest finally registered. Tristan Mabley's alluring little sister.

Christ.

The early morning hours flooded back to him. After he got as much out of Gemma as he could about her friend, they'd sat companionably on the couch while they finished their whiskey. The alcohol made them both sleepy despite the turmoil, and they'd lounged against the cushions. They must have fallen asleep, but how she ended up draped across him, he did not know.

But now that he was aware she was pressed against him, he was also aware he had a desperate need to get out from under her before she awakened to find what her warm, sleepy body was doing to his.

He had no idea how he would accomplish that feat,

though. She had her head pillowed on his chest; her full, soft breasts were crushed against his upper abdomen. His legs scissored her lower body and his hands rested on her hips while hers encircled his torso and hugged him like a body pillow.

He wrapped an arm around her waist and attempted to slide her off while he slid out from under her, but she immediately tightened her arms around him and grumbled sleepily. Ben tried again, only to get similar results. He let loose a sigh of defeat. He was going to have to wake her.

Brushing the chestnut waves of her hair away from her face, he curled his fingers around the back of her head. The feel of the silky curtain muddled his brain, and he forced himself to remember why he touched her in the first place. "Gemma. Darlin', wake up."

She grumbled again, and Ben attempted to shift them both into a more upright position. "Gemma," he tried again.

"It's too early," she growled. "Go back to sleep."

His fingers flexed in her hair. That was such a tempting prospect. "Gemma, as comfortable as this is, I'd rather your brother not walk in and find us like this."

That seemed to penetrate her sleepy mind. She stretched against him like a cat. Ben gritted his teeth to keep from holding her tight to his body and doing all the wicked things that ran through his mind.

He could tell when she became aware he was her bed and not what he was sure was a very comfortable mattress in her bedroom. She stiffened and her fingers curled into his shirt. Pushing up on her arms, hands against his chest, her eyes flew open.

"Oh my God!"

Ben's hands immediately latched onto her waist to steady her as her sudden movement threatened to topple her off the couch. It also, unfortunately, put the fly of his jeans right in line with her hips and held it there. Those wicked thoughts in his head screamed louder, wanting him to give them free rein.

He cursed himself and his wayward hormones. He should not be feeling this way about this woman. She was more than a decade his junior and a forever-type of woman. He was not a forever-type of man. His parents' and siblings' succession of marriages had taught him forever wasn't something his family did.

Their gazes collided. Ben watched as her sapphire eyes darkened to a midnight blue. Desire shot through him in another fierce blast at her unconscious reaction to him, making his already tight jeans tighter. He gripped her waist as he fought the urge to drag her down and see if she tasted as sweet as her personality.

She saved him from himself, though, as she scrambled off of him and backed away from the couch. Ben sat up and swung his feet to the floor. She mumbled something about going to get dressed and then practically ran from the room.

He ran his hands through his hair and willed the ache in his pants away. This was not the way he envisioned this day starting.

When he was sure he could stand without walking funny, he made his way to the kitchen in search of coffee. He needed a jolt to clear his head.

Tristan leaned against the counter, arms crossed, as he sipped a mug of steaming coffee. There was a hard glint in his eyes, telling Ben that he saw them on the couch.

As Ben reached for a mug from the cupboard, Tristan's free hand shot out to land on Ben's chest. "Care to tell me why you were sound asleep and wrapped around my little sister like ivy on a tree?"

"We fell asleep." Ben looked down pointedly at the hand resting on his chest.

Tristan scoffed, his scowl still in place, but lowered his

hand. "And that explains why your hands were splayed over her ass like you owned her, how, exactly?"

Ben suppressed the urge to deck the younger man. He reminded himself Tristan was just looking out for Gemma's welfare, but it still rankled that Tristan would equate him with some sleaze out to cop a feel.

"We did a lot of talking last night and fell asleep on the couch. I don't know how she ended up on top of me. She certainly didn't start out that way. End of story." Ben reached for the coffeepot. "She may have broken our case wide open, though."

That drew Tristan upright, his ire forgotten. "What?"

Ben filled his mug and took a big gulp of the hot brew, not caring as it scalded his mouth. He needed the pain to wash away the feel of Gemma's supple body pressed to his. "I was too wired to sleep, so I sat down at the table to look over the file again, trying to jog some facts loose from what I remembered of the other cases. She heard me moving around and got up. She saw the closeup of our victim's face and recognized her. Her name's Diana Lowell. Her son is one of your sister's patients."

"Shit."

Ben's sentiments exactly. He didn't know why, but he didn't like that Gemma was involved in this case. He had a bad feeling about it, and he learned early in his military career never to ignore those feelings. It wasn't often they were wrong.

Gemma lingered over her morning routine as long as she dared. She was not the type to take forever getting ready, and her brother knew it. She also knew that he knew she was an early riser. If she didn't surface soon, Tristan would come looking for her and then demand answers as to why she was hiding out in her room.

She swiped her damp palms on her light green capris and straightened her spine. So she'd fallen asleep on Agent Davidson—Ben. It was innocent enough. Especially after the night's revelation.

But there was nothing innocent about the way he made you feel. Or his body's reaction to you. Gemma grimaced and told her conscience to stuff it. She couldn't stop the shiver, though, as the memory of how his rock-hard body felt beneath hers came flooding back. The moment her gaze collided with his, she'd had the insane urge to run her hands over the powerful muscles beneath her hands and press her body back down onto every inch of his. She'd scrambled off of him before she could act on that desire. The man had at least ten years on her, and he wasn't exactly local. Lusting after him was the last thing she needed to be doing. It would only bring her heartache. Her body would do well to remember that.

Pep talk done, Gemma exited her bedroom and wandered into the kitchen. Both men were seated at the table discussing their game plan for the day. Ben had showered and changed, his hair still slightly damp. Her fingers itched to comb through the spiky strands.

Gemma clenched her fists to keep from doing that very thing and pasted a smile on her face in greeting. She went to the fridge to pull out items to make omelets, thankful for once that her brother couldn't boil water without burning it. It gave her something to occupy her hands, and it took her mind off her growing obsession with his former commander. She still didn't understand why she found him so attractive. She normally went for men more like David. Effervescent, good ole boy types. Not polite, authoritative types.

But there was just something about Ben that called to her, and her body was responding with a hearty, "Here I am!"

It needed to quit.

He wasn't staying around, not to mention she had a feeling he saw her as a bit of a kid. She was twenty-eight, but when Tristan told him those stories about her, she would have been in her late teens and early twenties. She was even younger in many of the stories he likely heard.

His body didn't see you as a kid, though, her conscience countered.

At the unbidden thought, Gemma's knife slipped off the onion she was chopping, and she nearly sliced her finger. Clenching her teeth, she took a deep breath, willing the memories of his firm body beneath her into the furthest recesses of her mind. She needed to stop thinking about him if she wanted to keep all of her fingers. Not to mention her sanity.

She quickly finished making breakfast and doled out plates before sliding into a seat next to Tristan. As she sat down, Ben stated he was going to head to Asheville to speak with Marcie Trent as soon as they were done with breakfast.

"I'm coming with you," Gemma said.

Ben frowned. "What?"

"Absolutely not." Tristan's firm voice nearly drowned out Ben's.

Gemma glared at her brother. She was still peeved at him for the other day and was not in the mood for his dictatorial tendencies today. She turned her attention to Ben.

"Caleb is going to be a wreck once he knows or suspects something bad happened. He's going to pick up on Marcie's emotional state once we tell her, and he needs someone there he knows while you talk to her. You won't get much out of her otherwise. She'll be too distracted trying to soothe Caleb. Besides, no one deserves to get that kind of news without some support. I'm coming with you," she repeated.

Ben stared at her silently as he weighed her words.

"Sir, you can't seriously be considering letting her—"

Ben held up a hand to silence the flow of words out of Tristan's mouth and looked at him. "First off, it's Ben. I'm no longer your commanding officer, and I'd like to think we're friends. Second, your sister is right. Mrs. Trent shouldn't have to face that kind of news alone, and that boy needs all the friendly faces he can get right now. Gemma not only knows the boy well, she's a trained therapist. She goes with me."

Gemma couldn't stop the grin that spread across her face. She tried valiantly to smother it, though, as Ben turned his hard stare back on her.

"But *only* to comfort Caleb and Marcie. You are not investigating this with me."

Gemma shook her head. "Wouldn't dream of it." And she wouldn't. She was a therapist. She left the detecting to her brother.

"Good. Eat. We need to get on the road."

She dutifully shoved eggs into her mouth. She had gotten what she wanted and wasn't about to argue. She chanced a glance at her brother. He sat with his back straight, expression tight as he ate. She could tell he didn't like Ben's decision. But there was also a speculative look in his eyes as he glanced between her and Ben.

Uh-oh. The cogs were turning, and with Tristan, that never boded well for her.

Had he picked up on her attraction to Ben?

Had Ben said something about falling asleep on the couch with her?

Gemma immediately dismissed that last thought. She didn't know Ben well, but she knew he wouldn't do something like that. It was none of Tristan's business what went on between the two of them. She sensed Ben felt that way too.

So why was Tristan looking at them like he was seeing something that intrigued him?

Four

Gemma stared hard at the front door of Marcie Trent's house through the windshield of Ben's SUV. She tried hard on the drive over here to keep her thoughts off of what was about to happen. She brooded over the couch debacle instead and tried to pretend things weren't awkward between them. Now, though, there was no avoiding what they'd come here to do.

"You ready?" Ben asked quietly.

"No," Gemma was quick to reply. She opened her car door, anyway. "But I'll never be, so let's just go."

He followed her to the door and rang the bell.

It swung open to reveal a woman in her mid-fifties, dressed in jeans and a t-shirt; her gray-streaked, ash-blonde hair pulled away from her face in a messy top knot. "Gemma? What are you doing here?" Marcie asked.

Gemma sucked in a breath. She felt Ben's hand rest on her back and was thankful for the show of support. "Marcie, this is Special Agent Ben Davidson with the FBI. We need to talk to you. May we come in?"

Confusion and fear ran across the woman's features as she opened the door wider. "Of course."

Gemma looked around for signs of Caleb, but saw none. "Marcie, where is Caleb?"

"He's up in his room, playing." She led them into the living room.

That was good. Hopefully, they could keep his world intact for just a little while longer.

Marcie lowered herself to the couch, worry plain in the pinched look on her face. "Why? Gemma, what's going on?"

Gemma settled on the couch next to the older woman. Ben sat in the adjacent chair. She looked helplessly at him. She just couldn't force the words past her lips. Grasping Marcie's hand, she held on for dear life.

"Mrs. Trent, you have a daughter? Diana Lowell?" Ben asked.

Marcie nodded and looked at Gemma. "Yes." Her eyes widened as she saw the expression on Gemma's face.

A tear leaked from Gemma's eye, and she tightened her grip on Marcie's hand.

"Oh my God! Has something happened to Diana?"

Gemma could only nod, another tear slipping free.

"She was found yesterday afternoon in the forest outside of Hot Springs." Ben's voice was low. "She'd been murdered."

A cry burst from Marcie. "No! No, no, no, no, no!" Gemma wrapped Marcie in a tight hug as the older woman cried. Tears rolled down Gemma's cheeks. She looked over at Ben, where he sat watching them stoically. She had no idea how he broke this kind of news on a regular basis. She didn't think she could do it, even if she didn't know the victim or their loved ones.

He reached out and placed a hand on her knee, oddly knowing she needed his strength. Gemma let it flow through her and took a deep breath, her tears subsiding as she got her focus back. They needed answers.

Gemma motioned to the box of tissues on the end table. Ben passed her a handful as she pulled back from Marcie.

"Marcie, I know this is difficult, but Ben needs to ask you some questions." She handed the grieving woman the tissues, saving a couple for herself.

Marcie wiped her eyes and sat back. "Of course." She turned watery brown eyes to Ben, trying to hold back the sobs.

"Mrs. Trent, Gemma mentioned your daughter met a man a few weeks ago. Andrew? What can you tell me about him?"

Marcie sucked in a steadying breath before she answered. "Not much, I'm afraid. Diana didn't date hardly ever, and when she did, she never brought her dates to the house. She always met them elsewhere. She didn't want to expose Caleb to anyone who wasn't going to stick around. Unfortunately, none of the men she dated ever made it past the first few dates. She mentioned Andrew, of course, and told me a bit about him. She really seemed to like him, but they hadn't been seeing each other long. Only a few weeks."

"Did she tell you his last name? What he did for a living?" Ben asked.

Marcie sniffed and wiped away more tears. "Yes. His last name is Emerson, and she said he was a day trader."

"Did she say what company he worked for? Or if he was independent?"

"She didn't say. I'm not sure if she knew."

"Was there anyone else new in her life?"

Marcie shook her head. "No."

"Other than the hospital where she worked and the equestrian center where she took Caleb for lessons, were there any other places she frequented?"

"Um, she took Caleb to a play therapy session once a week,

and they spent a lot of time on the weekends in the forest. Caleb likes the birds."

"Did you ever accompany them on their walks?"

Marcie shook her head. "No. I broke my ankle a decade ago, and it never healed quite right. I can't walk long distances."

Ben nodded thoughtfully and stood abruptly. Gemma frowned up at him.

"Excuse us a moment, please," he said.

Marcie nodded.

He motioned for Gemma to follow him. Perplexed, she excused herself and did as he asked. He walked several feet away, where they were out of earshot.

He bent his head low. "I need to talk to the boy. He may have seen something in the woods. I don't like that they spent so much time there, and that's where she was found. It's sounding all kinds of alarm bells in my head. The kind you don't ignore."

Gemma nodded, pressing her lips together thoughtfully, weighing his request. "You have to get Marcie to agree to it, and you have to let me lead the questioning. You're much too imposing of a figure for him."

She could see the inner debate going on in Ben's head. They had agreed she wouldn't do the investigating, but if she took the lead on questioning Caleb, it would put her square in the hot seat.

Finally, Ben nodded. "Okay. You're the expert here. I have no clue how to handle a child like him."

Gemma nodded and walked back to Marcie. She kneeled before the older woman and took her hand. "We need to ask Caleb some questions. He may have seen something or someone in the woods. We won't bring up Diana's death. We'll leave that to you to break to him when and how you see fit."

Marcie looked up at Ben, where he loomed over them. "I don't know. You know how he is, Gemma. He's not crazy about men, especially ones so... intimidating. No offense, Agent Davidson."

"None taken, ma'am. I'm well aware of how imposing I can appear. But it would be really helpful if we could ask Caleb a few questions."

Gemma pressed her lips together as they waited for Marcie's answer. She could only imagine what was going through the woman's head. Upsetting Caleb was the last thing any of them wanted.

"All right," Marcie relented. "But please tread carefully."

"We will," Gemma promised. "Why don't you go get him, and we'll wait down here? I have an idea to help Caleb feel more comfortable."

As soon as Marcie left to fetch the boy, Gemma grabbed Ben's hand and hauled him across the room to where a child-size table and chairs sat in one corner.

She pushed him down to the floor at the back of the table. "Sit here. Whatever you do, stay seated. You're so large you'll frighten him if you stand. From what Diana's said, his father is a big man, and he wasn't nice to them. It's left Caleb wary of large men. We don't want him to equate you with his dad or we'll get less than nothing out of him."

Ben nodded and tried to make himself as small as possible.

"And give me your gun and put your shield away. He doesn't need to know you're a cop. As far as he's concerned, we're just asking questions about the woods."

Ben hesitated slightly before handing her the weapon.

"I feel naked, just so you know," he muttered as he pulled his badge off his belt and tucked it into his pocket.

Gemma's cheeks heated, her thoughts turning to that morning. She quickly shoved them away. They weren't helpful right now. "I promise I'll give it back as soon as we get to the car." She stowed the gun in her purse out of sight just as they heard footsteps on the stairs.

Quickly, Gemma grabbed some sheets of paper and a box of crayons from the shelves beside to the table and kneeled next to Ben, between him and where Caleb would sit. She knew the boy loved to draw, and she hoped she could use that to help him open up to them.

Marcie walked into the room with a blonde-haired eight-year-old beside her just as Gemma got settled.

"Hi Caleb." Gemma greeted him with a cheerful smile. "I just stopped by because I heard you had a great place to go hiking where there are lots of birds. My friend, Ben," she gestured to Ben, "and I love to go birdwatching, and we were curious about where you went. Can you come sit down with us and tell us about your favorite birds and the best places to see them?"

Marcie hovered behind the boy as he decided. Gemma could see him sizing up the man sitting quietly in the corner. Ben, bless him, had his knees drawn up and his arms wrapped around them, his shoulders hunched, trying to appear non-threatening. Gemma offered the boy another smile, willing all the nerves out of her eyes. Caleb cautiously made his way over and sat down in the chair next to Gemma. Marcie kneeled at the very end of the table, opposite Ben.

Gemma held out the crayons. "I thought maybe you could draw us some pictures of the birds you see frequently, so we can watch out for them."

The boy nodded and took the box, immediately beginning to draw. Words flowed from his mouth—all about birds. Gemma knew from their sessions together that Caleb had an obsession with birds at the moment and could go on for days.

The adults listened for a while as Caleb described the bird he drew.

When he finally took a breath, Gemma quickly jumped in.

"Can you tell me the best place to see this bird? We want to make sure we find the right place to go so we can hopefully see it."

"They like the water because there are a lot of bugs there," he replied.

"Water? You mean near a river?"

The boy nodded. "I always see it there along with this one." Caleb grabbed another sheet of paper and started drawing another picture.

"Do you remember which river, Caleb?"

"I don't know the name, but Mom always takes me to a wildlife preserve."

Gemma smiled. "That's great, Caleb. These will really help. Do you ever see anything besides birds?"

The boy shrugged. "I don't really look for anything else."

"So how did you find out the wildlife area was the place to see these birds? Did you just hike there one day and see them, or did someone tell you it was a good place to go?" Gemma asked, switching tactics.

"Ranger Jack showed us the spot. He also showed me where to find woodpeckers and blue jays." Caleb launched into dissertations on both birds that would put the Audubon's bird guide to shame.

Gemma listened intently, knowing how important it was to be interested in what he was saying. She didn't want him to feel like he was being ignored.

"Wow! That's great, Caleb. I didn't know you knew so much about those birds. Did Ranger Jack teach you all that?"

Caleb shook his head. "I read most of it in books, but he told me some."

"That's great. What does Ranger Jack look like?" Gemma asked. Maybe they could track this ranger down and find out if he'd seen anything unusual. "Ben and I will look for him on our hike and ask him to show us the birds too."

Caleb nodded enthusiastically, eager to share his hobby with others. "Yellow hair, but darker than Mom's."

Gemma nodded. "Does he have brown eyes or blue?"

"Gray."

"Gray?" That was a very distinctive color and should make finding the right ranger easy.

The boy nodded.

"Is he taller than your mom?"

Caleb nodded.

Gemma tried to think of another man Caleb knew who was tall. "Is he as tall as my brother, Tristan?" Her brother often donated his time at the equestrian center to teach some of their older children and adult riders horsemanship skills.

"No."

"Okay, that's very helpful, Caleb. I think we'll know him if we see him now." Gemma was about to thank the boy for helping when he began talking again.

"If he's not in the woods, sometimes I see him at school."

Gemma frowned. "So, he comes to your class to talk about the park?"

Caleb shook his head. "He's in a car by the playground."

Alarm bells went off in her head. Maybe they wouldn't be asking Ranger Jack about unusual activity in the park. Maybe *he* was the unusual activity. She looked at Ben. He was watching Caleb with an intense stare. Marcie sat clutching her hands together, trying not to touch Caleb and distract him.

"Do you ever talk to him when you see him at school?"

Caleb shook his head, drawing another bird, this time a hawk. "He usually just sits there watching."

"Watching you?" Gemma asked softly.

Caleb nodded, not looking up from his picture. Gemma saw him draw a breath, likely about to launch into a detailed history of the hawk he drew. She quickly cut in, wincing a bit at how rushed she sounded. "What color is his car, Caleb? So we can look for it when we go hiking," she added, softening her words.

Caleb paused in his drawing and frowned, clearly trying to shift gears. Gemma repeated the question, and he answered. "Dark green."

"Was it a car like your mom's?" Gemma asked. Diana drove a late-model sedan.

Caleb shook his head. "Bigger."

"Was it an SUV?" she asked.

Caleb looked up questioningly.

"A big boxy looking vehicle, like my friend Ben's car out there." Gemma pointed out the front window where Ben's black Explorer was visible.

Caleb looked out the window and nodded.

"So, were the park and the school the only places you saw him?"

Caleb nodded. "He'd sit there till I left with Mom and then follow."

Gemma had to suppress the urge to gasp. Marcie couldn't, and Caleb glanced at her.

"Caleb, did the man follow you home?" Gemma kept her voice gentle.

The boy nodded, but didn't look up, intent on coloring in the hawk.

"Did he follow you anywhere else?"

Caleb shook his head and started talking about his hawk. Off topic now, Gemma couldn't see a good way to steer him back. She looked over at Ben and wordlessly conveyed that she was at an impasse. He nodded.

Gemma looked at Marcie, who was trying to keep it together, and mouthed, "Okay, Marcie." They listened to Caleb educate them on the red-tailed hawk for several more minutes before Marcie managed to cut in and distract the boy with the promise of a snack.

Caleb got up and scampered toward the kitchen.

Gemma grabbed Marcie's hand before she could follow her grandson. "Thank you, Marcie. He did great. We'll see ourselves out. If you need *anything*, please call. Day or night."

Marcie nodded and gave Gemma a watery smile.

Gemma's heart broke as she watched the woman leave the room. She could only imagine the depth of that woman's pain.

Ben's warm hand curving over her shoulder brought her back. She offered him a tremulous smile and retrieved her purse before walking outside. Once ensconced in the car, Gemma couldn't hold back the tears any longer.

She sank gratefully into Ben's chest as he pulled her as close as he could across the center console, her earlier awkwardness with him forgotten. She needed his strength.

Ben wove a hand through Gemma's hair and wrapped the other around her back as she wept against his chest. He was amazed she held it together this long. He had delivered a lot of bad news and conducted a lot of interviews in his day, but what transpired in that house had to be one of the most intense experiences of his adult life. Marcie's pain was palpable as she sat there and listened to her grandson describe the man who could very well be her daughter's killer.

And Gemma. Gemma was amazing. She kept her head through it all and extracted some very useful information out of what could have been a rather reluctant witness. Now, she wept for the child and his grandmother. For her friend. He just hoped she wept for herself too.

He continued to stroke her back as her sobs died down until she was just sniffling against his chest. Ben wrapped her rich chestnut hair around his hand and pulled slightly to tip her head up. "I know it doesn't seem like it, but it will get better." He knew that firsthand. He'd lost more than one friend to violent acts on the battlefield. It always felt like someone ripped the heart from his chest and stomped it to pieces in the dirt. But the pain eventually dulled to the point he could take a deep breath again.

She sniffed and nodded. "She was such a sweet person. Why would someone want to hurt her? Hurt her son by taking away his mother?"

"I don't know, darlin', but I intend to find out." Ben dropped a kiss on the top of her head. "I will find him."

FIVE

The next day, Ben pulled open the door to the equestrian therapy and riding center's front office, where Gemma worked. He had an appointment to see the director about getting a list of current and former employees and to interview the staff about Diana. Ideally, he'd like a list of clients as well, but at this point, he didn't have enough to get a warrant for that list. He gave his name to the receptionist, and she showed him through to Mara Roth, the center's director.

"Thank you for taking the time to see me, Mrs. Roth." Ben sat down in the guest chair she offered him.

"I'm happy to help you in any way I can. And please, call me Mara."

Ben nodded, flipping open a small notebook and clicking his pen. "Can you tell me when you last saw Ms. Lowell?"

Mara thought briefly. "I think it was Thursday for Caleb's regular session."

"And it went well?"

Mara nodded. "As far as I know. Gemma could tell you more."

He figured that was what she would say. Gemma hadn't

mentioned anything out of the ordinary the other night, but he made a note to ask her about it again, anyway, just to be safe. Maybe she'd remembered something.

"Did you notice anyone hanging around during Caleb's session who shouldn't have been?"

"I didn't see anyone, but I spend a lot of my time in here." She gestured to her office. "Particularly now. It's the end of the quarter, so I'm busy preparing reports for our board of directors."

Ben tapped his pen against his notebook. "What about unusual cars in the mornings or evenings?"

She shook her head. "No. I'm usually the first one here, and the lot is always empty. In the evenings, it's just staff vehicles."

"Okay. If you do notice anyone or anything unusual, please contact me or the lead detective from the sheriff's department, Gemma's brother, Tristan."

Mara nodded. "I'll be keeping an eye out. We all will. Is there anything else I can do for you today?"

He sat forward. "Actually, yes. I'd like to interview your staff. If you could draw up an interview schedule for today, so I cause the least amount of disruption, I would appreciate it. And point me to an empty office I can use to conduct my interviews."

"Of course. You can set up in our conference room just down the hall." Mara tapped a few keys on her keyboard, pulling a pad of paper close. "I'll get that schedule to you shortly. You can start with the grooms now, though, if you'd like. We're in the middle of sessions, so they should just be doing barn chores until the riders are done."

Ben nodded, flipping his notebook closed, and rose from his seat. "I'd also like a list before I leave today of all your former employees going back a year."

"I'll make sure Pam compiles a list and gets it to you."

"Thank you, Mara. I appreciate your cooperation."

"You're welcome, agent. If there's anything else I can do to help, please let me know."

"I will, thank you." Ben left Mara's office and headed down the hall to the conference room. He really hoped today garnered some information. This case left him uneasy, and he wanted to solve it as quickly as possible.

Ben threw his pen down in disgust as the final person left the conference room later that afternoon. He now had a full-blown headache and was no closer to having any answers than he was that morning. No one had seen the car or either of the men hanging around. He felt like he was chasing his tail on this case, just like with the previous victims. None of his leads seemed to go anywhere. No car. He couldn't find Andrew Emerson or Ranger Jack.

And to top it all off, Tristan called earlier to tell him the autopsy yielded few clues Ben hadn't already anticipated. Her legs were crushed, just as he predicted, and she died from asphyxiation. Dr. Tate was still waiting on toxicology reports, but Ben knew the lab would find ketamine in her system, just like the other victims. The only thing new they got was some fiber evidence that came off the ground near where the rope was tied and from her hair. Until they had something to match the fibers to, though, they had nothing.

Ben walked out of the small meeting room and down the corridor to the arena. He hadn't talked to Gemma yet. He was holding out hope she'd seen the car hanging around the center. But she didn't mention it yesterday on their drive back to Foggy Mountain or that evening over dinner, so he was doubtful.

That was an awkward affair. Gemma hardly spoke through the meal, and Tristan eyed them both speculatively. Ben tried to ignore the tension and just eat, but it had been damn hard. After Gemma finished her meal, she quietly excused herself. Ben and Tristan didn't see her again for the rest of the night.

He retired shortly after her. Dog-tired from the night before, he'd been in no mood to sit there while Tristan gave him the big brother stare. As far as Ben was concerned, what happened between Gemma and him was none of Tristan's business. Not that anything *was* happening or was going to. Still, in the mood he was in, if Tristan pressed the issue, Ben likely would have punched him.

Reaching the end of the hall, Ben pushed open the door that led to the arena and walked up to the corral fence. Gemma was on the far side of the arena, leading around a child with braces on her legs, atop a gray horse. He watched quietly, marveling at the ease with which she put people. The child astride the horse couldn't be more than six, yet she looked completely relaxed and happy as Gemma gave gentle guidance. She was a natural with kids. People in general, really. He was still in awe of her after watching her work with Caleb yesterday.

She came around the end of the arena and up the side where he stood. He knew the moment she noticed him. Her posture stiffened and her smile became a little strained. He hated that he put her on the defensive, but he had a feeling it had more to do with the attraction they felt for each other than any animosity toward him. She'd been nothing but polite. And he knew he certainly felt more defensive when she was around. If he didn't raise the shields high and bolt them down, they would soon finish what they started on the couch.

Gemma nodded at him as she passed, but didn't stop. He waited patiently as she finished her session with the young rider and handed the child off to her waiting mother. Ben hopped the fence to help as Gemma led the horse back to its stall to be groomed and tucked in for the night. They worked in silence until the horse was taken care of, then he followed her back to her office.

She was the first to break the silence. "I'm assuming you're here to interview the staff?"

He nodded. "Already done. I don't suppose you've noticed that green SUV Caleb talked about, have you?"

She shook her head. "No. I wracked my brain all evening for either the men or the car, and I can't remember seeing either before. I'm sorry."

Ben sighed, frustrated. "I figured as much when you didn't mention it."

Awkward silence descended again. Ben's patience snapped. This was ridiculous. They were staying in the same house. Even if he checked into a hotel, they'd still see each other frequently.

He stepped forward until he was close enough to touch her. "Listen, about the other morning. I don't know how we ended up the way we did, but it's not a big deal. We just got caught off guard, and we were still half asleep."

Keep telling yourself that, Davidson. Maybe you'll eventually believe it, his conscience countered. He couldn't help but scoff at his own thoughts. He knew he was probably deluding himself, but still, he had to try.

She wouldn't look at him, but she nodded. "Right."

He ran a hand through his hair. Deciding it wasn't worth the argument, he let it go and just tried to pretend they were past it. "Tristan got caught up in another case and said he'd grab a bite in town tonight. I have a bunch of case files from the previous victims to go over again. How about we go grab some dinner before I closet myself away?"

She looked at him then. After a moment of assessing him, she finally nodded.

Elation he shouldn't have felt flooded his veins. Maybe dinner was a mistake.

He opened his mouth to make up an excuse when she smiled softly. Any coherent thought or excuses he would have made fled his brain.

Dinner was definitely a mistake, but now Ben couldn't bring himself to care.

SIX

He had followed that damn FBI agent after the press conference and ended up at the equestrian center where that woman he'd strung up in the woods took that son of hers. He watched as the agent finally exited the building with one of the therapists, a hand resting on her back as he guided her to the car. Agent Davidson had certainly been in there long enough.

It had given him plenty of time to think. How the feds got to the crime scene so quickly was beyond him. It usually took the FBI several days to get involved. And he was in a new state. This shouldn't even have been on the cops' radar as a serial killing.

Someone must have flagged his M.O.

Dammit! He couldn't let anyone stop him. Not until everyone got his message.

That meant he needed to stop Agent Davidson. Which wouldn't be easy. The man was a brute. And tenacious.

As he watched Davidson interact with the therapist, an idea formed. Maybe there was another way...

He'd need to get some supplies first.

Seven

Gemma tried to relax as she sat down across from Ben in the booth at the Mexican restaurant they chose. Like it or not, she was going to see a lot of him until this case was either solved or it went cold. She didn't want to live on eggshells until that point. She'd go nuts.

Just don't think about that morning. Don't think about how hard his chest was or the way his hips felt pressed to—Gemma quickly cut off that train of thought. She bit back a groan of frustration, repeating like a mantra in her head that he was her brother's former commanding officer, was too old for her, and wasn't local.

It several more times of saying that in her head until she could look at him without remembering what his body felt like and how his clear blue-green eyes darkened to the color of the turbulent ocean when aroused.

Argh! She was thinking about it again. Gemma picked up her menu and hid behind it. She stayed there until the waiter came to take their orders. Then she had to face Mr. Tall Dark and Gorgeous.

She cleared her throat. Maybe conversation would distract

her. At least it would make her focus on something other than those broad shoulders that filled his side of the booth. "So, where are you from, Ben? You have a drawl." Gemma noticed the southern lilt to his voice the first time he spoke.

"Virginia," he answered. "I was born and raised just outside of Richmond."

"Where do you live now? You're investigating this case, so I'm assuming you're close."

He nodded. "I work out of the Richmond field office. I got lucky. When I got out of the academy, there was an opening there and I applied for it. It made my mother happy to have me home after so many years."

She noted the fondness in his voice when he spoke of the woman. "You're close with your family?"

He shrugged. "Some more than others. My dad and I have our issues, and my brother and I don't always see eye to eye, but we get along."

"How many siblings do you have?"

"Two. I have a sister as well. I'm the oldest."

The waiter came with their drinks. Gemma took a hearty gulp of hers, savoring the coolness. It was hot again today. The barn and arena were air-conditioned, but it was such a large space, it was always just a touch warm in the summer.

"So, how did you end up sharing a house with your brother?" Ben asked.

Gemma smiled. "When he came back after his stint in the Army, he joined the Asheville Police Department, but he wanted to be in Foggy Mountain. It's home, you know? Anyway, when a detective position opened up here with the county, he applied. It was about the same time I finished up my degrees and took the job at the center. Our parents decided they wanted to travel the country and offered us the use of the house. It didn't seem logical for Tristan and me to rent apartments or buy our own houses while our parents' house sat empty. We'd still have to do the upkeep on it while they were away."

"So, your parents are off gallivanting around the US?"

Gemma nodded. "They bought a fancy RV and go where they feel like. Right now, they're in Arizona exploring the Grand Canyon. They come home for holidays and our birthdays, or if they just need a rest, then they head out again."

The waiter appeared again, this time with their meals. Gemma finally felt herself relax, and they fell into easy conversation as they ate. When they finally left the restaurant, Gemma was surprised to see how low the sun had sunk in the sky. She didn't realize they sat and talked for so long.

Ben drove them back to the equestrian center so Gemma could get her car. He pulled up next to her Wrangler, and she climbed out. Ben came around the vehicle.

"Thank you for dinner," Gemma said as she craned her neck to look up at him. She wasn't short at five-foot-seven, but he had at least half a foot on her. "I had a nice time," she said, her voice soft. The waning light made his eyes look like liquid silver and cast shadows on the hard edges of his face. He looked like he'd been carved from granite.

"Me too." His voice rumbled low and washed over her senses. Gemma pushed the unlock button on her remote and fumbled for the door handle behind her. She needed to get in her car and drive away or she was going to do something foolish. Like lean into that hard body and kiss him.

He reached around her and grabbed the door handle. It brought him much too close. She could smell his spicy scent all around her as his cheek brushed her hair. Gemma gulped and closed her eyes against the onslaught of desire.

Eight

The car door snicked open and Ben stepped back.

"Goodnight, Gemma." His voice was gruff, but he was glad he could talk at all around the lump of desire in his throat.

After a brief hesitation, she cleared her throat and backed up a step. "Goodnight." Turning, she slid into the car. Ben closed the door quietly. With a final look, she turned over the engine and put the car in gear, pulling out of the parking lot and leaving Ben standing beside his car, wondering why the hell he tortured himself.

Getting so close had been a terrible idea, but he'd been in as much of a rush to get her on her way as she'd been to go. The low sun turned her chestnut hair to a halo of coppery fire around her head and gave her skin the warmest glow. Getting her door open for her seemed like the fastest option to remove temptation. It worked, because she was gone, but now he just had her scent stuck in his head and a need for a cold shower.

He was forty-two years old, but he felt like a goddamn teenager. Disgusted with his lack of control, he climbed back into his SUV and headed to the sheriff's office, where the files on the other murders waited for him.

Once he was back at his desk, he immersed himself in his case files, determined to put Gemma out of his mind. Pen in hand, he jotted down details from his other cases on a yellow legal pad, hoping to make some sense out of the clues he had. When his vision started to blur and his eyes grew scratchy, he laid his pen down and rubbed his face, biting back a yawn.

"You're still here?"

Ben looked up from his desk, startled to see one of the night shift deputies standing in front of him.

He sat back in his chair and stretched. "What time is it?"

"Just after eleven."

Christ. He'd lost track of time trying to find some commonalities. He closed the case file and thrust it back into the box on his desk, along with the legal pad. "Not anymore." He stood. It was past time he went back to the Mabley's and at least attempted to sleep.

Gathering the box—because he knew himself and would just end up driving back here to get them at three a.m. when he couldn't sleep—Ben bid the deputy goodnight and headed out of the station to his car.

Ten minutes later, he walked into the Mabley home, box in hand. The TV playing quietly in the living room reached his ears. Curious, he poked his head around the corner to see Gemma dressed for bed and curled up in one corner of the couch, watching the news.

She glanced up and muted the TV when she saw him. "Hey."

"Hi."

"You're as bad as Tristan." She motioned to his box. "Bringing work home with you."

Like a moth to a flame, he walked into the living room and set the box on the coffee table, then settled onto the far end of the couch. "Reading material to lull me to sleep," he quipped with a sigh.

"You look like you're stuck."

Ben frowned. "What do you mean?"

She gestured to the box again. "On your case. I swear, the military gives you guys a course on facial expressions. You and Tristan are two peas in a pod. He gets that same look when he's stuck on a case."

Ben grinned. Maybe it was the quiet or the late hour, but he felt himself relaxing. "You didn't hear? It's called Facial Etiquette for the American Soldier 101," he teased. "All officers are required to take it so they can adequately intimidate their troops."

She giggled. "I almost believe you."

Their shared laughter served to dispel the last of the tension he always seemed to feel around her. He didn't want to fight tonight. Not her and not himself. Not after rereading all those damn files and remembering how depraved some people could be.

"So, do you want to share?"

"My case?"

She nodded.

He studied her momentarily, sorely tempted after having watched her work her magic on Caleb. What the hell. It wasn't like it would hurt. Fresh eyes were never a bad thing, and Gemma had the advantage that she didn't think like a cop. Maybe she would see something he and Tristan hadn't.

"The only commonality I've got between them is that they were all single mothers. They came from different walks of life. None of them had similar jobs or lived in the same areas. They didn't frequent the same grocery stores or other public areas —" Ben leaned forward to rest his elbows on his knees. He ran a hand over his jaw. "I've got nothing."

Gemma reached for the box. "May I?"

He hesitated, not expecting that. He figured she'd ask questions, not want to see the files. Telling her about the case was one thing, but actually letting her look at the case files was quite another. She was a potential witness.

But he didn't have to give her all the details. She could look at the women's lives and possibly see something he missed.

He reached into the box and quickly flipped through the folders, pulling out the pertinent papers and thrusting them at her. "Here. This is everything on their daily lives and backgrounds."

Deciding not to hover while she read, he excused himself to shower and grab a beer. When he returned to the living room fifteen minutes later, she was nearly done and had, at some point, retrieved a pad of paper and a pen. As he sat down, she flipped the last sheet onto the stack with the others and looked up.

"Anything?" he asked.

"Maybe. Did you notice that all the children were undergoing treatment for an illness or condition?"

"Yeah. We checked them out. None of them went to the same doctor or hospital. These women literally never crossed paths."

"Do you have any notes on the kids' treatments? The doctors and clinics?"

Ben nodded and started rummaging again. He handed her papers as he found them.

After he gave her the information on the third child, she suddenly clasped his arm. "Did the fourth child stop or diminish traditional medical treatment?"

Nonplussed, he blinked once, then leafed through the folders more quickly, soon locating the information. "Yes. He had an illness that affected kidney function, and the victim took him off many of the traditional drugs in search of a more natural way to regulate his kidneys."

She stood abruptly and looked at him wide-eyed. "Ben, that's it! All five victims used a non-traditional approach to treat their children. That's why the women were targeted."

Ben stared at the sheets of paper spread across the coffee table. All this time and *no one* had seen this connection.

No one but Gemma.

He finally had a solid lead. Because of one incredible woman.

Ben jumped up and grabbed her. Arms circling her waist, he lifted her free of the ground. "You. Are. Amazing!"

Then, because he couldn't have stopped himself if he tried, he kissed her.

He intended it to be a congratulatory kiss. Just a brief contact, but the instant her mouth touched his, he knew a short kiss wouldn't be enough. His entire body stilled, his excitement fading as arousal replaced it.

He drew her closer.

Gemma's body tingled from head to toe. Every point of contact between her body and Ben's felt like fire touched her skin. After a brief moment of surprise at his kiss, she wrapped her arms around his neck, her fingers sliding into his hair as she sank into his embrace. His mouth was firm under hers. When his tongue begged entrance to her mouth, Gemma opened for him.

Her feet touched the floor, but he didn't let go or break contact. Instead, his hands started to roam. Gemma whimpered as he cupped her hips and pulled her closer. She could feel every ridge of muscle he possessed pressed against her softer curves. It was heavenly. She wiggled, trying to get even closer, and was rewarded with a growl.

His hands left her hips to slip under the hem of her pajama top and roam the smooth skin of her back and sides. Intense heat raced along her nerve endings until her knees felt like Jell-O. The kind that hadn't quite set yet.

All of a sudden, Ben jerked his mouth from hers and stepped back.

Breathing hard, Gemma locked her knees to stay upright. She stared at him, confused why he stopped and appalled that she wanted to drag him down to the couch and strip him naked. She'd never been so hot for a man so fast. She'd never been so hot for a man, period.

"We can't do this," Ben said, voice rough.

Knowing he was right didn't make the words hurt less, and Gemma had to turn away to keep the tears at bay.

"You're right," she whispered. "I'll see you tomorrow. Good night." Gemma made a hasty escape to her bedroom before she did something really silly. Like beg him to join her.

Nine

Gemma walked to the parking lot, weary after a long day. There had been something in the air today. Riders and horses alike had been ornery. But she was done, and she was going to go home and soak in a nice hot bathtub. She rifled through her bag in search of her keys, coming up empty. Had she left them in her desk?

Her shoulders slumped in defeat as she remembered exactly where they were. She glanced over at the empty parking spot where she'd parked her Jeep this morning. Her colleague, Stacy Mathis, had her car. In the craziness of the day, Gemma forgot she'd handed over her car keys this morning so Stacy could attend her night class in Asheville while her car was in the shop.

And she'd also completely forgotten to call Tristan so he could pick her up.

Well, no time like the present. Gemma pulled out her cell phone and dialed her brother.

"Hey. Can you come get me?" she asked when he picked up.

"What's wrong with your car?" She could hear the frown in his voice.

"I loaned it to Stacy and forgot. It's been a hell of a day, Tris."

"I'm tied up at the moment and will be for a while." She heard voices in the background, one calling his name. He shouted back before returning his attention to their conversation. "Is there anyone there who can give you a ride?"

"No. I walked out with Mara. We were the last two to leave. And before you ask, she didn't notice I was without a car because we parked on opposite sides of the building."

A long sigh came across the line. "Give me a few minutes to work something out. Someone will be there soon to get you."

Gemma thanked him and hung up. She leaned against the side of the building and settled in to wait for her ride. Knowing her brother, she would be escorted home in the back of a police car.

When her phone rang several minutes later, she expected to see Tristan's smiling face pop up on the caller ID, so the unfamiliar number that came up was a surprise.

"Hello?"

"Gemma! Oh, thank God! This is Marcie Trent. I didn't know who else to call. The therapist's office is closed and Caleb's really not doing well at the moment. I need help."

Gemma could hear the desperation in the older woman's voice and rushed to reassure her. "I'm waiting on a ride right now, but I'll be there as soon as I can."

"Thank you, Gemma," Marcie whispered.

Gemma hung up, her heart in her throat. It ached for that poor family. She willed her ride to show up sooner rather than later. When it finally did a few minutes later, she couldn't despair the fact that it was Ben pulling into the lot to pick her up.

She raced toward his SUV and was pulling open the door almost before he'd come to a complete stop.

"What's wrong?" he demanded as she jumped inside, an intense expression on his face.

"Marcie called. Caleb's having a hard time, and she needs some help."

She clicked her seat belt in place as Ben swung the car around and pulled out of the parking lot without a word.

"Thank you," she said softly, several minutes into their drive. She looked over at him. "Not just for picking me up, but for understanding."

He reached over and covered her hand with his. "Anytime, Gemma." He glanced her way for a long second before turning his eyes back to the road. "I mean that. Anytime."

Gemma turned her hand over in his and squeezed. They still needed to talk about what happened last night and what they were going to do about this crazy attraction they had for each other, but in that moment, Gemma didn't care. Because no matter what else Ben was, he was her friend.

It was dark when Ben pulled into Marcie Trent's driveway for the second time that night. He'd dropped Gemma off hours earlier, eliciting a promise from her to call him when she was ready to go home, before he left her to go back to the station.

Fifteen minutes ago, she kept her promise and called.

Ben had barely put the car in park when the front door opened and Gemma stepped through. He watched her turn and hug Marcie before she made her way down the sidewalk and climbed inside the car. The glimpse he got of her face in the interior light showed him a haggard, exhausted woman.

"How's he doing?" Ben asked softly as he backed out of the drive.

Gemma sighed, eyes closed as she rested her head against the seat. "A mess. But we managed to get past the panic and calm him down. He was asleep when I left. Marcie's going to call his therapist first thing in the morning."

Ben slid his hand over hers, wordlessly offering support.

They rode in silence back to the Mabley's house, hands entwined. He should have pulled away, but in all honesty, he didn't want to. She settled him as much as he did her. The sense of contentment was nice.

Halfway there, Ben felt Gemma completely relax. He glanced over to see her passed out against the window.

She looked like herself again now that she was asleep. He hadn't realized just how stressed she was until now, when he could see the difference. He suspected she hadn't given herself a chance to properly grieve for her friend yet. Instead, she'd thrown herself into her work and into helping Caleb, ignoring her own well-being.

He knew how that went. He'd done much of the same during his time in the Army. And it always came back to bite him in the ass, just like he knew it would for her too.

But no matter when it finally overwhelmed her, he would be there for her. The woman pulled at every emotional string he had, and he couldn't sit by and watch her suffer without suffering right along with her.

Ben shifted in his seat, not entirely comfortable with his thoughts. She was undermining all the defenses he'd erected to protect himself. She'd already slid firmly into the friend category and was quickly headed for the one he kept behind multiple locks. He didn't do attachments to women past friendship. He'd seen how messy it was when it all went to pieces. He had no desire to ever go down that road.

But her perseverance and drive rivaled any of the men he'd served with, and her compassionate nature echoed his own drive to do some good in the world. It made him want to watch her work her magic on people as she helped them cope with whatever ailed them, whether it be emotional or physical impediments. Now that she was hurting, he wanted to help her heal. He wanted to see her smile again, all bright sunshine and shining eyes. He wanted to be the one to hold her when she cried and to wipe away her tears. The shoulder she leaned on when she needed strength.

Those were scary thoughts for a man who had no desire to have a woman occupy a permanent role in his life.

Ben blew out a breath as he pulled into the drive at the Mabley's and shut off the engine. Any serious thoughts about the situation and decisions on it would have to wait, though. He was as exhausted as Gemma.

He stared at her in the darkened interior of the car. She looked so peaceful that he hated to wake her. He hit the switch to turn off the car's interior lights, got out, and walked around to Gemma's side, opening her door slowly so she wouldn't topple sideways. She shifted to settle more deeply into her seat as the door moved away from her. Quickly, he unbuckled her seatbelt and put her purse in her lap, gently scooping her off the seat and kicking the door shut. She stirred in his arms, and he stopped, waiting for her to settle or wake. After a moment, she burrowed into his chest, her breathing becoming soft and regular again.

A wave of tenderness hit him, quickly followed by a sudden flair of desire at the feel of her soft body cuddled into his chest and her warm breath heating the skin of his neck. She might tug at his emotions, but he absolutely could not give in to the desire. He knew without a doubt that if he had any chance of keeping Gemma out of the innermost recesses of his soul, he could not give in to the hunger running through his veins.

Teeth clenched at the feel of the woman in his arms, Ben carefully made his way up the drive to the porch. He managed to get the door open without jostling her too much. Thankfully, closing it was easier.

Just as he was heading down the hallway to deposit her in her bedroom, Tristan poked his head out of the den.

"What happened?" he asked, bounding to Ben's side.

Ben quickly shushed him. "She's just really tired. She had a hell of a day, Tristan." He resumed his walk down the hall. "I'm going to put her in bed, then I'll catch you up."

Tristan followed, but hesitated in the doorway to Gemma's room. The fierce look Ben sent his way had the younger man nodding reluctantly and heading back down the hallway.

Ben laid Gemma on her bed. She huffed at the change in position, but quickly settled into the pillows. He deposited her purse on the nightstand and tugged off her shoes. He knew she'd be more comfortable without the jeans she wore, but there was no way he was taking them off of her. Not with the heat that flared between them every time they made eye contact. Seeing her in just her underwear could prove to be the catalyst to send them over the edge. Instead, he pulled her t-shirt free of her pants and slid the belt she wore from its loops. Gently, he pulled at the covers until they slid free of her body, then pulled them up over her.

He couldn't stop himself from running a gentle hand over her cheek into her hair. She was beautiful. With the moonlight shining on her smooth skin and the waves of rich hair splayed on the pillow, she looked like a sleeping goddess. His whole body ached to climb into the bed with her and just hold her. She stirred his blood, but more than that, she stirred his protective instincts. For the first time in his life, he ached to protect and cherish a woman.

Ben silently cursed and snatched his hand back. He didn't know why a woman he met four days ago could have such a stranglehold on him, but she did. Maybe it was because he felt like he already knew her from all the stories he'd heard from Tristan over the years. Her zest for life and the compassion she had for others that Tristan described had made her someone he admired, even though he'd never met her. Now that he had experienced Gemma first hand, he couldn't help but want to keep someone like her in his life. She made the world brighter just by being in the same room.

God, how he wanted her.

With one last long look, Ben turned and swiftly left the room. Because, no matter what, he couldn't give in to this attraction. She deserved a man who would stick around, and he knew he wouldn't.

TEN

Ben scrubbed a hand down his face, weary after a long day of staring at files and reports. His search for Ranger Jack and Andrew Emerson was going nowhere. After giving the description of Ranger Jack to the supervisory park rangers, Ben had a whole host of candidates. They'd all said the same thing: they had several rangers fitting that bill, but none by the name of Jack.

Hoping to find something to narrow down the pool, Ben requested all the personnel files for the area's male rangers. He didn't realize there were so many. And not all of them had physical descriptions on file, so he was having to run those names against DMV photos. So far, none of them matched. His next step was to run background on the men who met the physical description, hoping that something would pop in conjunction with the name "Jack."

And Andrew Emerson was in the wind. If the man lived in the area, he had an out-of-state license, because he hadn't shown up on any DMV searches.

His frustration level wasn't helped by the fact he couldn't get a certain chestnut-haired beauty out of his thoughts, either. As a result, Ben was irritated and tense and ready to shoot something.

His phone vibrated on his desk. He snatched it up. "Davidson," he snapped, not bothering to look at the caller ID.

"Please tell me Gemma's with you." Tristan's frantic voice came over the line. Ben immediately sat up straight, the personnel files forgotten. He'd never heard Tristan like this. Not even in their most dire situations when their missions went south.

"No. I don't know where she is. Why? What's going on?"

"I just got a call from the neighboring sheriff's office. They found Gemma's car off of highway seventy, just north of Weaverville. It was crumpled against a tree and on fire."

Ben was on his feet and headed for the door before Tristan finished talking, the wheels in his brain spinning furiously as he took in what Tristan said. "*Just* her car?" he asked.

"Yep." Ben heard the tremor in Tristan's voice and felt an answering one vibrate through him.

Shit! That was not what he wanted to hear.

"You've tried calling her?"

"No answer."

"Are you at the accident site?"

"Headed there."

Ben's mind raced as he climbed into his SUV. Something didn't feel right about this, and it wasn't just the fact she was missing. Why was she on the highway to Asheville? The Mabley house was north of Foggy Mountain—the opposite direction.

"I'm going to call the FBI tech department. Have them ping her phone and see if we can get a location," Ben said, slamming the car into drive and peeling out of the parking lot. It was a long shot, because it could be a lump of melted plastic in the car. But if she had her phone on her person when the car crashed, it might lead them to her. "I'm headed your way now."

"See you there." Tristan hung up.

Ben immediately dialed FBI dispatch and requested to be put through to the tech department. He quickly outlined his request and had a location of her phone just as he came up on the accident site.

The answer, though, didn't make much more sense. It was in downtown Asheville. Ben pulled off behind a sheriff's cruiser and flashed his badge to the officer maintaining the perimeter. He was let through and pointed in the direction of the officer in charge of the scene. Tristan stood next to him.

Tristan spotted him walking up and broke away from the deputy. "What did you find out?"

Ben glanced at the smoldering wreckage of Gemma's Jeep. The flashing blue and red lights of the emergency vehicles cast an eerie glow through the smoke lingering in the air and reflected off of the smashed car. The sight of the twisted metal and the acrid smell of smoke turned his stomach. Stark fear for Gemma threatened to overwhelm him. Ruthlessly, he tamped it down and forced himself to focus. "Her phone pinged at a location in downtown Asheville."

Tristan's frown only deepened. "Why would she be in Asheville?"

"I don't know. Has there been any sign she walked away from the crash?"

Tristan shook his head. "Not yet. They're bringing dogs in to search the woods."

Ben nodded. "Good." He put a hand on Tristan's shoulder. He could see the younger man was trying to hold it together, but the situation was taking its toll. "I'm going to head to Asheville and see if I can find her there. Text me a recent picture so I can show it around. You stay here in case the dogs turn something up. I'll call you if I find anything, and you do the same."

Tristan nodded. "We have to find her, Ben."

"We will." Because Tristan was right. They *had* to find her. He didn't know how either he or Tristan would get on without her.

Ben drove as fast as he dared to Asheville, thankful his SUV was retrofitted with lights and sirens. As he entered the city limits, he called the tech department back so they could guide him to where Gemma's phone pinged. He pulled up outside a row of restaurants and shops in the swanky part of downtown. This was as close as the tech could get him, so Ben now found himself having to search six buildings—three on either side of the street—that were within range of the ping. He swung his SUV into an open parking space and quickly climbed out.

He eyed the businesses around him, searching for a target where she would likely be if she were here voluntarily. There were two restaurants, a bookstore, and several high-end clothing boutiques. He didn't even want to think about the private residences above the stores. He'd go there once he exhausted all other options.

Quickly disregarding the clothing shops as too expensive for a woman of Gemma's means, Ben headed for the closest restaurant. At first glance, he doubted she was here. Unless she had a date. It screamed elegance and romance. Ben didn't know if she was dating anyone, but he doubted she would kiss him the way she had and then go out on a date with someone else.

Still, Ben flashed her photo at the maître'd and asked to wander the dining room. He made quick work of the room without spotting her.

Back on the street, the bookshop was next. He quickly discovered it was closed and made his way to the remaining restaurant, a pub-style place that catered to Asheville's young, career-minded crowd. If she wasn't in here, he was seriously going to consider calling in backup. Worry edged the lines of his body as he pulled open the heavy door.

"Welcome to Smith's Grill. How many?" The young hostess quickly greeted him, a bright smile lighting up her face.

Ben showed her his badge. "I'm actually here looking for a woman." He pulled up Gemma's picture on his phone. "Have you seen her come in here tonight?"

The hostess studied the picture. "Maybe. Why? Did she do something?"

Ben shook his head. "No, she's not in any kind of trouble. She's just missing, and I'm out exhausting every possibility trying to find her."

The girl looked at Gemma's picture again before she shrugged. "Honestly, it's been hopping in here all night, so she could have come in and I just don't remember, or one of the other hostesses could have showed her to a table."

Ben sucked in a deep breath, trying to corral his frustration. "Do you mind if I take a look around? See if she's here?"

"Go right ahead. I hope you find her."

Ben smiled his thanks and wandered further into the packed restaurant. The bar was the first area he came to, and he scanned through the women. Not seeing her, he moved into the dining room. Every table was crammed full of people, and Ben had to pay almost as much attention to where he was going as to the faces in the crowd. He made it three-quarters of the way through the room when his hopes started to fade. There were only a handful of booths at the back of the room behind the pillar he had yet to check.

Not hoping for much, Ben rounded the column.

～

Today, Gemma had been prepared. Well, after the fact, but still, she didn't have to worry about bumming a ride from Tristan or Ben tonight. When Stacy asked if she could keep the car one more night because she had another class that evening and her car still wasn't ready, their boss, Mara, piped up, suggesting a girls' night for Gemma and herself. Gemma readily agreed. It had been far too long since she and Mara had been out on the town together. It had the added benefit of removing the possibility that Ben would be her ride home again. A win-win in any situation.

Gemma watched the people milling around the restaurant from her limited view behind the wooden pillar. Her obstructed sightline didn't really matter, though. She wasn't really seeing anything, anyway. Instead, her mind was elsewhere. She kept remembering Ben's eyes last night when she jumped into his SUV. He had immediately noticed something wasn't right. Concern and determination had shone glaringly bright from the clear, blue-green depths of his eyes. He had wanted to help her and would do whatever he could to do so.

She shivered under the remembered intensity of his gaze. He was working his way under her skin at an alarming pace. He'd handled the Caleb incident last night with no hesitation or disdain when he could have easily argued. She knew he was a busy man tracking a killer. His willingness to take her where she needed to go endeared him to her all the more.

And when she awakened this morning fully clothed in her bed, she'd known it was Ben who put her there. Tristan would have just dumped her on the mattress and thrown the blanket over her—*maybe* removing her shoes. He certainly wouldn't have untucked her t-shirt and removed her belt. She loved that Ben was considerate, but at the same time, she didn't. It made him all the harder to resist.

That in mind, Gemma was determined to stay away from

him. If she wasn't sure she could resist him, she would be damn sure to avoid him.

"You're awfully quiet," Mara said, startling Gemma from her musings.

"What? Oh. Yeah. It's been a nutty few days, and I'm just trying to make sense of it all, I guess." Gemma sat straighter in her seat.

A knowing smile turned up one corner of Mara's mouth. "You sure about that? You sure it's not a certain astonishingly gorgeous FBI agent that's monopolizing your thoughts?"

Gemma felt her cheeks flame, but didn't respond. She sipped her drink to keep her mouth busy so she wouldn't blurt out the truth.

Mara chuckled. "You think I didn't see the two of you dancing around each other the other day? You guys were practically shooting sparks."

Gemma's face flamed hotter.

Mara did a double take. "Oh my God! What happened? Did you sleep with him?"

"No!" Not in the sense Mara was thinking, anyway. She willed her blush away. "Of course not! I've only known him a few days."

"Honey, sometimes that's all it takes. But I'm guessing you kissed him, if the color of your face is anything to go by."

Gemma silently cursed her fair skin. What she wouldn't give to have swarthy coloring right about now.

Mara chuckled again. "You did, didn't you! Oh, you have to give me details! Please tell me a man who looks like that can set your undies on fire with just a kiss."

Gemma couldn't stop the laugh that bubbled out. "Holy crap, Mara! Really?"

Mara's grin only grew. "What? I'm living vicariously through you. I remember what it was like when Blake and I first started dating. I kept spare underwear in my purse because he could heat me up with a look."

"Does this mean you're ready to jump back into the dating pool?" Mara's husband, Blake, died in a car accident two years ago.

She shrugged. "Maybe. But we're not talking about me."

Gemma sighed. "Mara, I know you want everyone to be as deliriously happy as you were, but Ben is not the one to make me that way. He doesn't even live in this state. And he's like a decade older than me," Gemma said, trying to discourage her friend. Mara was wrong. Ben might heat her up, but he wasn't the one for her. There were just too many obstacles in their path.

"Gems, his age is a bonus, trust me. A seasoned man knows a lot of tricks in the bedroom. And one of you could always move. As much as I'd hate to see you go, I wouldn't begrudge you moving to be with him."

Everything Mara said was true. But could Gemma really move and leave everything she knew behind? That was a question she wasn't ready to answer yet. Thankfully, she was saved from having to say anything by the arrival of their entrees.

She was downing a mouthful of fries when a man entering her field of vision drew her attention.

"Gemma! Do you not answer your phone anymore?" As if magically conjured from her thoughts, Ben stood over the table. But the expression on his face was not the tender and caring one she'd been remembering. He was absolutely furious. His blue-green eyes were the color of hardened steel, and the tight clench of his teeth made the muscles in his chiseled jaw and cheeks jump.

Gemma gulped down the suddenly heavy mass of potato and just stared.

"Tristan and I have been trying to get a hold of you for over half an hour now! And here you are, plowing through a plate of fries and a burger like you haven't a care in the world." He gestured at her half empty plate.

Gemma's hackles rose. "I'm sorry. I wasn't aware that my free time was being monitored. I'll make sure you get a detailed itinerary of my day from now on, down to when I think I'll need to use the bathroom."

Her comments only seemed to make him angrier.

"You could have at least called him to let him know you were going to Asheville."

She lifted one eyebrow at him, barely hanging on to her temper. She was so tired of the men in her life treating her like a child. "Again, I wasn't aware I had a keeper. And I honestly thought I'd be home before him. Mara and I didn't intend to stay out late. You should know by now that I would *never* worry Tristan unnecessarily."

Once he looked slightly chagrined, Gemma continued. "Now, care to tell me what crawled up your butt?"

Ben's gaze bounced between her and Mara, who looked on with avid attention. Gemma just knew she was soaking all this up for future reference and speculation.

Finally, he took a deep breath and Gemma watched his anger fall away. He motioned Gemma to scoot over and sat down. "You really didn't know we called?" he asked.

Gemma shook her head and grabbed her purse from beside her. She pulled out her phone and groaned. "I left it on vibrate. It's so noisy in here I never heard it. I'm sorry, Ben. What's going on? Why are you here? And how did you find me, anyway?"

"I had the FBI techs ping your phone."

Gemma felt her eyes go wide, her anger flaring again. And she thought Tristan was bad. Ben took the "keeper" thing to a whole new level. "You *what*? Why would you do that?"

He sighed and closed his eyes. When he opened them, she could see the fatigue he was trying not to show. "Because

Tristan got a call from the neighboring sheriff's department saying your car was wrapped around a tree and on fire and we couldn't find you."

All the air fled Gemma's lungs along with her anger. Stark fear replaced it. *Oh my God*! Her gaze flew to Mara, who looked equally shocked. "Stacy." Gemma's voice was a mere whisper, but Ben heard her anyway.

"Stacy?" He frowned at her and looked at Mara, who'd turned white. "The woman you work with?"

Gemma nodded. "Her car still wasn't ready, so she asked if she could keep mine another night, because she had another class. I didn't see why not. Then Mara suggested we go out and that she would take me home afterwards, so I just went with it." She grabbed his arm as the implications completely sank in. "Is she okay?"

Ben covered her hand with his. "We don't know. There was no one in the car, which is why Tristan was calling you incessantly and why I tracked you down."

Gemma frowned and looked at Mara, who had an equally puzzled expression on her face. "Not in the car? Was she ejected in the crash?"

"The sheriff's department brought out some dogs to search for her, but I haven't heard anything yet. If she didn't get ejected, then we have no idea where she could be." Gemma fought the urge to lean into his touch as his hand came up to cup the side of her face. "I saw your car, Gem. If she wasn't thrown and she did indeed walk away from that, she wouldn't have gotten far."

Gemma bit her lip to keep the tears at bay. This was *not* happening. Stacy had to be okay.

"There's another possibility we have to consider," Ben said softly, looking at both women.

"Another possibility?" Mara asked through her shock.

He nodded. "She could have been taken."

Both women visibly started at his suggestion. "Can either of you think of anyone who would want to hurt her?"

Mara and Gemma quickly shook their heads.

"No," Gemma said. "Stacy's the sweetest person. Everyone loves her."

"She's a joy to be around," Mara added. "All her clients and their relatives can't get enough of her."

Gemma felt the weight of Ben's gaze settle on her. He stared at her silently, mouth opening and closing several times before he managed to get anything out. His fingers flexed where they laid against her head. "Would anyone want to hurt you, Gemma? Could they have mistaken Stacy for you?" he asked quietly.

Gemma inhaled sharply. Oh, God! Could she be the reason Stacy was missing, possibly hurt or worse? She couldn't hardly bear the thought.

Schooling her thoughts so she could function, Gemma thought quickly. "No one comes to mind. I don't tend to go around making people angry, Ben. And short of you and Tristan, I haven't argued with anyone lately."

He nodded. "Okay." He slid out of the booth, breaking contact with her. Gemma felt the loss deeply. His touch had anchored her. She fought for control.

"We need to go," he said, offering her a hand. Gemma quickly grasped it, thankful for the strength it offered. Later, when she could think straight, she'd contemplate how co-dependent she was becoming on him for her peace of mind. Right now, though, she needed to focus on finding Stacy. She had to be okay.

Ben found a server so she and Mara could settle their tab, then led both women out of the restaurant. He had luckily parked not far from Mara. Gemma opted to ride back with Ben. Mara followed closely behind.

The miles sped by quickly. Ben made calls on the way to

inform the others he found her and that they were looking for the wrong woman. In what felt like seconds to Gemma, they were at the accident scene.

"Oh my God," she breathed, getting her first look at her car. It was a burnt shell of what it used to be. All twisted metal and charred paint. The front driver's side was crumpled back to the door frame. The driver's door bent in slightly where the car spun into the tree after its initial impact.

"Gemma!"

She tore her gaze away from the car at the sound of her name. Tristan barreled toward her. He scooped her off her feet and hugged her tight.

"Thank God you're okay," he said into her hair.

Gemma hugged her brother for all she was worth. She was so sorry she'd put him through so much worry. He might drive her crazy, but she loved him. She knew if the situation was reversed, she would have been a wreck too.

"I'm so sorry, Tristan. I didn't hear the phone."

He pulled back. "It's okay. You're safe and that's all that matters." Gemma didn't miss the nod of thanks he sent Ben's way. "Now we just need to find your friend."

"There's still no sign of her?" Ben asked, moving up behind Gemma. She felt his presence with every fiber of her being and just wanted to lean into his solid strength. She didn't dare, though. It was too much temptation, and right now she felt very vulnerable.

Tristan shook his head. "The dogs have come up with zilch so far. If she got out of the car, it wasn't under her own power and there's no sign she was ejected from the vehicle."

"So, she's been kidnapped," Ben stated.

"Looking that way," Tristan answered.

Gemma felt her heart plummet. *Poor Stacy!* Why would anyone want to kidnap her? Gemma prayed they could find her before anything worse happened.

Eleven

S tupid bitch! Why did she have to lend out her car? Now he had an unforeseen complication and no leverage on that damned FBI agent.

He stared hard at the bound woman lying unconscious on the back seat of his car. He'd drugged her as soon as he'd come upon her in the vehicle before he realized he had the wrong woman.

He needed to decide what to do with her.

He wasn't into killing the innocent, and he had no quarrel with this woman. Could he take the chance and let her go? Use her as a warning for what would happen to the woman he was really after if Agent Davidson didn't back off?

Hmm... that had possibilities...

TWELVE

Gemma stumbled bleary-eyed into the kitchen the next morning. Not even the shower she just took had managed to wake her up much. When she returned home around one a.m., she'd fallen into bed, sure that she would soon be fast asleep. Instead, she laid there wide awake until she had heard Tristan and Ben come in. Only then did she drop into a restless slumber. Her alarm clock had blared entirely too early for her liking.

She didn't have the luxury of staying home today, though. With Stacy gone, the therapy center was down one therapist. She knew Mara was going to shuffle as many of Stacy's appointments as she could between Gemma and the third therapist, Liz Callahan. The upside to all of it was Gemma wouldn't have time to think about how tired she was or Stacy's fate.

She poured herself a cup of coffee and stared into the cupboards, trying to come up with breakfast. If the guys expected a big, hot meal this morning, they were going to be sorely disappointed. She was not in the mood to cook today.

Deciding that simple was the way to go, Gemma pulled

down the box of instant oatmeal packets. She dumped two in a bowl and added water before tossing the mixture in the microwave.

When Ben entered the kitchen, Gemma was staring numbly at the appliance, waiting for it to beep. She mumbled a greeting just as her oatmeal finished. Ben poured himself a cup of coffee and settled against the counter. Gemma was almost—*almost*—too tired to appreciate the view. His biceps bulged beneath the hunter green oxford shirt he wore as he crossed his arms while sipping the hot brew. Those powerful, broad shoulders of his strained the fabric. Dark denim clung to his strong thighs.

Gemma turned away to stir her oatmeal and to regain her equilibrium. She didn't have enough energy to resist him today. She added a splash of milk to her bowl. "Do you want some?" she asked, reaching for the oatmeal box again.

His hand on hers stilled her. "You don't have to cook for me all the time, Gemma."

She smiled and used pulling two packets of oatmeal out of the box as an excuse to remove her hand from his. "This hardly counts as cooking."

"True." He took the packets from her and shooed her toward the table. "Go sit. I can handle instant oatmeal."

Gemma wasn't going to argue, and sank into a chair with her breakfast. "So, did you find out anything last night after I left?"

Ben shook his head. He shoved his bowl in the microwave and started it up. "No. Everything led us to a dead end. I'm hoping the forensic guys can pull something from the car that will help."

She felt like crying into her breakfast. It was all so surreal. She hadn't stopped praying that her friend was safe since Ben crashed her dinner last night.

Tristan wandered in just then. He took one look at

Gemma and Ben munching on oatmeal and grabbed his own bowl from the cupboard. Gemma was thankful for the measuring lines on the packets. It was Tristan-proof cooking.

Finishing her breakfast, she rose, intending to say goodbye and be on her way before she realized she didn't have any transportation. Tears welled in her eyes, and she blinked furiously. Dammit! She was stronger than this!

Gathering her emotions, Gemma turned to the men who were silently eating, each lost in his own thoughts. "Um. I need a ride to work," she said softly.

Tristan cursed while Ben just frowned.

"I'll take you," Ben said, rising with his empty bowl and mug. "We need to talk, anyway."

Flutters started in Gemma's belly. She prayed he wasn't going to bring up their kiss from the other night. He short-circuited her brain on a good day. Today, she was exhausted and her emotions had been put through the wringer. No, today was not a good day for her to talk about her feelings with this man. He'd get much more than he bargained for if he tried.

Ben did his best to keep his eyes on the road on the drive into Foggy Mountain with Gemma. He really did need to talk to her, but dreaded the conversation. She wasn't going to like what he had to say, and he didn't want to argue with her. He was too tired. He hardly slept last night. When he arrived back at the Mabley's, he did little more than strip down to his boxer briefs before sliding between the cool sheets of his bed. He had been bone-tired, but sleep was still elusive. He had willed his mind to shut off, but to no avail. Details of Stacy's disappearance continued to run through his head.

Something about the whole thing bothered him. It was

too close on the heels of Diana Lowell's murder. Especially considering that Stacy and Diana knew each other. His gut screamed the two were connected. He just didn't know why. Stacy didn't fit the profile of the other victims, but he knew somehow her disappearance was related. They'd spent hours combing the woods for signs and calling all her known friends and family, hoping they'd heard from her.

They still had nothing.

His thoughts shifted back to Gemma. If Stacy's connection to Diana Lowell bothered him, her connection to Gemma—and the fact it was Gemma's car—bothered him even more. If Stacy's disappearance really was connected to his serial killer case, then it made more sense that Gemma was the target. She'd been more involved in the investigation than Stacy.

The thought that Gemma was the real target terrified Ben. When he found her safe and sound yesterday evening, the relief nearly made his knees buckle. He'd wanted to grab her and kiss her senseless, then hide her away where he knew she would be safe.

He knew he'd been a little harsh on her in the beginning, but the thought of something happening to her had a stranglehold on him and he'd taken his frustrations with himself out on her. Thankfully, she forgave him, even if she had kept her distance. She'd joined a search party soon after they arrived at the scene. He hardly saw her after that until he and Tristan dragged her away hours later when they finally called off the search. They'd covered nearly a mile in each direction on foot, looking for Stacy. The sheriff's department even sent up a helicopter with infrared to try to track her that way. They found a bunch of small game, but no people who weren't already there searching for the missing woman. Ben had sent Gemma home after threatening her with arrest if she didn't cooperate.

Which brought him back to what he needed to talk to her about. Christ, this was gonna suck.

"Gemma." She looked over at him and he almost lost his nerve. She was struggling with so many emotions right now and he was going to add a new fear to them. "Until we figure out why Stacy was taken, I don't want you going anywhere alone. I don't like that it was your car she was in when she was kidnapped. It has me wondering who the real target was."

He watched her eyes widen as his words sank in. "You think I'm in danger? That I was the reason Stacy was kidnapped? Someone thought she was me?"

Ben grabbed her hand. "I'm just saying it's a possibility. You two share a passing resemblance. I'd rather not take any chances and have to be looking for you too. If you have to leave the center, call me or Tristan. If neither of us can get free, we'll send an officer to escort you. Don't even go outside by yourself." His tone brooked no argument.

He could feel her eyes on him as she studied him. Finally, she nodded. "Okay."

He frowned. Well, that went much easier than he had expected. "Okay? You're not going to argue?"

She shook her head. "No. I just want you to find Stacy and catch the guy. If you're worried about me being on my own and something possibly happening to me, then you're not focused on Stacy or the investigation. I just wish there was more I could do to help you."

Ben felt his heart thud, trying to break out of the box he'd built around it. This woman was incredible. Her number one concern was always for someone else. She was willing to live life in a fishbowl if it meant her friend could be safe sooner.

He cleared his throat. "You just stay safe. That's plenty."

Thankfully, he was saved from having her create more chinks in his armor as they arrived at the equestrian center. He pulled up right next to the back door and put the car in park. "I'll walk you in," he told her before she could say goodbye.

Gemma used her keys to let them in. Mara's car was already parked near the door, but for safety purposes the back door was always locked, he learned the other day. Only Mara, the three therapists, and the office manager had keys and the alarm code, for which Ben was grateful. It made the building that much more secure. But, now with Stacy Mathis missing, Ben was going to recommend Mara call the alarm company right away and have Stacy's passcode removed.

He walked Gemma to her office, where he told her to stay put until he checked out the building. Once he heard the door lock behind him, he headed to Mara's office to check on her.

He knocked softly on her door, which was slightly ajar, before pushing it open to see her sitting behind her desk, papers in hand.

"Agent Davidson. What a surprise. Is everything okay? Any news on Stacy?"

"No, not yet. I brought Gemma in, and I just wanted to check out the building before I left. Did anything look out of the ordinary to you when you came in?" he asked.

She shook her head. "No. It was all locked up tight and nothing seemed amiss, but I haven't been out of the administrative area yet. Are you expecting trouble?" she asked. Ben could see the intelligence lurking in Mara's eyes as she probed. He was glad this woman was here. She'd be a good lookout for anything unusual.

"I hope not. We're just being cautious since Stacy is missing. I'd appreciate it if you could keep an eye out for anything suspicious and tell your employees to do the same. You should also call your alarm company and have Stacy's passcode changed or removed from the system." He handed her a business card. "If you notice anything, give me a call. If I don't answer, just leave a message, and I'll call you back as soon as I can."

She took the card and nodded. "For all our sakes, I hope it's just precautionary."

"Me too. I'm going to go finish my walk-through, then I'll be on my way." He headed for the door.

The front offices were small and all the doors were locked tight. Ben scanned all probable hiding places before moving toward the arena. He pushed open the door to the cavernous space and slapped at the wall for the light switches. Without the barn doors open, and the lights off, the place was pitch black. He walked along the wall toward the stables while the stadium lights warmed up. Curious snickers greeted him as he walked between the rows of stalls. Soft snorts of annoyance at his lack of treats followed him down the aisle.

Stables cleared, he walked back into the arena and stopped dead.

In the center of the arena, naked and dumped in a heap like garbage, was Stacy Mathis.

THIRTEEN

Ben raced to the center of the arena, vaulting the fence in an easy leap. He skidded to a halt in front of the woman and landed on his knees, praying she wasn't dead. He placed two fingers against her neck. His own heart racing as he realized she still had a pulse.

He took out his phone and dialed 911. After identifying himself and requesting an ambulance and police, he hung up and raced back to the door to the front offices. Pulling it open, he yelled for Gemma, then grabbed the first aid kit off the wall. He needed a space blanket. Stacy's skin had been like ice under his fingers and she was gray.

Finding what he wanted, he ran back to the unconscious woman, reaching her just as Gemma and Mara came through the door.

"Ben? What's—oh my God!" He could hear the women coming through the gate in the fencing as he spread the thin, crinkly blanket over Stacy's unconscious form.

"She's alive," he said, turning to them. "I called for paramedics and backup. They should be here soon."

He motioned to the barn doors on the side that led to the

parking lot. "Can one of you open those?" It will be quicker for the ambulance crew to pull right up to the barn than come in through the front entrance.

Mara immediately fled to do as he asked.

Gemma knelt next to Stacy and tucked the space blanket more securely around her friend. That done, she sat back on her haunches and wrapped her arms around herself.

Ben tipped her chin up so she'd look at him. "You okay?"

She shook her head. "No."

Ben enfolded her in his arms, aching to take away Gemma's pain.

"Agent Davidson!"

Ben turned at the sound of Mara's frantic call from twenty yards away. She pointed to the dirt.

"You need to see this."

Gemma in tow, they quickly made their way to Mara's side. He heard Gemma gasp as she read what was written in the dirt. Ben felt his blood boil. *Son-of-a-bitch!!* The bastard was getting bold.

He stared down at the message, willing it to change or show him the identity of the psycho. Instead, it just stayed there. Steady. Taunting.

Next time, Agent Davidson, I'll get the right one, and she won't be as lucky.

~

Gemma stared restlessly at the crime scene techs from her perch in the bleachers at the far end of the arena. They swarmed the enclosure, looking for clues to help identify the person who kidnapped and then dumped Stacy so callously.

She shifted, impatient. She needed to *do* something. As soon as Stacy had been carted off to the hospital, she'd helped

Mara, Liz, and the office manager, Pam, call all the patients on the schedule for today and tomorrow to inform them the center was closed. With the four of them working, it only took a few minutes to make all the necessary calls. Now, she just had to sit here and wait for Ben or Tristan to finish so she could leave. Sitting around twiddling her thumbs was not her forte. Anyone who knew her could attest to that. Gemma hated to be idle. But right now, she didn't have a choice.

Her eyes wandered over the men and women canvassing the arena until they landed on Ben. He stood next to her brother and another detective, their heads together as they talked. He'd told her in no uncertain terms she was to stay where he could see her at all times until he could set up a protection detail full of people he or her brother trusted implicitly.

So, here she was. Twiddling her thumbs. She just wanted to go home and go back to bed. Gemma couldn't help but think that if she went to sleep, she'd wake up and this would have all been a terrible nightmare.

She scoffed at herself. *Yeah. And the sun will rise in the west tomorrow.*

Sighing, she leaned back against the uncomfortable bleacher seating and settled in to wait.

Gradually, the sights and sounds faded as she drifted off. It wasn't until the sound of heavy footsteps on the metal stairs that she snapped awake. Wincing, she sat up and turned toward the sound as she stretched her neck to relieve the kinks.

Ben climbed the bleachers, eyes locked on her. She cast a quick glance behind him at the rapidly emptying arena. "Are you finished?" She stood up as he reached her. "Have you heard anything about Stacy? Is she going to be okay?"

He didn't respond. Instead, he just stood there and stared at her, his blue-green eyes coated in a sheen of silver in the harsh lighting. Just as she was about to ask again, he grabbed her and pulled her against him. His mouth slammed down on hers. Gemma froze, stunned. After about two seconds, though, her hormones kicked in and she was kissing him back.

She threaded her fingers into his hair and tugged at the short strands, trying to hold him closer. Ben's hands roamed her back before he banded one arm tight around her waist while the other snaked up her spine to her neck where he cupped the back of her head, holding her steady as he ravaged her mouth. Gemma's knees turned to Jell-O. She clutched his shoulders to hold herself upright.

Just when she thought she really would combust, he gentled the kiss and pulled back. She was grateful for the steel band of his arm around her. Her legs had gone past the Jell-O stage to water. She stared up at him, stunned by the fire that had erupted between them. This kiss was nothing like the one from the other night. That one had been the release of all the raw hunger building between them since they met. This one was full of an intense heat brought on by the emotional roller coaster of the last twenty-four hours. Gemma felt a hint of desperation and relief when he first kissed her.

He rested his forehead on hers. She watched the muscles of his jaw flex as he fought to tamp down the riotous emotions she could see coursing through his eyes.

"That was not my intention when I came up here," he finally said, voice gruff.

Gemma smiled softly. "I'm not complaining." God, but how she wasn't complaining. He could do that anytime he wanted.

His answering chuckle finally broke the tension between them. He straightened, but didn't release her. "How are you holding up?"

She caressed his jaw with her thumb as she rested her hand against his neck. "Better now. And not just because of the...

that." She gestured between them. "I seem to always feel better when you're near."

She felt his fingers bite into the flesh on her hips at her words. His jaw flexed beneath her touch and his eyes closed. Gemma felt a moment of elation that he seemed as affected by her as she was by him.

He swooped in and kissed her hard one more time before releasing her to grab her hand. "Come on." He led her down the bleachers. "Tristan and I set up a protection detail for you. I'm going to take you home now."

"You never did answer my questions, you know," Gemma said, following him down the bleachers and through the arena to the parking lot.

He glanced at her, frowning.

"Stacy? How is she?"

The frown disappeared, and he nodded. "I got off with the hospital a little while ago. She's got a concussion and a broken arm from the accident. A few other assorted bumps and bruises, but otherwise she's fine."

Relief flooded Gemma. "Thank God. Is the concussion why she was unconscious?"

Ben shook his head. They had reached his SUV, and he opened the passenger door so she could climb inside. "She'd been drugged. Ketamine."

Gemma halted in the process of fastening her seatbelt. "Ketamine?" That was a powerful tranquilizer. Coupled with her head wound, Stacy was lucky to be alive.

Ben nodded. "This guy's smart. She won't remember a thing about what happened, so even if she did see his face, she won't be able to tell us a damn thing."

Fourteen

Ben wasted little time getting Gemma settled in at home. After introducing her to her guard, he all but ran from the house like the Hounds of Hell were on his heels. That kiss and her confession left his emotions raw. He needed time to think. And some distance. When she was near, he forgot his resolve not to get involved with her as well as his oppositions to permanency.

He pulled into the police station lot and quickly headed inside, switching mental gears. His relationship with Gemma could wait. He had a more pressing concern, and that was finding the person threatening her.

Once again, he had to tamp down the blind rage that threatened to overwhelm him at the idea of someone wanting to hurt sweet, beautiful Gemma. If it weren't for the fact he knew she would refuse, he would hide her away until he could catch the bastard behind all this. He might make her do it anyway.

Tristan was waiting for him as soon as he stepped into the squad room. "The crime lab finished with Gemma's car. The brake lines were cut. It's a miracle Stacy made it as far as she did and that she didn't careen over an embankment."

Damn. Ben scrubbed a hand down his face and rubbed his jaw. That was not what he wanted to hear. "Can't say I'm surprised. He must have cut the lines while the car was parked at the equestrian center, then followed her when she left. He likely mistook Stacy for Gemma when Stacy left in Gemma's car. From a distance, and with all the trees shading that parking lot, it'd be easy to mistake one woman for the other. What about the center? How did he get inside? Mara said all looked well and that the alarm was on when she got there."

"He bypassed the alarm at the rear arena door. Used some kind of gadget to fake the system into thinking someone entered the code. Techs found scratch marks inside the alarm box where he hooked it up. Otherwise, we might not have figured out how he did it."

Fantastic. A tech-savvy sociopath. No wonder the guy had eluded law enforcement for so long.

"Why is he targeting my sister?" Tristan stepped closer. "That message in the dirt was for you. Personally. Why is Gemma involved in a personal vendetta against you? Is there more to your relationship with her than what either of you have let on? I saw that kiss you laid on her earlier."

Ben straightened at Tristan's tone. He couldn't blame the man for being angry and accusatory. Hell, he was angry at himself for getting Gemma involved. If he were in Tristan's shoes, he'd be feeling and acting the exact same way.

"I admit, there's something about your sister that gets to me. She's like no other woman I've ever met. But other than that kiss today, we've done nothing to suggest to others we're anything but friends."

Tristan's eyes narrowed. "To others? That mean you've done stuff that would suggest otherwise when others weren't present?"

Ben's face hardened. "I told you once before that what happens between Gemma and me is none of your damned business. She is an adult capable of making her own decisions. Butt out, Mabley."

"She's my sister, Davidson. I'm not going to stand by and watch her get her heart broken. Or in this case, worse." Tristan refused to back down. He still stood toe to toe with Ben.

Ben clenched his teeth. "You know I will do everything humanly possible to protect Gemma."

"Even leave her be?"

He sincerely wished it was that easy. Or that he'd stayed far, far away from her, like he'd been telling himself to do from the moment he awakened to her warm weight sprawled across his body. "I think it's a little late for that. No matter what our relationship is, this guy believes she means something special to me. I don't think we can convince him otherwise."

Tristan ran a hand through his hair, anger and frustration crisscrossing his face. He stalked several paces away before turning around to face Ben again. "We have to get her out of here. Hide her somewhere."

Ben scoffed. "Have you met your sister? She'll agree to protection because she's not stupid, but there's too much going on here—too many people who need her help—for her to turn her back and hide."

Tristan paced away again.

"She's got a round-the-clock guard in place. We'll both be in the house at night. She's not going to be alone. Ever," Ben argued. "We've got new leads now." He put a hand out and grasped Tristan's shoulder as he walked past for the third time. "I know us. I know how we operate. You and I make a good team, Tristan. We'll catch this bastard. And we can take turns nailing his ass to the wall when we do. Okay?"

Some of the fight leached out of Tristan's body. He nodded. "You're right. We do make a good team. This sicko messed up when he decided to target my sister. But I'd still feel better if she left town."

Ben wholeheartedly agreed on all counts. By targeting Gemma, their killer had upped the ante and made both men more determined than ever to catch him. He didn't stand a chance now. And Ben would breathe easier too if Gemma wasn't in immediate danger. "We can suggest that she leave, but you and I both know she'll likely refuse to go."

Tristan nodded. "Doesn't mean I'm not going to try my damnedest to convince her otherwise first."

Ben sighed. That was a conversation he was not looking forward to.

~

"Holy shit, Sis!"

Gemma whirled around at her brother's exclamation. He and Ben were staring at the array of baked goods lining the counters of the kitchen. After Ben dropped her off, she'd taken a short nap before nightmares awakened her. Unable to go back to sleep, she tried to watch some television to distract herself, but it hadn't helped. Working with her hands had always been the best way for her to sort through her feelings and take her mind off her problems, so she'd decided to bake something. One something turned into two somethings and then many somethings. She'd used up every bit of the baking ingredients she had in the house.

"I got bored," she said in reply. It wasn't a total lie. That had been part of her problem. She wasn't used to so much free time. But there was no way she was going to tell the two of them the truth. If she thought they were overprotective now, it would only get ten times worse if they knew how scared she really was.

Tristan inspected the fruits of her labor. "What are you going to do with all of this?"

She shrugged. "I figured the two of you would eat some of it and the rest you could take to work."

Tristan laughed. "How many people do you think work for the county sheriff's office? Geez, Gems."

Gemma blushed even as she straightened at his words. She glanced over at Ben, who stood in the doorway silently watching her and Tristan. "Maybe so, but when have you ever brought back leftovers?"

"Good point." Tristan grabbed a chocolate chip cookie off a plate and shoved the entire thing in his mouth. He moaned in ecstasy. "God, I love it when you bake. Ben, you need to try these." He shoved another cookie in his mouth.

One corner of Ben's mouth crooked up in a smile at Tristan's obvious delight. "I'll pass for now, thanks." He looked at Gemma. "We need to talk."

Gemma gulped, nervously. Even with the smile, his words were ominous.

He pulled out a chair from the table and motioned for her to sit. She sat on the edge and folded her hands in her lap to keep them busy. He pulled another chair closer and sat in front of her. Gemma could hear the scrape of a third chair behind her as Tristan brought a chair around to sit at her back.

"What's going on?" she asked, suddenly nervous. She looked from one man to the other. They wore matching expressions of wariness.

Ben's hand covered hers and held tight. "We got the report back on your car. Someone cut the brake lines."

Gemma felt her eyes widen. "I knew it wasn't a simple accident, but it never occurred to me there would be sabotage."

Ben glanced over at her shoulder at Tristan. Her eyes narrowed as she realized they were ganging up on her.

"What?" she asked, her voice dropping.

Ben took a deep breath. "We want you to take a vacation. Maybe go out west and visit your parents."

Gemma was shaking her head before he even finished. "I'm not hiding. No." She stood and walked across the kitchen to the cookies she'd been removing from their pans when Ben and Tristan came home.

"Gemma, we're talking about your life," Tristan said.

She looked back at him with a glare. "You think I don't know that?" She stepped toward him. "But I'm not going to run away. I trust the two of you and the entire sheriff's department to protect me. If I go into hiding, you may never catch this guy, and I have responsibilities I can't just abandon." She shook the spatula in Tristan's face.

He closed his eyes, frustration apparent on his face. "Gems—"

Ben waved him off. A silent argument waged between the two before Gemma watched in amazement as her brother huffed, then stomped out of the kitchen.

As soon as Tristan exited the room, Ben walked up to her and took the spatula from her fingers. He tossed it behind her, where it clattered on the granite counter, before he backed her up until her butt met the counter's cold surface. His arms framed her on either side, and he bent close. Gemma's pulse skittered wildly without her permission at his nearness. She cursed her unruly body. She knew he was trying to intimidate her. He wasn't having that effect, though.

"Ben—"

"No," he muttered. "Gemma, this is about your safety. You're not safe here. You need to leave."

She agreed, partially. But she wasn't leaving.

She tilted her head and studied him. There was a wariness in his eyes that had nothing to do with her involvement in his case. He *wanted* her to leave, she suddenly realized. Like a bolt of lightning, she recognized that she made him nervous. Nervous that she was getting too far under his skin. He was attracted to her and it wasn't welcome.

She knew how he felt. But she was tired of fighting it. What he made her feel was too good, and it was worth taking the risk. She'd realized that this morning when he kissed her senseless in the arena. He needed to realize that too.

No. She definitely wasn't leaving.

She straightened. With the way he was leaning toward her, her face lined up perfectly with his. "You're scared of me."

His eyes widened. He straightened and dropped his arms. "Gemma, this is not about us. This is about the lunatic after you."

"Not entirely," she countered. "You want me to leave, so I'll be safer. But there's no guarantee he won't follow me. And you want me to leave so you can ignore what's happening here." She waggled a finger between the two of them.

He tried hard to hide his feelings, but Gemma saw the flare of fear flash through his eyes before steely determination replaced it.

"No. What's going on here is irrelevant. This is about getting you away from a killer."

"Nope," she said, popping the *p*.

"Gemma," he growled.

She threw her arms around his shoulders and pressed her body against his. She felt every one of his muscles tighten as he fought not to touch her. She nuzzled her nose into his neck and along the outer shell of his ear. "I'm not leaving, Ben, so you better come to terms with this—" she sucked lightly on his earlobe, eliciting a low growl. "And with the fact that I'm here to stay."

He pulled away to look at her then. She let her feelings show, not bothering to hide them anymore. If there was one thing this situation with the serial killer was teaching her, it was that it just wasn't worth fighting feelings like these. Something this strong should be embraced. The rest would work itself out later.

"Dammit, Gemma," he growled. If possible, his body felt even more rigid under her hands than before as he fought harder for control.

Damn military training...

Determined to break the iron grip he had on his emotions, Gemma cupped his cheek. She fluttered a soft kiss over his lips, igniting the fire. His breath puffed over her face as it grew unsteady. She ran her hand up to his hair and tugged the soft strands, her lips hovering millimeters from his. "My only question now is when are you going to stop being afraid of what you feel for me and realize this is worth fighting for?"

She kissed him then, immediately begging entrance to his mouth. He didn't resist, his arms going around her as he kissed her back.

Gemma felt a moment of weightlessness as he wrapped his hands around the backs of her thighs and lifted her onto the counter. Pans clattered. The thought that the noise might bring Tristan running was quickly squelched as Ben stepped closer, pressing his body to hers.

Automatically, she wrapped her legs around him, holding him close. She had certainly snapped his control. His hands were trailing fire across her body. They dove beneath her shirt, ghosting over her skin and ratcheting up her arousal. She jerked at the intense pleasure that shot straight through her at the feel of his hands on her bare skin. His mouth plundered hers, sending fire straight to her core.

Eager to feel his skin beneath her fingers, she tugged his shirt from his pants and slid her hands under it to run them over his abs. Her fingers explored the ridges and valleys with their fine dusting of hair, the muscles jumping beneath her touch. She skimmed her hands up the hard planes to tangle in the whirls of hair covering his chest. Gemma ached to see and feel him against her.

Suddenly, cold air washed over her as Ben pulled away. She scrambled to hold on to the counter as he unwrapped her legs and stepped to the side.

Mouth opening to ask why he stopped, Gemma heard the footsteps coming down the hall from the living room. Understanding dawned, and she hastily pulled her clothes back into place. There was no way Tristan wouldn't know something happened, but they could at least minimize the shock value.

Ben yanked her off the counter and in front of him to hide his aroused state just as Tristan rounded the corner.

"Gemma, you have—" Tristan started, then stopped as he took in their disheveled appearance and Ben's arm wrapped around Gemma, his hand splayed over her belly.

He shook his head. "What? Are you trying to butter her up to get her to leave?"

Gemma's eyes widened, and she whirled around. "Is that what that was about?"

Ben stared at her, incredulous. "You started it, not me. I tried to deny this." He gestured between them with one finger. "You wouldn't let me. Remember?" Anger tinged his voice, and Gemma blushed furiously.

"You're right. I'm sorry. I'm a little out of sorts at the moment—for numerous reasons."

He nodded, then turned his gaze to her brother. She watched the anger in Ben's eyes turn to fury.

"And you're an ass, Mabley. You know me better than that."

"I thought I did. Then you started making out with my little sister in my kitchen." Tristan's furious expression matched Ben's.

"That's enough!" She stepped directly in front of Tristan and stuck her finger in his chest. "Every time I like a man, you do this. You attack him like he's a worthless piece of scum. And I know you know he is not." She pointed at Ben. "That man saved your life more than once and you're practically accusing him of assaulting me. For your information, he tried to keep his distance, but I forced the issue to get him to admit how he felt. I'm tired of the overprotective bullshit—from both of you!" She looked between the two men, who now looked chagrined; Tristan rightly more than Ben.

"Now," she poked Tristan in the chest again. "You owe Ben one hell of an apology."

She whirled around and pierced Ben with a heated look. "And we're not finished with this." She marched to the door, pulling her anger around her like a cloak. As she passed through the doorway, she tossed one last pronouncement over her shoulder.

"And I am *not* leaving!"

Fifteen

Gemma let out a sigh of relief as she shut herself in her office at work on Monday. Things had been tense at home since her argument with Ben and Tristan several days earlier.

They both ignored her for the most part, except to tell her who was driving her where and who her guard was for the day. Tristan glowered at her anytime she was in sight and spoke to her only when necessary. She knew she'd upset him by refusing to leave and by calling him out on his crap, but she was truly sick of being treated like a child. Things were going to change. He'd softened some over the weekend after Ben left to go back to Richmond to pick up more clothes and give a full briefing to his SAC.

Ben wasn't glowering at her, but he was avoiding her, leaving Tristan to take over chauffeuring her around. The only time he came back to the house was to shower and sleep. When he left Saturday morning, she had to fight the urge to throw herself at him and beg him not to go, or to take her with him. She hadn't slept well all weekend with him gone, which was saying something, because she hadn't slept well since this whole ordeal began over a week ago.

The men made up the same night as the argument, though. They were joking and laughing like nothing was wrong when she walked into the kitchen the next morning.

She blew out a frustrated breath as she put her things away and booted up her computer. Ben couldn't avoid her forever. With the heat they shared, he'd cave eventually. Military training or not, he was still a man. And a hot-blooded one at that.

Gemma fanned herself as memories of the other night flooded her brain.

Enough! She shoved those thoughts aside. If she dwelled on them, she would be a quivering mass of goo for Mara to scrape off the desk chair.

The one saving grace for the week was Stacy's progress. She was recovering well and went home on Saturday. Gemma visited her a couple of times at the hospital and at home. She felt so guilty for her part in the accident that she baked more cookies and pastries and cooked several easy to reheat meals to stock Stacy's freezer. Stacy told her repeatedly she didn't hold any hard feelings against her, for which Gemma was grateful. Things could have turned out so differently in so many ways.

Mentally slapping herself to shake off her musings, Gemma gathered what she would need for her first few sessions and locked up her office. Time to pull her head out of the clouds and do her job.

~

Ben pulled his cell from his belt as it vibrated. Gemma's number stared back at him, mocking him for the coward that he was. He had run back to Richmond over the weekend like a rabbit from a wolf. Gemma had been spot on with her accusations last week. She absolutely scared the shit out of him. He always told himself he didn't do permanent, and he'd never been tempted to even think otherwise.

Until her.

Now, permanent didn't seem like such a bad thought, and that was what scared him. He knew his track record and his family's track record with relationships, and it wasn't pretty. He didn't want to enter into something "permanent" with Gemma, only to have it end up being temporary and hurt her in the process. She deserved better than that. She deserved someone who knew how to do permanent.

He slid his thumb over the screen of his phone and reluctantly answered. "Yeah, Gems."

"I just wanted to let you know I'm taking a group out on a trail ride at Biltmore this evening. I should be done about seven-thirty."

Alarm bells clanged in his head. "Wait. When did this happen? Where's your guard? Did you clear this with Tristan?"

"Just a little bit ago. He's right here. And no, I haven't talked to Tristan since he dropped me off this morning," she said, answering his questions succinctly.

He sighed. She was still angry. "Gemma, we've talked about this. You can't go off gallivanting around in public."

"I'll be fine. It's not like I'm going to be alone. A guy I know from my riding club called to ask if I could show some of his family around the trails near Biltmore. He was going to do it, but he hurt his knee playing tag football a few days ago and can't ride. They came to town over the weekend for a family wedding and are leaving tomorrow. They really want to see the estate. I need to get out for a while, Ben. I've been cooped up in either the house or the office for nearly a week, and I'm going crazy."

Ben sighed. "What about your guard? Is he going with you?"

She hesitated, and Ben knew he wasn't going to like the answer.

"I asked. He said he doesn't ride."

Yep. He didn't like it. "You have to have a guard. I can't get away yet. I'm still playing catch up from the weekend."

"Well, Tristan's not answering his phone and I need to leave. I already loaded up my horse, Jasper, and Deputy Maxwell is going to drive me to the estate and wait with the truck."

He muttered a few choice expletives under his breath. He'd seen Tristan walk in with a suspect from another case about fifteen minutes ago. He was going to be tied up for a while. "Gemma—"

She cut him off. "I'll be fine. I just called to give you a heads-up. Unless you plan on locking me in my room and standing guard, I'm going."

He bit back a growl of frustration. He was sorely tempted. But she was right. The danger was minimal. It was unplanned and she would be in a group. He was overreacting based solely on his feelings for her. "Fine. But you check in with Maxwell every fifteen minutes and you call me as soon as you're done. I'll meet you back at the equestrian center and help you get Jasper settled, then I'll take you home."

"Sounds like a plan. And seriously, Ben, don't worry. I'll be fine."

His head knew that, so why was his gut screaming otherwise?

Sixteen

Gemma blinked, trying to bring the world back into focus. Why were things spinning? The leaves on the trees above her swirled wildly in her field of vision. A face appeared over her, and she tried to draw back, startled, but met resistance against her back. All of a sudden, she realized she was on the ground, staring up at a man who kneeled over her.

Panicking, Gemma struggled to scramble away. Hands grabbed her to hold her still. She screamed. "Let me go!"

The hands immediately released her, and Gemma tried to back up. Splitting pain in her skull stopped her. She grabbed her head and rolled to her side, moaning.

Why does my head feel like Wile E. Coyote set off one of his Acme bombs inside it?

"Gemma? Gemma? Can you hear me?"

She nodded and pain split her skull again. Her stomach rolled. "Oh, God. I'm going to be sick." Choking back the bile rising in her throat, Gemma tried to take a deep breath. Pain rushed through her torso, making her gasp.

What the hell?!

Unable to draw a decent breath, she started hyperventilating. Black spots dotted her vision, and the pain in her head increased again. She fought to stay conscious, terrified. *I can't let him take me!*

The black spots solidified and started crowding out the edges of her vision. Unable to stop it, Gemma prayed this was all just a nightmare and that she'd awaken safe in her bed.

Her limbs went limp as the blackness finally consumed her.

Ben and Tristan pushed through the E.R. doors at a near run. People scattered as they barreled past. Those in line at the admissions desk wisely stepped aside to allow the two men up to the window.

"Gentlemen, you can't just barge up here like that. There is a line for a reason," the clerk behind the Plexiglas informed them.

Tristan slapped his shield against the window. "Sheriff's department. We're looking for a patient who was brought in not long ago. Gemma Mabley."

The clerk quickly looked up the name. "She's still in the treatment room. If you'll have a seat in the waiting area, someone will be with you as soon as possible."

It was Ben's turn to show his badge, knowing it would carry more weight. "FBI. We need to get back there. She's under police protection. We need to know what happened and to find out if this is connected to our case." It wasn't a lie—they did need to know if what happened today was connected to the case—but he figured this information would get him further than telling her that Tristan was her brother, and that he was—whatever he was to her.

"Sir, I can't let you past the doors without a doctor's approval. If you'll have a seat, I'll call the exam room and have them send someone out to talk to you." The clerk, a woman in her mid-sixties, stared them down with a stare Ben was sure she had perfected on her children and grandchildren. He'd seen the same look on his mother's face often enough to know they weren't going to get anything out of her. He wasn't in the mood for the flak that would come with forcing his way into the treatment area, so he nodded reluctantly.

"Tell them to hurry," he told her. He put a hand on Tristan's arm and motioned for the man to follow him to the waiting area, satisfied to see the woman reaching for the phone as he walked away.

Ben settled against the wall while Tristan paced.

Tristan barely did three turns of the room before a man in blue scrubs and an air of authority pushed through the doors leading to the treatment area and zeroed in on them. "Are you the ones asking about Gemma Mabley?"

Tristan was at the man's side in two long strides. Ben was close behind.

"She's my sister," Tristan said. "What happened? Is she all right?"

The doctor eyed Ben.

"Friend," Ben said at the questioning lift of the man's eyebrow.

The doctor nodded. "I'm Dr. Thompson. Ms. Mabley was thrown from her horse. She likely sustained a concussion and some bruised ribs. We're getting ready to send her up to CT now."

"Can we see her before you send her up?" Tristan asked.

The doctor hesitated slightly. Ben put on his most intimidating agent face and silently stared the man down. Neither he nor Tristan would relax until they had seen her and verified for themselves that she was okay. And where was her damned police guard? They hadn't seen hide nor hair of the man yet.

"Okay," the doctor finally replied. "But only for a minute."

Ben followed behind Tristan and the doctor as they swept through the doors to the E.R.'s inner sanctum. Emotions roiled through him—fear, relief, anger. Each was vying for the top spot. They really needed to stop getting these calls about Gemma. If the woman wasn't so damn stubborn and would just leave like they asked, then they probably would.

Or at the very least, she could stay inside, where she was safe behind four walls and a bodyguard. That would alleviate the problem as well.

The doctor swept aside a curtain to reveal a bevy of activity. Nurses bustled to and fro, papers and medical paraphernalia in hand. Ben's eyes paused on the man leaning against the back wall, trying to stay out of the way—Deputy Maxwell.

Well, that answers that question.

He nodded at the man in recognition, then continued his perusal of the room. His gaze finally landed on the frightfully pale woman lying on the gurney in the center of the activity. Her chestnut hair stuck out in multiple directions, with leaves and twigs poking through the strands. Dirt streaked her too white skin.

Ben hovered near the entrance to the cubicle while Tristan hurried to his sister's side.

"Gemma! Are you all right?" Tristan asked, grasping her hand.

Ben watched, alarmed, as her head lolled toward his voice. He hoped that was a side effect of painkillers and not her head wound. Her eyes were wide and frightful. "You can't let him get me, Tristan! You have to stop him! Where's Ben?! He'll help you."

Ben's heart stuttered at the abject fear in her voice. In a few long strides, he was at her side, holding her other hand. "I'm right here, Gems. You're safe."

Her head swung around drunkenly at the sound of his voice. She winced, and he watched her fight back a bout of nausea. Ben bent low and twined the fingers of his free hand in her hair. "Baby, you're okay. You're at the hospital. You fell off your horse."

A frown wrinkled her brow as she tried to focus.

Tristan followed Ben's lead and bent in close. "Sis, do you remember what happened? Why did Jasper toss you?"

Her frown intensified as she struggled to remember. "Noise. There was a loud noise, and he reared."

Ben caught the frown Tristan sent his way. "You're sure?" Tristan asked.

Gemma nodded slowly. Her eyelids were starting to droop.

"We're ready to take her to CT now." One of the nurses had sidled up next to him and spoke softly. Ben nodded at her.

"Tris," he said quietly.

Tristan looked up and Ben motioned toward the nurse. He nodded as he caught Ben's meaning. "Sis, the doctors need to run some more tests on you right now, but Ben and I will see you later."

Ben felt her hand tighten around his briefly before she nodded. The nurse unlocked the brake on the gurney and slowly started to wheel it out of the room. Ben let Gemma's hand slide free from his, leaving a bereft feeling in its wake.

Tristan stepped close as they watched the medical team take her away.

"It doesn't make sense," Tristan said, staring after the disappearing gurney.

Ben looked at his old friend. "What doesn't?"

Tristan looked at him. "Jasper spooking at a loud noise. He is the most unflappable horse I've ever run across. He's naturally steadfast, but he's been well-trained on normal stressors, too, because he doubles as a therapy horse. Loud noise—commotion of any kind—shouldn't have startled him. Not like that. No, something else besides a noise spooked that horse. I want to talk to the people she was with and have a look at him. See if we can't piece together what happened."

Ben nodded, trusting Tristan's instincts. They'd saved his ass more than once. He wasn't going to doubt the man now. Not with Gemma's safety on the line. "Might as well start with him." He gestured to Deputy Maxwell, who still stood near the wall, watching them patiently.

Ben motioned the man over. "Tell us what you know," he ordered.

"I'm afraid I don't know much. I was with the truck when one of the other riders came barreling out of the woods on her horse about the same time an ambulance screamed into the parking lot.

"I asked what was going on, and she said Gemma fell off her horse. She took one of the medics back with her on horseback while the other one and I ran behind. When we reached the group, Gemma was unconscious and the medic was assessing her."

"Did she miss a check-in?" Tristan asked.

Deputy Maxwell shook his head. "No. She'd been texting me regularly to tell me she was safe. She was due for another check-in about the time the ambulance showed up."

"You're sure it was Gemma texting you?" Tristan asked.

Maxwell pulled out his phone and looked up the messages. He handed it to Tristan. "Read those and tell me that doesn't sound like her. I may not have known her long, but I've quickly learned she's got a wicked sense of humor and she's none too happy about being followed around 24/7."

Tristan grunted in agreement as he read. "It was definitely her." He glanced at Ben. "These have her brand of sarcasm all over them." He handed the deputy back his phone.

"All right. Is there anything else you remember or noticed?" Ben asked.

Deputy Maxwell shook his head. "No. That was about the extent of my involvement. Once the paramedics and I arrived on scene, the rest of the group backed away so we could do our jobs. I left with Gemma, so I didn't get a chance to talk with any of them."

Ben led the way out of the cubicle, the others following. "Maxwell, I want you to stay with Gemma as planned. We'll talk to hospital security so they know you're supposed to be hanging around."

He stopped at the central work desk for the E.R. staff and found Dr. Thompson.

"Dr. Thompson, this deputy needs to stay close to Ms. Mabley. Does he need an escort to get to CT?"

Dr. Thompson looked at Maxwell. "Have you been cleared with hospital security yet?"

"Haven't had time, doc," Maxwell said.

The doctor rose. "Then yes, you'll need an escort." He flagged down an orderly. "Can you show this officer to CT, please? He needs to stay with a patient. Gemma Mabley."

The orderly nodded and Maxwell followed him from the E.R.

Dr. Thompson turned to the two men who had invaded his sanctum. "Is this all really necessary? That man was terribly disruptive when Ms. Mabley was brought in. He refused to leave and threatened to arrest anyone who tried to remove him from the area."

Ben clenched his jaw, trying not to deck the arrogant physician. He thrust an arm out across Tristan's chest to halt the step he took toward the man. "Ms. Mabley is the target of a violent man. I assure you, the precautions are very necessary."

Dr. Thompson frowned. "Well, please clear your officer with hospital security, so there aren't any more incidents." Clearly finished with them, the doctor spun around and grabbed a chart off the desk.

Ben shook his head and pulled Tristan from the E.R. "Let it go, Mabley. He's an arrogant prick, but he's not worth the paperwork."

A plan began formulating in Ben's mind for what they needed to do next as they headed back to the waiting room. After they talked to hospital security, he needed to get his hands on Gemma's cell so he could contact the guy who asked her to take the trail ride in the first place and track down that group.

Headed for the corridor that would lead them to the hospital security office, a man stepped in his path.

"I heard you asking about Gemma. Is she going to be okay?" The man's worried gaze bounced between Ben and Tristan.

"Who are you?" Tristan asked, stepping forward.

"Robert Cassidy. I was part of the group Gemma took out," the man replied.

"Can you tell us what happened, Mr. Cassidy?" Ben asked. He took stock of the man before him. About fifty, the man was fit and several inches shorter than his own six-foot-three. Hair more gray than brown anymore was still thick on his head and cut well. Lines bracketing the man's eyes and his dark tan indicated he spent a lot of time outside. His dark brown eyes looked genuinely worried about Gemma.

Cassidy stared at a point beyond Ben's shoulder, not seeing the present. "Um, we were just riding along the trail, laughing and talking, when we heard a loud bang. Gemma's horse reared. She tried to calm him, but he was freaked. We heard another bang, then her horse bucked hard, and she went flying. She landed against a fallen tree." He looked at Ben and Tristan then. "I've never seen anything like it, and I've been on the back of a horse nearly my entire life. She was so still we all feared she was seriously hurt or worse. Is she okay?" he asked again.

Tristan nodded. "A few bumps and a concussion, but nothing that won't heal in time. So, you said you heard two bangs?" he said, echoing the question foremost in Ben's head.

Cassidy nodded.

"You're sure?" Ben asked.

Cassidy nodded again. "Definitely. I don't think the horse would have tossed her without the second one. She almost had him under control when the second one occurred."

Ben frowned and exchanged a glance with Tristan. He didn't like where this was headed. "Mr. Cassidy, can you describe the bangs?"

The man frowned. "Sharp, like the retort of a rifle, but a little more muffled, I guess."

Ben exchanged another look with Tristan, this one more alarmed. "Where is the rest of your group, Mr. Cassidy?"

"Back at the hotel by now, I would imagine. I followed the ambulance here to wait on word about Gemma's condition while the rest of the group took care of the horses."

Tristan wrote down the name of the hotel where the group was staying and their names before promising that someone would be by tonight to interview them all.

"I don't like this," Ben said to Tristan as they headed down the corridor.

"Me neither. I want to get a look at that horse. My gut says he got shot with a BB gun. Unless the gun went off right beside him, rifle fire would not startle that horse like that, and even then, he'd only sidestep."

After informing hospital security of the situation and the

need for an armed guard, Ben and Tristan headed to their cars, the need for Gemma's phone gone now that they'd located the group.

"Let's head to the hotel and find out what happened to Jasper, then go take a look at him," Tristan said.

Ben nodded in agreement. "I'll follow you."

The hotel wasn't far, for which Ben was thankful. He didn't want to be alone with his thoughts and emotions at the moment. They were a jumble of frustration, rage, and a more tender emotion he refused to name. Seeing Gemma so out of it was frightening. She was such a strong woman that it was hard to see her vulnerable like that.

As he pulled into the hotel parking lot, he forced his mind back on task. They needed answers, and he hoped the riding group could shed some more light on what had happened. It could all just be a coincidence. The horse could have spooked from the noise, like Mr. Cassidy said. But Ben had a feeling there was more to it than that. He prayed he was wrong, but his gut said otherwise.

SEVENTEEN

"Anything?" Ben asked Tristan as they met up later in the hotel lobby. They had split the list of names and just finished interviewing everyone.

Tristan shook his head. "All their stories were consistent with Cassidy's. Two sharp, muffled retorts and Gemma landing against the tree. No one saw or heard anything out of the ordinary except the noise."

Ben clenched his fists in frustration. "I got the same thing. I think it's time we go look at Jasper."

Tristan nodded. "You drive. Since he was taken to the Biltmore stables with the other horses, the equestrian center's truck is still there. After we look him over, we can take him and the truck back where they belong."

On their drive over, Tristan called the Biltmore's stable manager, asking the man to meet them there to let them in. Ben followed Tristan's directions, and they were soon pulling onto the massive estate. A truck with a single occupant met them at the front gate and led them back to the stables.

Ben parked next to the pickup, and both men climbed out.

"Mr. Jenkins?" Ben asked.

The man nodded as he closed his door.

Ben held out a hand. "Special Agent Ben Davidson, FBI. This is Detective Tristan Mabley, Gemma Mabley's brother."

Mr. Jenkins shook both their hands in a firm grasp. "I'm real sorry to hear your sister got hurt, detective. How is she?"

"Concussed and bruised, but otherwise okay," Tristan replied.

"Good, good. So, you're here to get her horse, right?" Jenkins started walking toward the stables. Horses whinnied as he pulled open the heavy barn doors.

"That's right."

"He's a fine animal, detective. It's obvious he's been well-trained and well-cared for. Must have been quite something that came out of nowhere to have spooked him like that." Jenkins led them down the row of stalls about halfway before coming to a halt. Gemma's horse, Jasper, poked his russet head over the stable door and nudged Tristan.

"Hey boy. You had quite the night, huh?" Tristan rubbed the horse between his eyes and patted him on the neck. "Let's get you home, all right?"

Jasper whickered softly.

"Did anyone check him over for injuries when he was brought back?" Ben asked. Tristan unlatched the door and stepped inside while Ben spoke to the manager.

Jenkins scratched his head. "We didn't, but I don't know about the riders in her group. They brought all the horses in and removed their tack. I had a groom helping to take them to their stalls, but he just put them in and closed the doors. No one said anything about any injuries to the horses, though."

Ben nodded and turned his attention to Tristan, who was inspecting the horse. He ran his hands slowly over Jasper's smooth coat from front to back, feeling for abnormalities. As he rounded Jasper's rear, he suddenly stopped.

"Hey, Ben. Come look at this."

Ben stepped inside, moving behind the horse to Tristan's side.

Tristan pointed to a spot very close to Jasper's tail. "If I hadn't been looking for it, I don't think I'd have seen it."

Ben peered closer. To the right of the tail were two small lumps with tufts of hair missing. His blood ran cold as the implications sank in. Their killer was much more adept at keeping tabs on Gemma than they thought, and he was well-prepared. Gemma's jaunt to Biltmore was last minute. Their suspect must have had the gun already with him. It also meant he was someone who blended in very well around here and wouldn't raise suspicion walking around. Or very good at hiding.

Ben looked up at Tristan. "You were right. He's been shot." His shock was brief as anger swiftly replaced it. He stepped back. "Let's get him loaded and get back to Foggy Mountain."

Tristan nodded. In minutes, they had the horse loaded and were on their way home.

While Tristan drove the truck and horse back to town, Ben headed back to the hotel to question the riding group again. Now that they knew foul play was involved, it was important to reconstruct the scene. He was hoping their stalker would be arrogant enough to believe Ben and the rest of the police would see this as an accident. It might have made him sloppy. Ben wanted to find the guy's sniper's nest and see if the sick bastard left any clues behind.

Inside, Ben explained the situation to the manager on duty, who gave him the use of the hotel's conference room without hesitation and instructed the desk clerk to call all the guests from the riding party downstairs.

Once they all arrived, Ben led them to the conference room and asked them to take a seat. "I'm sorry to have to call you all down here at this hour, but we've done some further investigating into Gemma's accident and it wasn't an accident. Someone deliberately shot Jasper with a BB gun. I need you to help me to reconstruct the scene so we can find where the shots originated."

Talking erupted all around him. He patted the air to quiet everyone down. "One at a time. Which direction were you headed when the horse first reared and you heard the first shot?"

"East," Robert Cassidy answered.

The room was equipped with a white board. Ben snatched up a marker and drew a set of parallel lines horizontally on the board. He put an X between them to mark Gemma's position. "All right, who was closest to Gemma?"

A teenager raised her hand. "I was."

"Which side of her?"

"The left," the girl answered.

Ben frowned at the board as he placed another X to the left of the first one. "Was anyone on her right?" He looked at the people assembled. They all shook their heads.

"The trail was only wide enough for two abreast," Cassidy said.

"He reared and then took off up the trail about twenty yards before she reigned him in," one of the other men said. "She started to get him calmed down when we heard the second bang and he reared again, then bucked. She wasn't ready for the buck, and she lost her seat and landed against the tree."

"Which side of the trail is the tree?"

"The right," the man answered.

Ben put an X off to the side of the trail on the right, slightly ahead of the others.

"And no one noticed anything off to the right of the trail?"

Again, they all shook their heads.

"We were all so focused on getting to Gemma and catching, then calming, Jasper that we didn't look around much," the mother of the teenager confessed.

Ben stared at the whiteboard. He needed to get out there and study the scene. He itched to walk through the forest to the right of the trail. "Was there any delay between the noise and when Jasper reared?"

His witnesses all looked at each other, frowning, and slowly shook their heads.

"No. It all seemed to occur at the same time," Cassidy replied.

That meant the shooter had been fairly close. He wouldn't have to search far from the scene for clues.

"Did any of the other horses spook?"

"We had a couple sidestep, but none of them reacted like Jasper," Cassidy replied.

Ben thanked the group for their help and sent them back to their rooms. He had a good idea of how things played out.

Now, he just needed some daylight so he could go hunting.

EIGHTEEN

Gemma opened her eyes slowly, wincing as pain lanced her skull at the light streaming through the window. She struggled through the fog in her brain to make sense of where she was and why she felt like she was wading through pea soup.

Yesterday's events came flooding back as she took in her surroundings. She fell off her horse. She was in the hospital.

Her eyes landed on the figure seated next to her bed. His dark head was bent at an awkward angle and resting on the arm stretched across the side of her bed, holding her hand.

Gemma felt her heart clench. He was here.

He could deny his feelings until he was blue in the face, but right now, right here, she knew he felt it too.

"Ben." Her voice came out a croak. She cleared her throat and tried again. "Ben."

His head lifted as he snapped awake.

She watched in the span of a second as he took in his surroundings and reality rushed back to him. His gaze swung toward her and collided with hers.

He immediately leaned forward and gently thrust his free

hand into the hair at the side of her head. "Gemma. How do you feel, baby?"

She smiled softly. "Like I fell off my horse."

He smiled back at her. "You did. Do you remember what happened?"

She frowned as she forced her sluggish mind to think about yesterday. "I remember hearing a loud noise and Jasper reared up. And I remember flying through the air, but nothing after that."

"According to the people with you, there were two loud retorts, and he reared both times."

Gemma frowned. That didn't make sense. Jasper wouldn't startle that much at a noise.

Ben nodded as he read her expression. "Tristan thought the same thing: Jasper's too steadfast. So, we took a look at him. He'd been shot twice near his tail with a BB gun."

"What?!" Gemma jerked up in bed and immediately regretted it. Fire raced across her chest and her head swam. Her stomach threatened to revolt.

Ben immediately stood and helped her ease back onto the pillow. He stroked her hair until she had the nausea and pain under control.

"How far did I fly? I feel like I fell out of a three-story building."

"The others said you only went about fifteen feet, but you landed against a fallen tree." Ben studied her as she tried to get comfortable. "Please don't do that again. After the car accident and now this—I don't think Tristan and I can take much more."

Gemma rolled her eyes. "I'll try. Is Jasper okay?"

He clutched her hand. "He's fine. And I mean it, Gemma. I want you to stay put until this is over. No more excursions. To and from work, that's it. I still really want you to take a trip out west to see your parents."

Gemma frowned, trying to follow the conversation thread with her muddled brain. "We've had this discussion, Ben. I'm not hiding."

He leveled an exasperated look on her. "Someone shot your horse yesterday, Gemma. You could have been killed in that fall. There is a killer after you." His voice rose with each point, his features hardening.

"I know all that, but it doesn't change the fact we'll never catch the bastard if I hide."

"Yes, we will," he growled.

Gemma's frown deepened. "This conversation will get us nowhere, and I don't want to fight, Ben. I'm not hiding, so unless you plan to chain me to the floor of my house, drop it. I won't take any unnecessary risks, but I'm not going to sit behind a locked door all the time, either."

Ben released her hand and abruptly stood. He paced several feet away before running his hands through his hair to grip them at the back of his head. He spun back to her, but was spared having to reply as Tristan entered the room.

He stopped just inside the door, taking note of the distance and tension between Gemma and Ben. "Um, am I interrupting something?"

"Yes," Ben said.

"No," Gemma replied at the same time, eager to shut down the conversation.

Ben frowned, but Gemma just stared at him, willing him to drop it.

"Later," he muttered before turning to Tristan. "You ready?"

"Yep."

Gemma looked between her brother and Ben. "Ready for what?"

"We're going out to the Biltmore trails to see if we can

gather any evidence of the shooter," Tristan said as Ben grabbed his phone from the nightstand.

In one swift movement, Ben leaned over her, one arm on either side of her torso, his face aligned with hers. She looked up into his intense gaze, startled at his sudden movements.

"We will finish this—all of this—later, Gemma." He leaned down and kissed her hard once before rising and quickly striding out the door.

Tristan cocked an eyebrow at her, a smirk crossing his face, before he followed Ben into the hallway.

Slightly dumbstruck, she stared at the empty doorway, wondering if he meant what she thought he did. If that kiss actually meant *something*.

Worn out from the short exchange and the range of emotions that flowed through her in the last few minutes, she let her body sink into the bed. Fatigue made her eyelids heavy. She grazed her lips with her fingertips, a soft smile curving them upwards. The emotions weren't all bad.

Ben threw his car keys onto his borrowed desk at the sheriff's department in disgust. He and the team he hauled out to the Biltmore estate had come up with absolutely nothing. Oh, they had found the shooter's hide out—as thick as the underbrush was in that forest, it was impossible not to leave some trace behind—but crumpled foliage and compressed detritus was all they found. No footprints, no fibers. Nothing. If it wasn't for what they found at the Lowell crime scene, he would think this guy was a ghost.

"Mail call, Agent Davidson."

Ben took the letter the young deputy handed him. He frowned down at the plain envelope. It had his name and the department address on it, but no return address. Ben glanced at the postmark. It had come through Asheville. Any mail he got should be coming from his office in Richmond, and he wasn't expecting anything.

Ben laid the letter on the desk and quickly pulled on some gloves. He carefully sliced the top of the envelope with a letter opener and pulled out the single sheet of paper inside and unfolded it.

Just like at the equestrian center, Ben felt rage make his blood boil as he read the short missive typed on the plain white paper.

That was just a little fun. When I finally decide to end her, it won't be so quick as a bullet.

"Mabley!" Ben bellowed across the bullpen.

Tristan came running from where he was in conversation with the sheriff about their investigation. The older man followed closely behind.

"I got another note," Ben said, gesturing to the letter lying on his desk.

Tristan read it quickly, an oath slipping past his lips as he comprehended the text.

"I assume this is referring to Gemma?" the sheriff asked.

Ben nodded.

"Why is our killer targeting her?" the sheriff asked, echoing the same question Tristan asked after Stacy Mathis was dumped in the arena.

Ben scrubbed a hand over his jaw. "Somehow, he got the impression she means something to me."

The sheriff cocked an eyebrow and looked up at Ben. "And does she?"

Ben sighed, unable to deny that he felt *something* for the beautiful therapist. He looked at Tristan as he spoke, finally able to put into words what he couldn't the other day. "Yeah."

Tristan's jaw tightened, fury igniting in his eyes. "I still say I ought to kill you myself. Save this psycho the trouble and save my sister in the process."

Ben gave Tristan a glacial look. While he might agree with the sentiment behind Tristan's words—he would be reacting the same way if it was his sister who was the target of a madman—it didn't mean he liked it. "It's not like I planned any of this. And, like I told you before, she was a target before any real feelings cropped up between us. He must have seen us together and assumed she was someone important in my life. Being your sister, and the therapist of our victim's son, she hasn't exactly been removed from this investigation."

"All right, simmer down, boys," Sheriff Raymond said, stepping between the two. "Taking pot shots at each other will not keep Gemma safe. She needs you both, and she needs you to focus on the case. Mabley, run down the letter. Send it off for prints and DNA, and see if you can find out where it was mailed. Agent Davidson, where are we with the list of rangers?"

Ben focused on the sheriff. Raymond was right. It would do no one any good if he and Tristan came to blows. They made a damned good team, and they needed to work together to find this son-of-a-bitch before he made good on his threats against Gemma.

"I've been over the list twice. There's no one with the name Jack. I talked with the chief about a few whose names could have Jack as a nickname. He confirmed they all go by their given name. Either the guy is pretending to be a ranger or he picked the name at random. I've separated out those who fit the physical description we got from Caleb Lowell, and I'm in the process of running more extensive background checks on them, but there's a lot of average height, blonde or light brown-haired men on that list. So far, nothing's popped." Frustration clawed at Ben. He'd never had a case so utterly vexing. Every time he thought he had something, he rounded the corner to find nothing.

"Keep at it. Something has to give soon. In the meantime, I'm going to add to the guard around Gemma. She now warrants a team." Raymond cocked his head, his gaze swinging between both Ben and Tristan. "Unless the two of you can get her to leave town?"

Ben barked out a laugh. "That's like trying to get rid of kudzu. Unless we lie to her and get her away from here before she realizes our plan—or we hog-tie her and take off anyway— she's not going anywhere."

Tristan nodded in agreement. "Ben's right, sheriff. You've met Gemma. She won't run. Not when she's convinced she's the key to bringing this guy down, and definitely not while there are others who need her."

Raymond nodded. "If this guy gets much bolder, you may just have to go with the kidnapping plan and sort out the consequences later."

Ben was sorely tempted to instigate that plan today. He was still struggling to shake off the fear he felt at the idea Gemma was in danger. While he staunchly refused to label what he felt for the woman, losing her would leave a lasting mark, one he wasn't sure wouldn't be fatal to his peace of mind.

"Agent Davidson?"

Ben turned to see the same young deputy who brought him the letter, walking up to him.

"Sir, there's a woman on the phone who says she's the mother of your victim, Ms. Lowell. She wants to talk to you."

A small flame of hope ignited. Maybe Mrs. Trent had thought of or seen something that could lead them to the killer. "Transfer her to my phone," he told the young man, pointing at the landline phone on his desk.

"Yes, sir." The deputy sprinted back to the front desk to transfer the call. Ben sat on the edge of his desk, waiting for it to ring.

He didn't have to wait long. He picked up the extension as soon as it jingled, putting it on speakerphone. Tristan and the sheriff listened avidly.

"Mrs. Trent?"

"Hi, Agent Davidson. I wanted to let you know I heard from Diana's boyfriend, Andrew. He saw on the news she'd been killed, and he called to offer his condolences. I told him the police wanted to talk to him. He said he would stop into the station today, but I wanted to make sure you knew. He didn't say when he would come in, just that he intended to."

While it was looking less like it was the boyfriend who killed Diana, his absence this past week was troubling. Ben was anxious to talk to Andrew Emerson. "Do you have caller ID, Mrs. Trent?"

"Yes. You want his phone number?"

Ben grabbed a pen. "I do."

She rattled off the digits. Ben quickly thanked her and hung up. He turned to Tristan and Raymond. "Emerson called Diana's mother after he heard the news about Diana's death. She said he intends to come in to talk to us. She gave me his phone number just in case."

Ben moved to his chair and pulled up the phone number in the database, hoping it was attached to an address. It came back as a cell phone registered to a Nathaniel Andrew Emerson Jr. with an Asheville address.

Ben grinned as he swiped the keys from the desk and stood. "Feel like going for a ride, Tris?"

"Hell yeah."

"I'll take care of the note," the sheriff said. "Go."

Both men spun on their heels and quickly headed for the exit. Outside, they climbed into Ben's SUV and headed south, making the half-hour drive in twenty minutes. In the city, Ben wove through the streets until he pulled up to the address listed with the phone number. It was a high-rise, high-end condo building in the downtown area. It towered outside the window of Ben's SUV. The red brick façade and reflective windows gleamed in the sun.

"Damn. There goes our element of surprise," Tristan muttered, staring up at the undoubtedly secure building.

Ben frowned, a contemplative expression crossing his face. "Maybe. Give me your radio."

Tristan passed it to him. Ben quickly radioed Asheville's dispatch and requested a squad car at their location.

"What are you thinking?" Tristan asked.

Ben stepped from the car, still looking at the building, scanning for exits. "Well, if we can keep the guard from alerting Emerson we're here, he won't have time to rabbit."

"Which is what the uniforms are for," Tristan surmised. "I'm glad one of us is thinking straight."

Ben stopped and stared at Tristan. Up until now, he hadn't given much thought to the younger man's ability to work the case. He'd never been anything but professional on their missions together, and it hadn't occurred to him that this case would be any different. "You okay to work this? I can call Raymond and have him assign me another detective."

"Hell no!" Tristan's face hardened. "I'll be all right. This is my sister. I have to be on this case."

Ben studied the younger man. Tristan had always been a little impulsive, but it had been tempered with rationality in the past. He was quick to decide, but he always thought things through. He hoped Gemma's involvement wasn't causing Tristan to lose his objectivity. Ben knew his own was threatened. "Just don't go all hotshot on me, all right?"

"I won't. I want to nail this son-of-a-bitch, and I don't want him to walk on a technicality." He held Ben's gaze. "And that works both ways, you know. Don't blow this because you fell for her."

Ben looked away and studied the building again, afraid Tristan would see the truth in his eyes—a truth he still refused to fully acknowledge. He couldn't deny Gemma made him feel something, but he absolutely refused to put a name to it. He knew it was futile to resist what he felt. That eventually he wouldn't be able to deny it—wouldn't be able to not put a name to it. But for now, he was determined to keep his distance in the vain hope it would help him keep an emotional distance in the case. He knew he was a bit delusional, but anything else threatened to open the floodgates on his emotions. He wasn't ready for that.

"I'll be fine," he finally replied. "Come on. We've got a suspect to question." He stepped off the curb and crossed the street just as the patrol car pulled up. The uniforms met them in front of the condo building. Ben quickly outlined what he wanted from the officers, and they entered the high-rise.

Ben stepped up to the security desk and explained who they were and what they wanted. He knew he'd made the right call when the guard eyed the uniformed officers warily as Ben explained they would be waiting in the lobby to make sure Mr. Emerson wasn't alerted to their presence.

Guard sufficiently neutralized, Ben and Tristan headed for the elevator and Emerson's apartment on the tenth floor. The building was small, holding only a handful of units on each floor, making it easy to find the correct apartment.

Hand resting on the butt of his gun, Ben knocked. "Andrew Emerson. This is the police. We need to speak with you."

Footsteps sounded inside, quick but not frantic. The door swung open moments later to reveal a man about Tristan's age, casually dressed in jeans and a polo shirt. A frown marred his features.

"Are you Andrew Emerson?" Ben asked.

The man nodded. "I am. Is this about Diana?"

Ben nodded and flashed his badge, identifying himself and Tristan. "May we come in? We have some questions."

Wordlessly, Emerson held the door wider and motioned them inside.

The apartment was what Ben would have expected from a seemingly well-off bachelor. Leather furniture was grouped around a large flat-screen television. Artsy photographs lined the white walls, bringing pops of color to the room. Books and magazines littered the coffee table, and a jacket was draped over the back of one of the chairs. The place was clean and tidy, but it looked lived in.

Emerson motioned to the couch and chairs. "Please have a seat. I was planning to come by the station later, after trading closed."

Ben and Tristan took seats on the couch while Emerson settled into an adjacent chair.

"You're a day trader, correct?" Ben asked.

Emerson nodded.

"Independent?" Tristan asked.

Again, Emerson nodded.

"Can you tell us where you've been for the last week, Mr. Emerson?" Tristan asked.

Ben sat back and let Tristan lead. He wanted to watch Emerson's body language. Right now, the man looked relaxed and ready to answer their questions.

"I've been out of town for a convention. I use trading software for my business, and the big name, online-trading companies hold a convention in New York every year to showcase their latest products and services and to get feedback from those of us who use their websites to run our businesses. I got back late Sunday evening and spent yesterday catching up on emails and what not. I watched the morning news today, and that's when I heard about Diana's death."

"Do you have receipts to corroborate your story?"

Emerson nodded. "They're in my office and on my computer. Let me go get them."

"We'll follow you, if you don't mind," Tristan said, rising.

Ben hung back and watched Emerson lead the way to his home office. As much as he wanted this to be their guy, he just didn't think he was. While he was obviously uncomfortable being questioned by the police, his countenance and expressions were open and honest. This was a man saddened by the death of his friend, but one who had nothing to hide. They would run down every part of his alibi, but Ben's gut was screaming that Andrew Emerson had nothing to do with Diana Lowell's death.

Nineteen

Frustration clawed at Gemma as she attempted to find something remotely interesting on daytime television. It had been three days since her accident and she'd been home for two. Boredom already threatened to drive her insane. She was at a loss for things to do. Reading made her head hurt. TV did too after a while, but she had a feeling that was due more to the quality of the programming than her head injury.

She couldn't even bake anything because it hurt her ribs to move that much. This next week was going to be brutal.

With as big of a sigh as her bruised ribs would let her muster, Gemma finally decided on a soap opera. At least the characters on the show still led more dramatic lives than she did.

Barely.

She rolled her eyes at herself. God, could she be any more melodramatic?

The sound of the front door opening and closing drew her attention. She twisted as quickly as her battered body would let her and was just in time to see Ben walk into the room.

She smiled at him, delighted to have something besides

terrible TV to entertain her. "Hi. What are you doing here? I thought you were going out to the Biltmore again to talk to the employees you missed the other day."

He came around the couch and sat down next to her. "I was, and I did. Now, I'm taking a much needed break and checking to see how you're doing."

Gemma rolled her eyes. "I'm bored, that's how I'm doing. Daytime TV is awful, and I can't read or do much of anything else without it hurting my head or my ribs." She sighed softly. "Basically, I'm wallowing in my misery."

He chuckled. "If it's any consolation, I know how you feel. Concussions are the worst injuries to recover from. Mental rest is torture, especially when you're used to being extremely busy."

She eyed him speculatively. "That sounds like the voice of experience. Just how many concussions have you had?"

"Four," he replied after a brief moment of thought.

Gemma's eyes widened. That was a lot.

He smiled at her expression. "Dangers of special forces."

"How long were you in?"

"Twenty years. I was a Ranger for over half of that."

"What made you leave?"

Ben sighed. "I got injured several years ago." He propped his left foot on the coffee table and pulled up his pant leg, revealing a shin and calf covered in a multitude of jagged scars. "I took some shrapnel from an IED. It shattered both bones and caused some fairly extensive muscle and ligament damage. There's almost as much metal in there now as bone." He rolled his pant leg back down. "It still functions, but I can't run on it for an extended period of time. It wasn't bad enough to medically discharge me from the Army, but it was enough to end my tenure on the Ranger teams. I was relegated to training new Ranger recruits."

"And you didn't like it," she said.

He shrugged. "It was all right, but I missed the action—the planning and solving the puzzles that made an op successful. Once I hit my twenty-year mark, I retired and joined the FBI."

"Are you happy with that decision?" she asked, genuinely curious.

"Absolutely. Being a Ranger—well, it's a young man's job. I was thirty-six, almost thirty-seven, when the IED nearly took my leg. I knew my days were numbered anyway before the explosion ever happened. My time on the teams just ended a little sooner and a little more abruptly than I originally planned."

Gemma suppressed a shudder. She remembered the fear that plagued her anytime Tristan called or emailed to say he was going off-grid for a while. A low-grade terror had been her constant companion until he returned safely each time. She was thankful all of his injuries were relatively minor in comparison to what some others endured.

She reached over and laid her hand over Ben's, where it rested on the cushion between them. "Well, I, for one, am glad that you—and Tristan—made it home safely, if not with a little extra hardware."

He smiled and flipped his hand over to hold hers. "Me too. Speaking of injuries, how are yours? I know you're still sore, but are you starting to feel better?"

Gently, she touched the lump on the side of her head. "I get a little light-headed here and there, but my head doesn't really hurt anymore except when I touch the bump or if I read. My ribs are more bothersome. I can't lift my arms up very far or move very fast. I just wish I could go outside and go for a walk. Tristan threatened to handcuff me to a chair if I dared step foot out the door, though."

"With good reason."

Gemma huffed. "I know. Doesn't change the fact I'm going stir crazy."

Ben glanced around thoughtfully before his gaze landed on hers. "I have an idea. It's only a temporary respite, but it's better than sitting here watching that." He pointed at the drama playing out on the television.

She frowned, intrigued. "Anything is better than that. What did you have in mind?"

He stood, holding his hands out to her. She took them and rose gingerly.

His eyes raked her form, making her cheeks heat. She was completely covered in her leggings and t-shirt, but under his scrutiny she was acutely aware she wasn't wearing a bra. It hadn't seemed like it was worth the hassle earlier, so she skipped it.

A gleam sprang to life in his eyes, letting Gemma know he'd noticed. She fought the urge to cross her arms. No use bringing more attention to her current state of dress.

Jaw clenched, he cleared his throat, briefly looking away. "Go change. Just something comfortable."

"Are we going somewhere? I thought I was on house arrest." She hadn't been kidding when she told Ben that Tristan had threatened to chain her to her bed. Her brother made it abundantly clear she was to stay inside, away from the doors and windows.

He rolled his eyes, one side of his mouth quirking up. "I'm giving you a pass. Go change." With a nudge, he urged her toward the hallway and her bedroom.

Eyeing him suspiciously, she headed down the hall. Once in her room, she pulled a pair of jean shorts, a t-shirt—and a bra—from her dresser. As quickly as her injuries allowed, Gemma changed clothes. The bruises on her ribcage protested against the band of her bra, but it was tolerable. Sliding her feet into a pair of sandals, she headed back out to the living room.

"I'm ready."

Ben looked up from his phone where he'd been texting. He fired off the message quickly, then stood, tucking the device into his pocket. "Let's go, then."

"You going to tell me where we're going yet?"

He grinned at her as he guided her out of the room. "Nope. It's a surprise."

Frowning, but nonetheless intrigued, Gemma let him lead her out the front door to his SUV. He opened the passenger door and helped her inside.

"I don't even get a hint?" she asked after he climbed into the driver's seat. She buckled her seatbelt as he started the car.

Ben waved to the officers stationed outside her house as he turned out of the drive. "No. You'll probably figure it out as we get close. Just relax, okay? Take in the scenery and enjoy the fact that Tristan will blow a gasket over this, but for once, it won't be your fault."

That drew a laugh from her. "You're going to make him regret he invited you to stay with us."

He slanted a heated glance her way. "He probably already does."

A blush stole over Gemma's face. She looked out the window. "Yes, well, that's his problem."

Ben chuckled. "That it is."

Gemma stared out the window pensively as he drove. While it was nice to be out of the house, she didn't know what to make of Ben's behavior. Since her accident, he'd been attentive, but there were no more kisses or heated touches. The conversation he promised her in the hospital never materialized. Not about her staying or leaving, nor about the feelings they had for each other. Their hand holding on the couch just a little while ago was the most he'd touched her since she woke up in the hospital. Now, he was giving her heated looks and acting like the attraction between them was completely normal. It was irritating and confusing.

Well, enough was enough. She wanted answers. They were going to finish at least one part of that conversation, like he promised. Turning in her seat, she faced him as best she could across the front seat of the car.

"Ben? What are we doing?"

He frowned and glanced at her. "I'm breaking you out of the house, remember?"

She waved her hand. "Not that. I mean you and me. This thing between us. What are we doing?"

Muscles worked in his face. His eyes remained on the road, but Gemma could see them dart around as he tried to think of an answer.

"Don't tell me there's nothing there. It would be a lie, and we both know it."

"Gemma," he started, an apology evident in his voice in just the one word.

Angered that he continued to deny what was so obvious, she laid into him. "Don't 'Gemma' me, Ben Davidson. I told you last week you needed to realize that what's between us is something worth fighting for. I wasn't just blowing hot air. I meant it, and I'm going to fight for it. For us."

He sighed. "I'm not arguing with you about feeling something between us. It just can't go anywhere."

She frowned fiercely, baffled. "Why the hell not?"

He looked at her briefly, his face expressionless. She was really starting to hate the soldier training. It made him difficult to read.

"I'll be forty-three in December. You're what? Twenty-seven?"

"Twenty-eight. I'll be twenty-nine in September," she retorted.

"Okay. That's still almost a fourteen-year age difference. How we grew up and the things that shaped us are vastly different. Not to mention the fact I've been all over the world and have seen and done things that most people never will."

She scoffed. "You may be older and worldlier, but your life experience mimics my brother's, and I've been dealing with him my entire life. As for how we grew up, everyone is different. I remember Tristan telling me you came from a privileged background. That initially he wasn't sure about you as the new CO of his unit because you were a West Point brat. Are you telling me that because I grew up middle-class, we can't be together? That you could never be with any woman who didn't come from the upper crust of society?" She frowned at him. "I may not have known you long, but I've figured out you don't have a prejudiced bone in your body, so that's all a load of bull. Next argument, please."

He growled at her in frustration and shot a highly annoyed look her way.

Gemma refused to relent. "What are you so afraid of?"

"Nothing," he quickly fired back.

"Prove it."

His head jerked toward her. "What?"

She crossed her arms gingerly and arched an eyebrow at him. "You heard me. Prove you aren't afraid of me."

He stared at her a moment before turning his gaze back to the road. "How do you propose I do that? I'm already taking you out of the house when I shouldn't be. I could just as easily have stayed away all day every day and left you to your own devices."

"This is you being a friend. I don't want a friend, Ben."

"Then what the hell do you want?" he asked, anger drawing his eyebrows down and putting a touch of red in his cheeks.

"I want someone who wants me back," she answered

honestly. "Who wants me in his life and wants to share mine. Someone to stand next to me and tackle whatever the world throws at us. Together. I want a partner. In this life and the next."

He clenched and unclenched the steering several times, his jaw working. "Well, I'm not that man."

That was such utter crap. He already wanted her—their interlude in the kitchen last week was proof of that—and she knew he would stand by her side for anything that came her way. He had too much integrity not to.

She did her best not to glower. "Why not?"

He was silent for so long, Gemma didn't think he was going to answer.

After several moments, his quiet voice broke the silence. "Because I don't know how to be that man."

Gemma didn't know what to say to that. After their angry exchange, it was the absolute last thing she expected him to say.

"Anyway, it doesn't matter." He signaled a turn and turned left off the highway. "We're here."

Conversation dead in the water for the moment, Gemma looked out the window and quickly realized where they were.

"The equestrian center?" She looked over at Ben, perplexed.

He shrugged as he pulled the SUV into a parking spot. "I thought a little horse therapy would do the therapist some good." He put the car in park and unbuckled. "I know you've been worried about Jasper, so I figured seeing him would help alleviate your concern. It has the added bonus of busting up your boredom."

She smiled broadly, her ire with him forgotten. "This is the best thing you could have possibly done." Eager to see her horse, Gemma unbuckled and opened her door. As fast as she could possibly move in her bruised state, she got out of the car, meeting Ben around front.

His eyes darted around the parking lot, looking for any unusual or peculiar activity, reminding Gemma that danger could very well be lurking just around the corner. The ache in her chest was proof of that.

Not wanting to remain out in the open any longer than necessary—she might protest being stuck inside, but she understood why—Gemma let Ben usher her into the building.

Pam, the receptionist, let out a squawk before scurrying around the front desk.

"Oh my goodness! It's so good to see you!" She extended her arms to give Gemma a hug. Thankfully, the woman remembered Gemma's injuries and only squeezed lightly.

"It's good to see you too, Pam."

The older woman perused Gemma's face, no doubt looking for signs of injury. "When Mara told us what happened, we just couldn't believe it. This business with the serial killer is just downright frightening." She turned her gaze to Ben, a frown turning down the corners of her mouth. "How close are you to finding this crazy person? He's getting a little close for comfort. Someone else is going to end up dead."

"Pam!" Gemma was shocked. She was normally such a mild-mannered, soft-spoken woman. All the trouble lately must really be getting to her for her to talk to someone that way.

Ben laid a hand on Gemma's arm. "It's okay, Gemma. She has a right to be concerned. This place does seem to be the center of the activity. And to answer your question, Pam, we're following leads and gathering information. Something will shake loose eventually. It always does."

Her frown didn't disappear at his words. It just turned more thoughtful. "Well, I hope it does soon. This whole situation is nerve-wracking." She turned back to Gemma. "What are you doing here? You're supposed to be resting."

"I was getting a little bored at home, so Ben brought me to see Jasper."

"Oh, he will be delighted to see you. I swear, he's been moping since Tristan brought him back."

Gemma laughed. "He probably just misses all the treats I sneak him."

They bid Pam farewell and continued down the hall toward the offices and arena. Gemma stopped in her office to get an apple from the bag she kept there expressly for Jasper.

Ben just shook his head. "You weren't lying when you told Pam he just misses his treats."

Gemma's mouth quirked. "Not entirely, no." She pushed through the arena door, welcoming the familiar sights and sounds of patient sessions. Stacy and Jennifer were both busy with their young, disabled riders, the children beaming from ear to ear at the freedom that came with being on the back of a horse.

Ben stopped at the railing and watched momentarily. "You guys do something special here, you know that?"

Stepping up next to him, Gemma smiled. "I know. Animals really are the best medicine."

He looked down at her, an intensity in his eyes that made Gemma's breath catch. She just wished she knew what it meant.

"Come on." He took her hand. "Let's go get you some medicine of your own."

Fingers entwined, they headed for the stables.

She led the way down the corridor to Jasper's stall. The beautiful animal saw her approach and neighed a greeting, tossing his head.

"Hey there, boy. Did you miss me?" Gemma smiled at the horse. Opening the bin on the outside of his stall, she pulled out a knife and quickly quartered the apple she brought him. Jasper hung his head over the half-door, trying to take the juicy fruit from her.

She turned her back and pushed him away with her shoulder. "You have to wait. Knives are bad for horses, silly." Finishing her task, she slipped the knife back into the box and held one of the quarters out on her palm for the eager animal. He quickly took it from her and ate it.

"You missed your treats." She gave him another chunk, which he also quickly gobbled up. She laughed at his eagerness. "Pig."

She offered one of the slices to Ben. "Here. Make friends."

He took the proffered slice and held it out to the horse. Jasper hesitated only a moment at taking the treat from someone new before he quickly gave into his desire for the apple and lapped up the fruit.

She passed Ben the last slice, and he fed it to the horse. Jasper nudged at her, looking for more.

She laughed and rubbed his face. "That's all there is, you goof."

Jasper tossed his head and stared at her balefully. She wrapped her arms around his neck and pressed her face against the side of his. "I know. I missed a few days. I'm sorry. I'll make sure someone gives you one until I can come back and do it every day." She continued to stroke the horse, finding a sense of peace that she hadn't known she was missing. Ben had been right to bring her here. She'd needed this.

Ben stood back and watched the exchange between woman and horse. He couldn't believe he was slightly jealous of the big animal, but he was. Jasper was getting all sorts of love and attention right now and absolutely loving it. Ben didn't have any right to be jealous of that. Not after what he told her in the car on the way over here. He'd rejected outright what she offered him. He wasn't allowed to be upset about to whom or what she bestowed her affections. And, honestly, he shouldn't care.

But, God help him, he did care. Where that left him, he had no idea.

His phone rang, saving him from his own thoughts.

"It's Tristan," Ben said when he pulled the phone from his pocket and saw the number on the screen.

An ornery smile spread over Gemma's pretty face.

Grinning back at her at the thought of how angry the man probably was right about now, Ben swiped to accept the call.

"Hey, Tris. Gemma's safe. She's with me. She was going a bit stir crazy, so I took her to the equestrian center to see Jasper."

"I know she's with you. The guards outside the house called to tell me when you left with her. That's not why I'm calling, though."

Dread settled low in Ben's stomach. He didn't like the serious note in Tristan's voice. "What happened?"

Tristan sighed. "There's been another murder."

TWENTY

"What have we got?" Ben asked as he stepped up to the cluster of people next to a group of sheriff's cruisers.

Tristan turned, a scowl on his face. "You get my sister home safe?"

Ben tipped his head once in a nod. He couldn't tell if Tristan was pissed because he'd taken Gemma out or if he was just ticked that they had another body. It was probably both.

Not wanting to argue, Ben's reply was succinct. "She's locked up safe and sound, guards posted in front and back." As soon as he hung up the phone with Tristan, he whisked Gemma back to the safety of her house, eliciting a promise from her that she would stay inside, away from the windows. Rattled by the second murder, she readily agreed. It killed Ben to leave her alone, so obviously distressed, but it couldn't be helped. If she ever had any hope of living a normal life again, he had to do his job.

"Good." Tristan motioned for Ben to follow and began walking toward the trees. They were at a city park that ran along the river this time.

"A couple of teenagers found her on their way to the park for a pick-up game of basketball. They cut through the woods as a shortcut from the neighborhoods on the other side."

"Jesus. Are you serious? How old are they?"

"Thirteen and fifteen. They're brothers. I got some cursory information from them about the location of the body, then called their mother to come get them. I told her we'd be by later to get formal statements."

Ben was glad they were in the care of a parent. That was a disturbing sight for an adult. He could only imagine what those boys were going through.

Tristan led them through the thick foliage deep into the woods. The swath of trees was only about ten acres thick, but it was dense, the river running through the center, feeding the plant life.

Sounds of people talking met his ears just before the crime scene came into view. Yellow police tape roped off an area around the victim who, like all the previous ones, swung by a rope around her neck from a tree limb, completely naked.

Ben stared at the body, horrified those two teenagers found this woman. She was in much worse shape than the other victims.

"He's escalating," Ben noted, stepping forward to get a closer look. Blood streaked her body in rivulets that had run off her feet and hands to pool beneath her on the ground. She had multiple lacerations to her arms and legs, some of them down to the bone. She looked like her killer had come at her with Freddie Krueger gloves.

"Anyone recognize her?" Ben snapped on a pair of latex gloves and slipped under the police tape.

Tristan shook his head, putting on his own gloves. They both signed the crime scene log. "No. Ben, what the hell is going on? I read your case notes. He's never killed two women so close together, and he's never dumped one so publicly before. I mean, he had to drive through residential areas, park in a public place and carry her—and the stuff to hang her with—in here without anyone seeing."

"I don't know. I think we threw off his game when we found Diana so quickly. I'm getting too close for comfort—which is why he's targeting your sister. He's trying to get me to back off. I don't know why he killed this woman, though. I can only think that maybe his rage at me, his attacks on Gemma, have combined to make his urge to kill stronger."

"Great. An unstable psychopath. I hope this scene yields some clues. We need to catch this guy before he kills a seventh victim."

Ben wholeheartedly agreed.

"Well, gentlemen, I can tell you that you will be happy," Dr. Tate said, having overheard their conversation. He and his assistant kneeled next to the pool of blood beneath the victim. "She presented quite the problem for her killer. We've found some bits of cloth on the brambles over there." He pointed to their right. "And judging from what I can see from here, it looks like she's got some defensive wounds on her hands. She either fought back when he kidnapped her or she was lucid when he started slashing. I imagine when we get her down, we're going to find some fibers and maybe even some hair stuck in all that blood."

Dr. Tate stood to face them. "Our guy was ticked this time. There's a lot of rage in those wounds."

Ben agreed. "Hopefully, it made him sloppy. As soon as you get her down, scan her prints. Maybe we'll get lucky and she'll be in the database."

"Will do, Agent." He turned his attention to his assistant and the other techs roaming around the crime scene. "Let's get the leaves and dirt from around her bagged. We'll sort through it back at the lab. Chris, did you get pictures yet?"

Ben turned to Tristan as the doctor walked away to do his job. "Let's canvass the area. See what we can find."

They headed for the brambles Dr. Tate indicated, eyes scanning in front, below, and around as they walked.

Nothing stood out, and they soon reached the tangle of thorny vines. Wild raspberries covered the bushes, plump and juicy.

A crime scene marker sat looped over a set of vines, the evidence it marked already bagged and with the forensic techs.

"Through there." Tristan pointed to where there was a break in the brambles.

Careful of the thorns, the men made their way down the narrow path. The thicket went on for nearly twenty yards before it gave way to just trees.

They stopped, looking for anything that shouldn't be there.

"What's on the other side of this?" Ben asked.

"The river goes through there." Tristan pointed to a thicker copse of trees about fifty yards to their left. "If we keep walking straight, we'll come to the street and I think the parking lot."

"What's on the other side of the river, past the woods?"

"Just houses."

Ben felt frustration mount. The ground was covered in dead leaves and other plant growth, which meant the killer hadn't left any footprints. He and Tristan weren't going to get anywhere tracking the guy without help.

"Call in your K-9 officer and have him come track the killer's path through the woods. We can't really canvass outside the park until we know where he went in."

Tristan nodded, pulling out his radio and calling for the K-9.

Ben turned in a circle, looking for anything that would

lead him in the right direction. Tristan scanned the woods right next to him.

"I hope we're searching in the right place. That fabric the crime scene crew found could be from anyone. People cut through here all the time." Frustration edged Tristan's voice.

"I know, but it's all we've got to go on at the moment."

While he was also frustrated, Ben felt a sense of anticipation brewing. The killer was getting bolder, willing to take risks. But those risks were going to get him caught. This murder seemed hasty, and hasty people made mistakes. Ben was going to find that mistake and take this bastard down.

"So, why did you break my sister out of house arrest?" Tristan asked later as they walked down the sidewalk outside the main parking lot of the park. The K-9 tracked their killer's path through the woods to the street, where it abruptly stopped. They were now going door to door to see if any of the residents across from the park had seen anything.

Ben shrugged. "You know what it's like to recover from a concussion. I was just trying to give her a little relief from the boredom."

Tristan made a humming sound, but didn't say anything.

Frowning, Ben stopped. "What?"

"Nothing."

He shook his head. "God, you're just as bad as she is."

Tristan grinned. "She giving you crap for avoiding her?"

Ben looked at him in surprise. "I haven't been avoiding her."

"Whatever," Tristan scoffed, rolling his eyes.

Ben planted his hands on his hips. "Explain how I've been avoiding her. I've been back to your house every night. I spend time with her. That's not avoidance."

Tristan faced Ben, amusement still stamped on his face. Ben was glad someone found this conversation amusing. He just found it annoying.

"Not physically. You're emotionally avoiding her."

Ben threw up his hands and started walking down the sidewalk again to the next house. "Just as bad," he muttered. Persistence must be a family trait.

"Eventually, you're going to have to face it, you know," Tristan remarked, catching up. They climbed the steps to the porch.

"There's nothing to face, because it doesn't matter how I feel. Nothing can ever happen between your sister and me." He knocked on the door.

"You tell that to Gemma. She sets her sights on something and it'll take a nuke to deter her. And you, my friend, are firmly within her sights."

Mouth in a firm line, Ben slanted an annoyed glance at Tristan. "I did tell her that."

Tristan's eyebrow rose. "Yeah? How'd that go?"

He huffed, uneasy. "I'm not sure yet. We got to the equestrian center, and she got sidetracked."

Tristan laughed, patting him on the shoulder. "You're screwed. She's had time to think about it now."

That was what he was afraid of. The woman wasn't one to be easily dissuaded. But he meant what he said. It didn't matter what his feelings were. He couldn't be the man Gemma wanted. The one she deserved.

The door opened and Ben pasted a smile on his face, shoving thoughts of his complicated relationship with Gemma to the back of his mind. He and Tristan flashed their badges.

The young woman eyed them curiously, the baby propped on her hip chewing happily on a plastic ring.

"Hi, ma'am. I'm Special Agent Davidson, this is Detective Mabley. We're investigating a crime that occurred last night in the park." He motioned behind himself at the expanse of green across the street. "Did you notice anything unusual overnight?"

She frowned thoughtfully, before suddenly her face brightened. "Actually, I did, but it might not be anything."

"Anything you can remember, ma'am. The smallest detail could be helpful," Tristan encouraged.

The woman readjusted the little boy before continuing. "Well, Cooper's teething and hasn't been sleeping well. He woke up around three-thirty, four o'clock fussing. I got up with him and brought him out into the living room. I was out here walking him around when car lights lit up the room. That's not normal for a car just passing by. You have to pull into our driveway for it to light up like that. My husband was home, so I knew it wasn't him." She shrugged. "It was probably just a car turning around. I know it was probably nothing, but it caught my attention."

"Did you happen to look out the window and see the car?" Ben asked.

She nodded. "I did. I was walking right by it when the car pulled in."

"Can you describe the vehicle?"

She looked at him thoughtfully. "It was an SUV, dark-colored. Maybe green or blue."

Ben shared a look with Tristan. That sounded a lot like the car Caleb Lowell said Ranger Jack drove.

"Could you tell what make or model the car was?"

She chewed her fingernail as she thought momentarily. "It was an older Chevy, maybe. Like a Tahoe or something."

"Did you notice anything else? Could you see the driver?"

She shook her head. "No. It was too dark. With the headlights shining, all I could see was the shape of the car and that it was dark-colored."

"Okay. Could we get your name and contact information?"

"Of course. My name is Allie Brannigan." She rattled off her phone number and address.

Ben recorded it in his notebook.

"Do you think the car is important? What happened, anyway? Should we be concerned?" She looked past him to stare at the park worriedly.

Ben hastened to reassure her. "A woman was murdered, but we don't think you or the public are in any danger. Your information about the car could be significant, but it could also turn out to be nothing."

Her eyes widened. "Wait, you said you're an agent. As in FBI agent? This has to do with that serial killer case I heard about on the news, doesn't it? Oh my God!"

"Ma'am, again, we don't think you're in any danger," Tristan reiterated. He pulled a business card from his pocket. "Thank you for the information about the car. If you think of anything else or you see anything suspicious, please call."

She took the card, worry pinching her brow. "You're sure my family is safe?"

"Yes, ma'am. You have a good day now."

Still looking slightly worried, she nodded before bidding them good day and closing the door, the lock clicking into place.

"Looks like your suspicion was right," Tristan remarked as they headed back down the porch steps. "We're looking for a ranger, or someone impersonating one."

"Let's just hope the forensics team can find something that links our victim to one of the names the park service gave us. We can't get a warrant for vehicle information on all the park ranger staff based on the word of an eight-year-old autistic boy and a late-night sighting of a similar car near our crime scene."

While he was hoping forensics found a smoking gun, he knew the probability of that was almost zero. This guy, while he was clearly becoming unhinged, was still too smart to leave something like that behind. The most Ben could hope for was something that led him directly to the ranger service so he could get warrants for information. He just hoped they found something worthwhile before their killer found another victim.

~

Files in hand, Ben walked into the Mabley's living room later that night. A sense of déjà vu struck him at the sight of Gemma sitting on the couch watching the news.

She looked up when he entered and smiled softly. "Hey."

"Hey." He sat down in the recliner opposite her. "I figured you'd be sound asleep."

She shrugged. "I took a nap after you brought me home. Now, I can't sleep."

Ben was in a similar boat. There was no way he would fall asleep any time soon. Not because he wasn't tired—he was exhausted—but because his mind refused to shut down. He had so many details about the case rattling around in his head he felt like he was trying to put together a five-thousand-piece jigsaw puzzle. That was all one color.

Although some new shades were creeping in. They had gotten lucky and the woman's prints were in the system. Her name was Amber Patakis. She'd been arrested five years ago on drug charges. She also had a four-year-old daughter and a one-year-old son who now had no mother. He just needed to figure out how she fit.

"Where's Tristan?"

Ben sighed and leaned back in the chair, rubbing his gritty

eyes. "He decided to go out with some friends. Said he needed to decompress. We found out who the victim was and had to go tell her husband she was dead. We also had to go talk to the two teenagers who found her and make them relive it all over again, so we could find out if they saw anything of significance on their trip through the woods."

"Oh, Ben. I'm sorry." She stood up and came over to him, sitting on his lap before he knew what she was doing.

"Gemma." He tried to gently lift her off, but she wrapped her arms around his neck and settled onto his lap, shushing him.

"I'm not trying to do anything or push anything right now. You just looked like you needed a bit of comforting."

Some of the fight leached out of Ben's muscles. He looped his arms loosely around her waist. He didn't have the emotional defenses tonight to fight her. Besides, she felt really good in his arms.

A bone-deep weariness stole over him. He was so damned tired. Gemma's warm weight was like a balm, helping to calm his turbulent mind.

He sighed, burying his nose in her soft, fragrant hair, and inhaled the floral scent of her shampoo along with something uniquely Gemma. It was intoxicating. He felt his eyelids growing heavy.

Grabbing the afghan in the basket next to the recliner, she tucked her feet up and spread the blanket over them. Her fingers toyed with the buttons on his shirt, her warm breath washing over his neck.

Some of the fatigue gave way as his body registered the soft female form curled up on top of it.

He looked down at her, tipping her chin up so he could see her face. "Why do you do this to me?" he asked quietly. He ran his thumb over her bottom lip, feeling its softness. "I can't be the man you deserve, Gemma, but it doesn't stop me from wanting you. God knows I shouldn't, but I do."

The hand resting on his chest slid up to cover his cheek. "I don't need a perfect man, Ben. I just need you."

More tenderness than he'd ever felt, as well as a good dose of another emotion he refused to name, poured over him. Unable and unwilling to fight their attraction tonight, he kissed her softly.

A slow burn lit his soul, pushing back the darkness that had descended on him over the course of the day. Whether he wanted to admit it or not, he needed her. She banished the chaos and the mayhem, the evil that he dealt with every day. She was the quiet place he hadn't known he needed until now.

Cognizant of her injuries, Ben kept the kiss gentle. His lips lingered on hers, taking the comfort she offered.

After a moment, she pulled back to smile up at him softly. "Feel better now?"

He returned her smile. "Yes."

"Good." She kissed him lightly on his nose before sinking into him and snuggling under the blanket.

Ben didn't care that they were in a chair in the living room with the lights blazing and the television still playing. Or that Tristan would find them when he finally came home. He closed his eyes and let the fatigue clawing at him take over, sinking into a blissfully peaceful sleep.

TWENTY-ONE

Warm sunshine bathed Gemma's face as she exited Ben's SUV and walked to the back door of the equestrian center Monday morning. Feeling much better after a week of rest, she managed to convince him and Tristan she was just as safe at the center as she was sitting at home.

She unlocked the door and quickly punched in her code on the control panel once inside. Ben made sure the door shut and locked behind him as he followed her in. The arena lights were already on and the grooms were exercising several of the horses that wouldn't be used in sessions today. Gemma waved as they greeted her and headed for the door that led to the front offices.

It felt great to be back doing something. Ben and Tristan left her to her own devices for much of the weekend while they were off chasing leads and gathering information. Thankfully, her head had healed quite quickly, and she was able to read some. She also managed to bake again and made enough cookies to feed all the law enforcement officers in the state. Tristan had just rolled his eyes and stuffed one in his mouth when she handed him the boxes to take to work this morning.

Gemma unlocked her office and flipped on the lights, crossing to her desk to deposit her things.

Ben followed her around the desk. "I will be back tomorrow afternoon. Early evening at the latest." He pulled her close, wrapping his arms around her waist and linking his hands at the small of her back.

She laid her hands against his chest, liking the closeness they'd developed the last few days. They still hadn't resolved where any of this was going, but he did seem to be softening toward having a relationship with her. For now, that was enough. One day, he would tell her why he thought he wasn't worthy of her, and then she would tell him why he was wrong.

That day would not be today, though. Ben had to go back to Richmond again for meetings later this afternoon and to brief his boss on the case as well as catch up on a couple of other cases he was working before the serial killer struck again. "Be careful driving. That's a long way and you haven't had much sleep lately."

"I've driven further on less."

She gave him a mock annoyed look.

He grinned. "I'll be fine. Do you think you can stay out of trouble until I get back?"

Gemma rolled her eyes. "I better. I don't know what trouble I could find when I'm either going to be locked up here or at home."

Ben scoffed. "You're a trouble-magnet, so nothing would surprise me. Just promise me you'll do your best not to go looking for it."

"Scout's honor." She held up three fingers.

His eyes narrowed. "Were you even in the scouts?"

"I was. I sold more cookies than anyone else in my troop every year."

He laughed. "Now that I can believe." His smile slowly

faded as he stared down at her. One hand came up to brush the side of her face. "Just be good until I get back, okay?"

Gemma covered his hand with her own, tenderness welling up at his concern.

He bent his head and kissed her gently, but with enough fire to curl her toes. Gemma locked her knees to stay upright.

Not quite ready to let him go when he started to pull back, she wound her arms around his neck and pressed closer.

He growled softly, his arms tightening around her as she deepened the kiss.

After a moment, he pulled back again. This time Gemma let him.

"Forget trouble-magnet. You're just trouble."

She giggled. She was okay with that if it meant he kept kissing her that way.

With one last quick peck, he released her. "I better go so you can get to work." He shook a finger at her. "I meant what I said. Behave."

Gemma rolled her eyes again and shooed him toward the door. "I will be fine. Now, go."

Acquiescing, he headed for the door. "I'll call you tonight. Be nice to your brother while I'm gone."

She laughed. "I'll try, but I make no promises." Tristan had a way of pushing her buttons like no one else. And he enjoyed it. They would likely argue at least once before Ben returned.

He grinned and waved before disappearing around the corner. His boots echoed on the hard floor as he headed down the hall.

Gemma sighed. It was going to be a long thirty-six hours until he got back.

~

A rap on her office door had Gemma looking up from a stack of files late that afternoon. Tristan stood in the doorway.

"Hey," she greeted.

"Hey, Sis. You about ready to head home?"

She nodded. "Just let me finish this patient report and we can go."

Sauntering into the room, Tristan sat in one of the chairs opposite her desk to wait. He propped a booted foot on his knee and pulled out his phone, no doubt reading emails and case notes. The man seemed to be always working anymore.

As quickly as she could, Gemma finished her report and stuffed the papers back into the file, stacking it atop the others on her desk. "All right. I'm done." She opened her desk drawer and withdrew her purse. "Let's go."

Tristan stood, putting away his phone and waited for her to exit before following her out, closing the door behind him. Gemma locked it with her keys.

"I parked out front," Tristan said, pointing to their left. "Pam let me in as she was leaving."

"What do you want for dinner?" she asked as they made their way out. "I'm starving. I think there's some chicken in the freezer."

"Why don't we stop for something so you don't have to cook? My treat. Or we could do sandwiches at home. I know you're probably tired after your first day back."

She shrugged. She wasn't going to argue about not having to cook. Besides, he was right. She was tired, and she had a headache blooming between her eyes. "Stopping for something sounds good to me. How about Daisy's?" Daisy's Café was a homestyle diner just down the street owned and operated by a local Cherokee woman. It had the absolute best food.

"Works for me." He pushed through the doors and headed

for his truck, which was parked along the sidewalk in front of the building.

Within minutes, they were pulling into the restaurant parking lot. Gemma's stomach growled. Lunch had been a long time ago, and she hadn't had time for a snack this afternoon.

The hostess quickly seated them, handing them menus and taking their drink orders before she left.

Gemma barely glanced at her menu. She already knew what she wanted. Instead, she watched her brother as he looked over the menu, the fingers of one large hand drumming the table. He looked tired. Not just, haven't-slept-well-for-a-week tired, but bone-deep-life's-wearing-on-him tired. The fine lines beside his eyes crinkled a little deeper, the dark shadows a little darker than she had ever seen them. His shoulders, while still broad and straight, seemed to sag just a little. Like the weight of the world sat on them.

In all the craziness, Gemma hadn't taken the time to really look at her brother lately. She had been so focused on first Diana and Caleb, then on her growing relationship with Ben, that Tristan had taken a bit of a backseat in her life.

Well, no more, she vowed. He might drive her up the wall, but he was still her brother, and she loved him. He didn't deserve the way she had treated him lately.

"Hey. Are you okay?" she asked, reaching out to cover his hand with hers.

He looked up from the menu, startled. "I'm fine. Why?"

She shrugged. "You just look rundown."

With a soft sigh, he set the menu down. Turning his hand over in hers, he gave it a quick squeeze before releasing it. "I'm okay. Just stressed. This case has me feeling like I'm a dog chasing my tail."

Gemma nodded. She had a feeling Ben felt the same way. "I'm sorry. I wish I could help in some way."

"No," he was quick to reply. "I don't want you anywhere near this. You're already much too close. Obviously." He motioned to her head, indicating her injuries. "I still wish I could convince you to go out west and spend some time with Mom and Dad."

Gemma had contemplated leaving after the second victim was found, but ultimately, she just couldn't. There were people here counting on her. Unless there was no other option, she intended to stay.

"I know you do, but you know why I can't. And you know you would do the same thing in my shoes, so don't argue with me."

Reluctantly, he nodded.

"Have you made any headway with the new murder?"

The waitress arrived with their drinks and to take their orders before he could reply. Once they told the young woman what they wanted, Tristan sat back and watched to make sure she was out of earshot before he replied.

"Some. We know who she is, and we got some forensic evidence at the scene—clothing fibers, mostly. He had a motive too. She was a major health nut. When she was arrested for drug possession, she was pregnant with her first child. Jail made her clean up her act, but she still had to give up her baby to the foster system until she could prove she was clean. She went on a health kick and never looked back. Her husband— who she met and married after she was clean—said they used a lot of alternative medicine on themselves and the kids and ate a mostly vegetarian diet. We just don't know how her killer knew that."

Gemma frowned and took a sip of her drink, thinking. "And her husband doesn't remember seeing anyone lurking around?"

Tristan shook his head. "Nope. We've been retracing her

steps in the time between Diana's murder and hers, hoping something will show up. So far, we're still drawing blanks."

Heart aching for the woman and her family, Gemma wished she could do more to help. Normally, she stayed well away from Tristan's cases, but this one drew her in no matter how much she tried to distance herself, and not just because the killer had made her a target. The psychological aspect of it was sending her brain into overdrive as it tried to solve the puzzle of what could make someone do something so heinous. It left her feeling slightly unsettled all the time. Like the answer was just out of reach.

The aroma of Daisy's wonderful cooking reached her nose, drawing her from her reverie as Daisy Featherhawk herself sidled up to their table, steaming plates in hand.

"Hi there, you two. It's been a while, so I thought I'd come say hi. Gemma, here's your usual—chicken and dumplings over mashed potatoes. And Tristan, your meatloaf." The older woman set the plates in front of them before straightening. She tossed her long salt and pepper braid back over her shoulder and propped her hands on her ample hips. "I hear you two have found some trouble. And that you," she pointed at Gemma, "found a man."

Tristan barked out a laugh while Gemma's cheeks heated. Apparently, the killer wasn't the only one who thought there was more to her relationship with Ben.

Picking up her fork, Gemma smiled. "Trouble, yes. The man thing? Well, that's a little more complicated."

Daisy's smile was wicked. "Ooo, that's a story I need to hear." She glanced around the busy diner. "But not tonight, because it's hoppin' in here. You two enjoy your dinner now." With a wave, she turned and headed to take another table's order.

Gemma smiled at her retreating figure. "She's such a whirlwind."

"Who can cook like an angel." Tristan's eyes rolled in ecstasy as he shoveled a bite of meatloaf into his mouth.

With a grin at her brother's antics, she tucked into her own meal. She was hungry after moving around all day and quickly polished off the food on her plate. A piece of Daisy's peach pie sounded really good, but Gemma was stuffed to the gills.

But it would make a good late-night snack.

Grinning to herself, she flagged down Daisy as she blew past their table on her way to the kitchen.

"Can I get a piece of your peach pie to go, please?"

Daisy pulled out her order pad. "You sure can, sugar. How about you, detective? Do you want some dessert to go?"

Tristan groaned and rubbed his stomach. "Oh, why not? Blueberry pie, please."

Daisy scribbled both items on their bill, then tore it off and laid it on the table. "Good choice. That's my granddaughter's favorite."

A vague recollection of a tall, dark-haired woman a couple of years older than herself crossed Gemma's mind. "How's she doing? I don't remember seeing her lately. Her name is Iris, right?"

Daisy's brow wrinkled in a disturbed frown. "She's doing all right, I guess. It's been a while since I talked to her. She's in the military, so she's busy. I can't remember the last time she was home." The older woman waved a hand and smiled at them, banishing the shadows that had crossed her face at the mention of her granddaughter. "But that's neither here nor there. I'll get your pie boxed up so y'all can get out of here." Spinning on her heel, she headed for the kitchen.

"Do you remember her granddaughter?" Gemma asked, watching Daisy scurry away. "She was a few years older than me. I think she might have been a senior when I was a freshman."

"Vaguely. She was two years behind me, I think. Quiet girl. Super smart, but very shy. I can't see her in the military. She just doesn't seem the type." He shrugged. "Maybe she changed. Or maybe she joined to help herself change."

Daisy returned with their pie. Tristan pulled some cash from his wallet and handed it to the woman, telling her to keep the change.

She smiled as she bid them farewell. "Gemma, you bring that man of yours in here one day soon, understand?"

Gemma nodded politely.

"And you, young man, be careful out there. That man you're after—he's evil." She shook a long finger at Tristan.

"I will, ma'am. Thank you."

Outside, Gemma quickly buckled herself into the passenger seat, cradling their pie.

Tristan started the truck and pointed them in the direction of home.

He drummed his fingers against the steering wheel, his tongue poking out from between his teeth.

Gemma knew that look. He had something on his mind, but he didn't think she was going to like it. She sighed. "Spill it."

"What?" He frowned over at her.

"Whatever it is on your mind. Just say it."

"Jesus, what are you? A damn mind reader?" His fingers stopped drumming.

She shook her head. "No. Just a Tristan reader. Are you going to tell me what's on your mind, or are you going to make me guess?"

He huffed and shifted in his seat, hesitating a moment before finally responding. "So, what is going on with you and Ben? I saw you the other night asleep in the chair. Do you think he's really the guy for you? I mean, he's in his forties."

Gemma shook her finger in Tristan's face, glaring. "Don't you start. He's a good man and you know it."

"I didn't say he wasn't. I just wonder if he's the right one for you."

"Well, that's not for you to decide, so butt out."

He looked at her thoughtfully for a moment before turning his eyes back to the road. "You really do like him, don't you? More than any of the others you've brought home over the last few years."

Gemma crossed her arms and settled back into her seat, relaxing a bit as his antagonistic tone disappeared. "I do. I just wish I could convince him we're worth it. He's got some hang up—thinks that I deserve better." She scoffed. "I don't know what put the idea in his head that he's not good enough for me, but he's dead wrong."

"He said something similar to me the other day."

Gemma sat up, intrigued. "He did? What did he mean by it? Did he say?"

Tristan shook his head. "I don't know. He just said you deserved better."

She sighed. "Why does he have to be so cryptic? Is that something else they teach you in Ranger school?"

Tristan laughed, relaxing into his seat. "They teach us many things." He waggled his eyebrows.

He leaned into the door to rest his arm on the sill at the same time the windshield spider-webbed. The headrest exploded in tufts of foam where his head had just been.

Gemma screamed.

Tristan cursed and swerved.

A loud pop sounded and the car veered toward the center line. Gemma stared out the intact section of the windshield in horror. A silver minivan was headed right at them.

"Tristan!" She grabbed the chicken bar and squeezed her eyes tight, waiting for the crunch of metal.

The truck swerved again, spinning one hundred eighty degrees on the road before coming to a jarring halt.

Her eyes flew open, looking around frantically. "What the hell was that?"

"Someone shot at us." He hooked a thumb at the headrest in pieces behind him. "Get down." He pushed her toward the foot well.

He didn't have to tell her twice. She unlatched her seatbelt and slunk to the floor.

Hunkering low, he grabbed his radio and called for backup, then cautiously opened his door, gun drawn.

The sound of a woman shouting reached her ears.

"Ma'am, stay in your car!" Tristan yelled as he slowly climbed out of the vehicle.

Gemma muttered a prayer as he cleared the door. Completely exposed, there was nothing to stop a bullet from taking him away from her forever.

What seemed like an eternity, but in reality was only a minute or two, passed before Tristan poked his head back in and told her she could get out.

Hands shaking, Gemma pushed herself up and looked out Tristan's open door. The truck had come to rest within feet of the minivan. She heard several small children crying in the van, and her heart leaped into her throat. If Tristan wasn't such a good driver, they very well could have hit that van full of kids.

She climbed out of the truck and came around to where Tristan stood talking to the driver of the other vehicle. Sirens wailed in the distance as their backup got closer.

As she leaned against the truck, surveying the damage, she couldn't help but think that Ben was going to blow a gasket over this. He hadn't been gone twelve hours, and she had already found trouble.

Twenty-Two

Cursing at himself, the shooter lowered his rifle. He had been so close! Why did the damn man have to move?

When Gemma and that cop brother of hers stopped for dinner, he realized it was the perfect time to get his hands on the woman. He had taken up a sniping position on their route home and waited while they ate.

He still couldn't believe he missed. Today had been the perfect opportunity. He'd followed Agent Davidson after he dropped Gemma off this morning, only to realize the man was leaving town. With Davidson away and Gemma's brother dead or incapacitated, he could have taken her and been long gone before anyone went looking.

He peered through the rifle scope again, wondering if he could get off another shot. Children began pouring out of the minivan that Detective Mabley's truck had barely missed. An obviously distraught woman attempted to corral them to the side of the road out of traffic. Other vehicles were now stopping to render aid, and the first rescue vehicle had arrived.

Even though it was tempting just to shoot the man now, it

would do him no good. With all the people around, he would never be able to get to Gemma.

Realizing he needed to be on his way before the good detective sent deputies into the woods looking for him, he slung the rifle over his back and climbed down from the tree. Gemma Mabley's day of reckoning was coming, and he would finally see to it that Agent Davidson was too crippled with grief to continue his investigation.

He just needed a better plan.

Twenty-Three

The sound of the car door closing echoed through the warm night air as Ben exited his vehicle. He'd driven like a madman back to get back to Foggy Mountain after Tristan's call earlier. He didn't care that it was after one in the morning. It wouldn't have done him any good to stay in Richmond overnight. He wouldn't have slept.

Using the key Tristan gave him the first night he was here, Ben let himself into the silent house, disarming the alarm system. He locked the door and reactivated the alarm before heading down the hallway to the bedrooms. He needed to see her. To make sure she really was all right.

The door to his left opened before he reached Gemma's door at the end of the hall. Tristan stepped out, gun in his hand.

Ben stopped abruptly, hands raised. "It's me, Tristan."

Tristan lowered the gun, eyes glowing a steely blue in the low light. "What the hell are you doing back already? I told you we were fine."

Ben shrugged, unable and unwilling to verbalize what drove him to make the six-hour journey back to the Mabley's so late at night. Especially to Tristan. "I just decided to come back."

Tristan rolled his eyes, letting Ben know he wasn't fooling anyone. "Sure you did. I'm going back to bed." He turned on his heel and went back into his room, closing the door with a soft snick.

Ben stared at the closed door. What the hell *was* he doing?

Acting like a lovesick fool, that's what. But he'd be damned if he could muster up the effort to care. All that mattered was the chestnut-haired trouble-magnet sleeping twenty feet away.

Drawn like a moth to a flame, Ben continued down the hall until he stood outside her door. Softly, he turned the knob and stepped into the doorway.

The glow from the nightlight in the hallway cast just enough light for him to see the lump in the bed buried beneath the comforter. She looked like she was hiding from the world. After what she'd been through, he wouldn't be surprised if that was exactly what her unconscious mind was trying to do.

As silently as he could, he crossed the room and sat on the bed next to her. She looked like a mummy. Sleeping on her side, she had the comforter pulled all the way up to her ears and tucked beneath her chin. He reached out and ran a finger along her cheekbone, needing to touch her to reassure himself.

She stirred at his touch, a soft sigh escaping. Her eyelashes fluttered as she slowly opened her eyes.

"Shh. I didn't mean to wake you. I just wanted to check on you before I went to bed."

"Ben?" She pushed the blankets back a bit and rolled onto her back.

His hand slid from her face to rest on her shoulder.

"What are you doing back so soon?"

He toyed with a lock of her hair. "After Tristan called, I knew I wouldn't be able to sleep, so I drove back tonight."

She sat up, her hands going to his chest. "I'm glad you're back."

Any pretense about why he'd driven back in the middle of the night vanished as she looked up at him with her sleepy, but happy, blue eyes. He had needed to touch her to know she was safe. To take her in his arms and show her how grateful he was that she was alive and well.

Palming the back of her head, he kissed her. Not a gentle kiss like they shared that morning before he left, but a soul-searing, mind-numbing lip lock that threatened his sanity and had him instantly aching for more.

It didn't matter that this was wrong. That their relationship could never go beyond his time here for this case. He was helpless to do anything except surrender to the woman in his arms.

Her fingers lanced through his hair, sending shivers down his spine. He curled his free hand over her hip through the blanket and pulled her closer. She came eagerly.

All coherent thought disappeared as she trailed her hands down his shoulders, leaving a blaze of heat in her wake. Nimble fingers slid beneath his t-shirt to flutter over his stomach. The muscles clenched in response.

In a vague moment of clarity, he remembered where they were and that he left the door wide open. Ben broke away and stood.

"No. Come back," she breathed, reaching for him.

"I'm just closing the door. I doubt you want Tristan listening to this." He crossed the room in three long strides and closed the door, throwing the lock with a quick flick of his wrist.

Three more steps had him back at her side. She flipped on the bedside lamp, illuminating the room in a muted glow. He whisked his shirt over his head and sat down to unlace his boots.

The soft tickle of her hands on his back and biceps nearly undid him. He moaned. She was tracing the tattoos he'd revealed.

His fingers fumbled with his bootlaces, but he managed to jerk them free. Toeing the shoes off, he turned to end the torture.

Urgency gripped him, and he grasped the hem of her sleep shirt, pulling it over her head and exposing her body to his view. Fading bruises marred the otherwise perfect skin of her ribcage, but it did little to diminish her beauty. He cupped one perfect, full breast in his hand, the pink nipple beading when he flicked it with his thumb.

She leaned into him, resting her forehead against his. His other hand skated gently up her side.

"I don't want to hurt you, Gemma." His eyes found hers in the soft light.

"Just don't squeeze me and I'll be fine," she retorted, nipping at his lips.

Growling softly at the contact, he tried to kiss her, but she pulled back to look at him. She trailed one nail down his biceps, tracing the lines of his tattoos once again. "These are beautiful. I had no idea you had them."

Goosebumps broke out on his skin from the light touch. "Most people don't. When I got them, per Army regs, they couldn't be visible below a t-shirt sleeve. Unless I take my shirt off, you can never see them."

She grinned wickedly. "That's fine by me. You can just wander around the house without a shirt now."

He laughed. "I think Tristan would disapprove."

"Mm. I don't care what he thinks."

He tugged on her hair, tipping her head back. "No?"

"No." She looked up at him, desire stamped all over her

face. Taking his head in her hands, she kissed him for all she was worth.

Ben's control snapped. He took over the kiss, plundering the sweet recesses of her mouth. Gently, he moved her over on the bed and laid down on his back, pulling her onto his chest. His hands roamed over her back and up her sides, caressing her breasts as he enjoyed the feel of her warm weight pressing into him.

She moaned and tossed her leg over his waist, setting herself astride his hips. Heat from her core scalded his abdomen, making him nearly cross-eyed with need. As much as he wanted this to last, he knew it wouldn't. Not this time. He was already near the breaking point and neither of them were naked yet.

Looking to rectify that, he hooked his index fingers in her panties and tugged. She moved to help him take them off, kicking them to the floor once he got them to her knees.

Before he could touch the new places he exposed, Gemma tackled the button and zipper on his jeans. With a quick rasp of metal, his erection sprang free, covered only by the thin material of his boxer briefs. Hot light speared him behind his eyes as she ran her palm down his length, squeezing him through his underwear. She was killing him.

Unable to take much more, he pulled her up his chest and fused their mouths together again.

Gemma felt like a live wire. Like she had been electrified with fifty thousand volts of pure energy. Tingles raced up and down her spine, making her entire body hum as Ben's hands and mouth roamed over her. Desperate for more, she pushed at his jeans and underwear, trying to shove them down. He lifted his hips so she could push the material down past his butt.

She didn't waste any time once he was free of his pants. As soon as the material cleared the tops of his thighs, she straddled him again and positioned herself over his erection.

He grasped her hips, holding her steady, a groan ripping free from his chest. "Please tell me you're on the pill."

She nodded, her voice lost in the sea of fire created by the man beneath her. Not waiting for him to respond, she pushed down and took him inside. They both moaned at the searing connection.

Heat swamped her body as he filled her, and she gasped as he thrust up. She rolled her hips in response, and they quickly found a rhythm that sent them spiraling toward paradise.

She tried to slow them down—she wanted this to last—but her body had a mind of its own. With a final roll of her hips, her body let go. Wave after wave of the most intense pleasure she'd ever felt rolled through her. She bit her lip, trying to keep the shout of ecstasy inside. A muffled moan escaped as she rode the surge of sensation rocketing through her veins.

Ben's body tightened beneath hers as his own climax hit. He pulled her closer, drowning a moan in her neck as he succumbed to the flames.

Body boneless, Gemma collapsed onto his chest, her breath sawing in and out as she tried to regain her equilibrium.

"Wow," she finally managed. "Why did we wait so long to do that?"

He groaned, tightening the band of his arms around her waist. "I don't know."

Passion ebbing, Gemma yawned. She shifted, curling into him as sleep pulled at her. Her toes hit denim, and she lifted her head, laughter bubbling up. "You want help with your pants?"

He chuckled and untangled himself from her. "Next time,

maybe I'll make it all the way out of them before you jump me."

She sat up and grabbed the waistband, tugging them down his legs. "I wouldn't be too sure about that." He kicked his feet, freeing himself from the dark denim.

Dropping the jeans to the floor, she looked up to see him propped on his elbows staring at her, his eyes liquid silver in the low light. Her heart sped up, and arousal flooded her system once more. The man was so incredibly sexy.

"Don't look at me like that, Gems. I'm no spring chicken anymore. My forty-year-old body can't recover that fast."

Grinning wickedly, she crawled back up his frame until she was stretched out along his side. She threaded her fingers into the whorls of hair on his chest. "You can make it up to me in the morning."

Truthfully, while her body hummed with desire, it was also running on fumes. It had been a long and arduous couple of weeks, and she was nearing the end of her reserves. She yawned again.

Ben pulled the sheet and comforter back up over them and placed a lingering kiss on the top of her head. "Mara won't mind if you're late, right?" he said with a smile.

She giggled sleepily. "If only."

He reached one long arm over to turn off the lamp before dropping another kiss on her hair. "Go to sleep."

Hooking her leg over his, she did just that.

∼

Sunlight filtered through the blinds over the bedroom window, waking Gemma the next morning. She raised her head to glance at the alarm clock on the nightstand next to Ben. It was still early.

Settling back down, she ran her hands over the warm male

body lying next to her. For a man his age, he was incredibly fit. No doubt a holdover from his Army days. Firm, supple muscles rose and fell beneath her as he breathed. His warm, golden, tattoo-covered skin felt like silk under her hands. She lightly traced the ridges of bone and muscle in his chest, moving up and over his shoulders to follow the outlines of the muscles in his arms. He was beautiful.

Her ministrations soon roused him from his slumber. His eyes fluttered open, and he smiled at her as he came awake. "Good morning."

"Good morning," she echoed, continuing to run her hands over his body.

He hummed a little. "That feels good."

She smiled. "Good, because I like touching you." She ran a hand down his arm. "And looking. I love that you have these," she said, fingering the ink on his arm. "I'm surprised, but I know I shouldn't be. You're edgier than your Hollywood looks imply."

He looked at her, aghast. "Hollywood?"

She giggled. "You look like a movie star. Until you take off your shirt and we see this." She touched the tattoo on his right pectoral muscle. "Tristan has the same one. It's your Ranger insignia, right?"

He nodded.

She ran a finger around the design. "I never thought I would be attracted to a man with tattoos. I've always gone for the more preppy types. Buttoned up, straight-laced. Professionals. My last boyfriend was an attorney who I don't think even knew how to hold a gun properly, let alone fire one."

"Now I see why Tristan was running them off."

She slapped his chest.

He crossed his arms, laughing, and gave her a fake pout. "Ow."

She rolled her eyes and sat up. "As much as I hate to admit

it, I'm kind of glad he did." She shook her finger in his face. "If you *ever* tell him that, I will deny it and then make you sleep on the couch for a week." Ben's eyes dropped to her naked chest. His pupils dilated, crowding out the turquoise as he became aroused. She felt her body flush in response.

"So why are you glad?" He sat up, slipping an arm around her waist to pull her closer.

She sighed, pressing her body to his. "Because we wouldn't be right here right now if he didn't. I'd probably still be attached to David Masterson and trying to deny that I found you intriguing and sexy."

He nuzzled her neck. "Remind me to thank him."

She sucked in a deep breath, goosebumps erupting on her skin.

The alarm clock on the nightstand buzzed, breaking the mood. Ben growled, releasing her to reach over and turn it off. Gemma sagged into the mattress with a groan. She did not want to go to work. She wanted to stay right here all day. If only it was the weekend.

He tossed the blanket back and stood. Every cell in Gemma's body went on full alert at the sight of the naked man standing next to the bed.

God, he was gorgeous.

Grabbing her hand, he pulled her off the bed before scooping her up into his arms. She let out a squeal at the unexpected move.

"Later, I'll thank him. Right now, we need to get ready for work."

She rolled her eyes, looping her arms around his neck as he headed for the attached bathroom. "I'm going to be late, aren't I?"

A grin quirked the corner of his mouth. "Maybe."

Twenty-Four

Frustration clawed at Ben's gut as he watched the surveillance footage from the construction business located near the shooting. A green Chevy SUV drove out from behind the business just minutes after Tristan's truck was shot up. Unfortunately, the video quality was too poor—even with the enhancement the FBI techs did—to see the license plate or the driver.

Tristan's fist slammed into the desk. "Dammit! What's the point in even having the cameras if you can't make anything out?"

Ben sat back and scrubbed his hands over his face before glancing up at Tristan, who leaned on his fists on the desk. "Well, at least we know we're looking for a green Chevy SUV like Mrs. Brannigan and Caleb described."

"It still doesn't help us get that warrant. We don't have anything to confirm that the killer is a park ranger." Tristan pushed off the desk and ran both hands through his hair, clasping them at the back of his head. "I swear, this guy is a damned ghost. If that car didn't keep showing up, I'd think he was a figment of our imagination." He dropped his hands. "How does he keep eluding us, Ben? Other than the clothing fiber evidence, we have nothing. Best guess is that he's white, approximately a hundred seventy-five pounds, and wears a size ten shoe. That's a majority of the men in the county. We can't cross reference them all with a green Chevy SUV."

"No. You're right. We've got jack all and we're running out of leads. If we're going to catch this son-of-a-bitch, I think we're going to have to go on the offensive." The bones of a plan began to take shape in his mind. If they played all their cards right, they could draw the bastard out.

Tristan's gaze sharpened. "You have an idea?"

"Maybe. But it's going to involve your sister."

"Seeing as she doesn't want to leave, I don't think we have much choice."

Ben agreed. If Gemma was ever going to be safe, they needed to catch this guy. Preferably before he became even more unhinged and killed his seventh victim.

"So, what do you have in mind?"

"He's fixated on her, thinking if he hurts her, he punishes me and hopefully gets me to back off of my investigation. I think that's what yesterday was about. With you out of the picture, and me out of town, Gemma was easy pickings. What if we give the illusion she's alone?"

"Set a trap, you mean? With Gemma as bait?"

Ben leaned back again. It sounded crazy when put so bluntly, but they were running out of options. "Yeah."

Tristan's eyebrows skyrocketed. "You seriously want to put her in harm's way?"

"No. But I don't have any other ideas. The longer this guy is out there, the greater the chance something happens to Gemma or to some other unsuspecting woman."

Tristan sank into a chair. "So, how do we do this and keep

her safe? She might be the pawn, but it doesn't mean we leave her defenseless."

Ben picked up a pen and twirled it through his fingers as his mind worked out the details. "We set it up some place we can control the access points and make it *look like* she's by herself—the house or the equestrian center most likely—then we make it clear she's alone. Hopefully, he'll show his face."

"And if he doesn't?"

That was the rub. For this plan to work, their guy had to take the bait. "We cross that bridge if and when we come to it." He sat forward, tapping the pen on the desk. "I'm not saying this is foolproof, but we have to try something, or we're going to have a third victim in as many weeks. *Or* he's going to find a way to eliminate one or both of us and get to Gemma. Neither of those scenarios is acceptable."

Tristan sighed. "You know, I've always hated it when you used that logical thinking crap on me. It's made me agree to some really hair-brained ideas in the past."

Ben grinned. "It never got you shot, though."

"True," Tristan answered with a short laugh. "Fine." He shook a finger at Ben. "But you get to ask her if she'll do it."

A frown creased Gemma's forehead as she listened to Ben and Tristan's plan to catch the serial killer. "Let me get this straight. You want to leave me 'alone'," she air quoted, "so the killer will make a move on me and you can catch him. How do you know he'll know I'm alone? We can't exactly call him up and tell him that."

Ben and Tristan shared a look before turning back to her.

"You and I are going to stage a public fight," Ben

explained. "If he's watching you like we think he is, then he'll know you're alone when I go storming off."

"That's a big if. What happens if it doesn't work? If he isn't watching me?"

Ben shrugged. "Then we try something else. The point is we can't sit around on our hands and do nothing. He's already devolving. It's time for a push."

Gemma chewed her lip and looked back and forth between the two men. She couldn't believe either of them was proposing such a thing. It went against every brotherly instinct Tristan had. And Ben—well, he had already stated that he wished that she would agree to let him spirit her away somewhere safe. They must be getting desperate for leads if this was the plan.

"I think the idea has merit, but I just can't see it working the way you envision it to," she finally replied.

"Why not?" Tristan asked, obviously perplexed.

She looked up at him. "Because of all the chaos he caused by trying to shoot you. He's going to be much more cautious now. Trying to take you out so directly was a bold move, and he's going to anticipate that you're going to step up the security surrounding me. Even if Ben and I stage a fight and I appear to be alone, he's going to wonder if I really am—which, according to your plan, I won't be. I just don't think he'll take the chance. Not without some extra incentive."

Tristan frowned. "What kind of incentive? We don't have anything on the guy to use to embolden him."

She grinned. "Sure you do. Me."

Ben waved a hand. "I'm confused. What are you talking about? We already want to use you as bait. If you're suggesting we really do let you go off alone with just a tracker or something, you can forget it. Using you as fake bait and real bait are two different things, and the latter is not going to happen.

There's going to be a team of deputies and agents surrounding you in the shadows. That is non-negotiable."

"Not that, no. What I mean is, what if I disappear for a few days? We make him wonder where I am and if I had really run away to safety. If he gets anxious about my where-abouts, it might just unhinge him enough that he won't think it through when I come back and we stage our fight. When you storm off 'angry,' he'll hopefully walk right into your trap."

Ben studied her, speculation in his green eyes, as he thought over her proposal. She was right about this. She could feel it in her bones. This guy had become obsessed with her quickly. If she removed herself from the picture—even temporarily—it would drive him absolutely nuts until he found her.

"What do you think?" Ben asked Tristan.

Tristan shrugged. "She's the one with the psychology degree. She may not use it to delve into the inner-workings of a criminal's thought process, but she knows how the human mind works. I say we give her plan a chance. It can't hurt."

"All right." Ben gave a short nod. "We'll do it your way, Gems. I'll have the FBI book you a plane ticket out west. I'm sure—"

Gemma held out her hand to cut him off. "Hold on there a minute. Who said I'm going out west? I have no desire to bring Mom and Dad into this. On the off-chance this psycho tracks me down, I don't want them anywhere near me."

"Okay." Ben crossed his arms and stared at her defiantly. "If not Arizona, then what did you have in mind? And I hope you plan on Tristan being with you if you aren't going to see your parents, because you certainly can't go without someone there to watch your back."

Gemma felt her hackles rise. He was going back to the heavy-handed crap again, thinking he knew best. Well, he didn't know her as well as he thought he did or he would be anticipating what she had to say to that.

She took a step forward and rested her hand lightly on his chest. "Oh, I definitely don't plan on going alone." She walked two fingers up his torso to trace his jawline. "You're going with me."

He frowned fiercely. "I can't. I have a case to investigate."

"And Tristan doesn't?" she quickly shot back.

"It's different. This is *my* case. You two wouldn't even be involved if it hadn't landed on your doorstep."

"Maybe not," Tristan argued. "But I think you'll have more success if you go with her. Both of you disappearing at the same time? Ought to drive our guy wild. You have a phone and a laptop. You can still run things from wherever it is she has in mind. I can handle the grunt work here."

"I think we both need a break from all this, Ben," Gemma argued. "And we definitely need some space from everything so we can figure out whatever this is between us."

His hand came up to cover hers. "Gemma—"

She cut in before he could voice an argument. "You've been trying to get me out of here since this started. Wouldn't it be nice to not have to worry about my safety for several days?" She freed her hand from his so she could circle his neck. She toyed with the hair at his nape. Desire darkened his eyes. Gemma pressed the advantage and leaned into him. His hands landed on her hips. "No one would bat an eye if you took a few days off. You've been working non-stop since you got here. This is a strategic move to draw out a suspect. We could go down to the Sea Islands outside of Charleston. A lot of them are gated. You can't even get onto the island without a pass or a boat."

She stared up at him and watched the muscles in his jaw work as his mind warred with his body's response to her.

Ben's eyes closed. If he clenched his jaw any tighter, he'd

break his teeth. "Gemma, I can't—" he took a deep breath and his eyes popped open. "I need to be here. I'm sorry. If you want to go, I'm all for it, but it's going to be Tristan going with you."

Gemma steeled her resolve. There was no way she was going anywhere with Tristan. She leaned closer. "I'm not going with Tristan. You and I have some things to talk about." She pressed her finger over his lips as he began to protest again. "I am well aware you don't think now is an appropriate time for us to discuss our relationship. But, knowing you and how scared you are of what you feel for me, there will never *be* an appropriate time. Tristan is right. He can handle the groundwork, and you can manage things from a distance. You're. Going. With. Me." She punctuated each word with a poke to his chest.

The steely resolve remained in his turquoise eyes. Deciding this called for the big guns, she grasped his face in her hands and pulled him down for a kiss.

His resistance only lasted a millisecond before he gave in to the kiss and took over. His tongue swept inside her mouth to tangle with hers, and he wrapped his long arms around her waist, lifting her against him.

Tingles raced through Gemma's body, making every touch, every whisper of contact feel ten times more potent. She circled his neck with her arms and wriggled closer until every inch of her body was touching his.

A sound of disgust penetrated her passion-fogged brain, reminding her that Tristan stood only feet away.

Ben heard it as well. Gemma had to reach out a hand to the wall to steady herself as he thrust her away from him at the sound.

She glared at her brother. "You can go away now."

He just grinned wickedly at her.

Ben scowled at them both. "This is insane. Why are we

arguing about this? And what happened to you not wanting me to lay a hand on her?" he asked, leveling a glare at Tristan.

Tristan shrugged and crossed his arms. "I'd say that ship sailed a while ago. I still don't trust you not to break her heart, but I can't keep you apart now. You don't back down like the others."

Ben's scowl deepened. Gemma could see he'd been depending on Tristan's support to get out of going with her. While she was thankful Tristan was taking her side, she couldn't help but scowl along with Ben at his admission that he had deliberately sabotaged her past relationships.

"If you won't go with her, then she doesn't go. We'll come up with some other plan." Ben fixed his eyes on her as he addressed Tristan.

She smiled sweetly. "That's where you're wrong. If you don't go, I go alone."

Ben growled while Tristan just laughed.

Gemma flattened herself against the wall when Ben advanced on her. "That's not going to happen, Gemma." His voice rumbled through her, low and dark, the anger in it palpable.

Her eyes narrowed to slits. She was through with over-bearing men. "Try and stop me." She pushed past him and stomped down the hall to her bedroom.

Ben watched Gemma retreat down the hall, her shoulders ramrod straight in defiance. The woman tried his patience like no other. He wanted to chase after her and strangle her for being so obstinate at the same time he wanted to go wrestle her onto the bed and keep her there, where she was safe in his arms. He couldn't ever remember being so conflicted over anything, and it was driving him absolutely crazy.

She slammed her door behind her, emphasizing just how angry she was at him. Tristan stepped in front of him, glaring.

"What?" Ben glared back.

The look on Tristan's face was identical to the one his sister had just leveled on him.

"Are you really going to stand there and let her leave?" Tristan gestured down the hall. "You know she'll find a way to go by herself."

Ben's eyebrows shot up, incredulous. "How the hell is she going to get away? She doesn't have a car, and the house is surrounded by cops."

"Oh, she'll get away, trust me. Gemma was the master at sneaking out when she was a teenager. She never once got caught, and I still don't know how she got away. I could lie in wait outside and never see her coming or going."

Ben crossed his arms, tipping his head back and closing his eyes. The muscles in his jaw clenched and unclenched. Why did she have to be so stubborn?

"She terrifies you, doesn't she?"

Ben opened his eyes and tipped his head down. Tristan watched him with speculation in his deep blue eyes. He swiped a hand down his face and opted for total honesty. All the half-truths sure weren't working for him anymore. "Like nothing in my life ever has."

Tristan shook his head and pinched the bridge of his nose. "I can't believe I'm about to advocate for a man to date my sister. She better appreciate this." He dropped his hand and looked Ben square in the eye. "Why are you so afraid? You obviously have some strong feelings for her, and she feels the same. And it's not like she's some whack job, stalker-type. So, what the hell is stopping you?"

"Because I don't do relationships. You know that. When

have I ever mentioned a woman as more than a passing fancy? I don't want to be tied down," Ben snarled.

"That's bullshit and you know it," Tristan tossed back. "You aren't afraid to be tied down. And if it's the right woman, it won't feel like a ball and chain. No, you're scared of *her*. Of what she makes you *feel*."

"Since when did you become Dr. Phil?"

Tristan smiled. "Ben, I've watched my parents for the last thirty-four years. They aren't 'tied down' to anyone. But the feelings they have for each other are intense. Gemma and I grew up knowing how much they love each other. It's a scary thought to imagine someone having that much power over you. Someone with the ability to knock you down and cut you off at the knee so you can't ever get up again. But, if the happiness my parents have enjoyed for the last four decades is anything to go by, it's totally worth it. I hope I'm one of the lucky ones who gets to experience it someday. You're a lucky man to have a woman like Gemma look at you the way she does. Don't run from that."

Ben paced several feet away before turning back to stare at his friend. Logically, he knew Tristan was right, but it didn't change the conflicted emotions coursing through him.

But Tristan was wrong about one thing. It wasn't fear for himself that left him quaking, not totally. He was mostly afraid he would let Gemma down. That he could never offer her enough to make her happy.

"Tris, I don't know how to love like that. I don't want to break her heart." He absolutely did not want to hurt Gemma. He feared that if they ventured down the relationship road, it would only lead to destruction.

"Man, if you haven't noticed, she's already head over heels for you. If you don't at least try, then you already have."

Ben's gaze turned back to the hallway. Was Tristan right? Did it matter anymore if he kept his distance or not?

"If you don't want her the way she wants you, then you need to tell her that. She deserves that much. And stay the hell out of her bedroom at night."

Ben looked at Tristan, who stared at him, thunderclouds in his blue eyes.

"And if I do want her as much as she wants me?"

Tristan crossed his arms, still glaring. "Just go talk to her."

Inhaling deeply, Ben squared his shoulders. Tristan was right. Gemma deserved an explanation for his behavior. She deserved a hell of a lot more, but he still wasn't sure he could give it to her.

Boots echoing on the hard floor, he headed down the hall.

Gemma pulled her phone from her pocket and texted Mara as soon as she closed her bedroom door, asking her friend to book her a condo on one of the Sea Islands. She was going to Charleston whether Ben and Tristan liked it or not. This needed to end, and the only way that would happen was if they antagonized the bastard enough, they pissed him off and he came after her. In order to do that, she needed to leave town for a few days.

Getting away from the house would not be a problem. She nearly made a career out of sneaking out of this house when she was a teenager. She knew how to elude people when she wanted to.

The only thing that gave her pause was that she was used to eluding the people she knew and could see. She didn't know what the killer looked like or even where he might be hiding. It naturally made her a little leery that he would be able to follow her once she slipped out of the house. She was banking on the fact that he wouldn't be expecting her to sneak out. In the end, it didn't matter, though. If leaving was the only way to catch the man, then leave she would.

Grabbing her suitcase from her closet, she laid it open on her bed. Moving to her dresser, she pulled out a handful of t-shirts and laid them in the open case.

She doubted she would have to resort to sneaking out, though, she mused as she packed. There was no way Ben would let her leave alone. No matter how he felt about her or how much he denied last night meant anything, he wouldn't let her be alone with a crazed killer stalking her. He cared that much she knew.

Gemma took a handful of underwear from her drawer and turned to toss it on top of the other clothes she'd haphazardly thrown into the suitcase. The door flew open, and Ben loomed in the doorway, larger than life.

Her breath caught at the expression on his face. It was wary, but not angry like it had been when she stormed out of the living room. Uncertainty shone in his eyes, along with something more intense.

He stepped inside and quietly closed the door. Gemma worked the lingerie in her hands until she realized what she was doing. She dumped it all on the bed and clasped her hands together to keep them still. He stopped in front of her and stared at her again, much like he did that day at the arena.

His eyes tracked to the open suitcase behind her. One eyebrow cocked, but he remained silent.

She crossed her arms and stared up at him defiantly. "What?"

He sighed. "You're not going to make this easy, are you?"

She just shook her head. He was dreaming if he thought she'd just throw her arms wide and let him back into her good graces with just a kiss. She was done with tiptoeing around their feelings for each other. After last night, he owed her more than that.

"God, Gemma." He scrubbed at his face with one hand, closing his eyes briefly before looking at her again. When he did, the naked emotion she saw there was enough to give her hope. "I barely know where to start. You have come barreling into my life and completely flipped it upside down. Not only am I dealing with a case that continually comes up to bite me on my ass, but I'm dealing with the killer coming after *you*. You. The one person in the world who has ever found a chink in my armor and wormed her way inside. You burrowed in and used every tool you had to just chip away at it until you finally ripped it free. Now, I'm exposed and—*feeling* things for the first time I never thought—never wanted—to feel for anyone."

He stepped close and wove the fingers of one hand into her hair, cupping the side of her head. His eyes burned, and Gemma felt herself sinking deep.

"The truth is, I don't think I can give you what you need to be happy and I don't want to hurt you. That's why I don't think we're a good idea," he said softly.

She touched his face. "I told you before. I don't need a perfect man, Ben. I just need you."

"You say that now, but—"

"I will say that *always*. You aren't the only one feeling things you've never felt before." She framed his face in her hands. "I just want you to give us a chance."

Emotions swirling in his eyes she couldn't quite decipher, he laid his hands over hers and pulled them down to clasp them between their bodies. "I can't promise I won't screw this up, but I can't just walk away from you anymore." He took a deep breath and let it out. "And, I don't want to."

Elation poured through Gemma. Finally, she had broken through his defenses. He may not have admitted he loved her—yet—but it was a start.

Standing up on her tiptoes, she pressed a kiss to his lips.

Holding her close, he deepened the kiss briefly before

gently pulling away. Arms looped loosely around her waist, he brushed the hair away from her face.

"So, I'm guessing by the haphazardly packed suitcase behind you that you were planning an escape?"

Gemma had the good grace to blush. She nodded. "I texted Mara as soon as I got in here and had her book me a condo on one of the Sea Islands."

When he just stared at her, she kept talking. "You said it yourself. We need to draw the killer out. If me going away entices him out of his hidey-hole, then away I go. With or without you." She poked him in the chest for emphasis.

"Well, at least you covered your tracks. Just out of curiosity, how were you planning on getting away? You don't have any means of transportation and there are two cruisers parked on either side of the property, watching for any sign of trouble."

She smiled coyly and shrugged. "They aren't watching for me, so slipping past them would be easy. As for transportation, my dad's truck is in storage."

Ben rolled his eyes and sighed. "I'm going to have to watch you like a hawk. You never miss a beat."

She giggled. "But you'll never be bored. I can promise you that."

His answering smile was joyful and unencumbered. He looked like a weight had been lifted off his shoulders. Gemma was glad to see that acknowledging his feelings for her had such a positive effect on him.

"No, I definitely won't." He nodded at her suitcase. "So, when does this reservation of ours start?"

"Tomorrow."

He groaned, his head falling back. "Well, at least that gives me a little time to put things in order before we leave."

"Tristan can handle it," she said, threading her fingers into his hair.

His eyes darkened as arousal flared. "I do believe you're right." He tightened his arms around her, pulling her flush against him.

"Of course I am."

He smothered her giggle with a kiss.

Twenty-Five

Warm, salty air brushed over Gemma's face as she leaned against the railing on the balcony of the small condo she rented in South Carolina's Sea Islands. It was shortly after seven o'clock, and a warm evening breeze blew across the dunes. The sound of waves crashing and seagulls crying reached her ears. Once they made it to the condo, she'd quickly changed for dinner before making a beeline for the balcony. The fresh air and waves crashing had called to her like a siren's song.

Closing her eyes, she took a deep breath, absorbing the atmosphere. Peace washed over her for the first time in two weeks.

Strong arms circled her waist, and Gemma leaned back into Ben's warmth. He pressed a kiss to her neck. "I know it's all temporary and the world will come crashing back around our ears the minute we drive back into Foggy Mountain, but right here, right now, I'm very glad you pushed me into this."

She spun around and looped her arms around his neck. "Mmm. Me too," Gemma murmured against his mouth as he settled a soft kiss on her lips.

All too soon for her liking, he broke the feather-light touch. "You ready to go grab some food?"

Gemma stepped away, suddenly eager to start their mini-vacation. South Carolina's coastal region was one of her absolute favorite places. It had some great places to explore and some of the best restaurants a person could find anywhere.

"Yes!" She grabbed his hand and led him back into the condo.

~

Ben found himself grinning at Gemma's enthusiasm for this little trip. It was definitely catching, and he felt a lot of the tension that had been his constant companion for the last couple of weeks start to melt away as he let her lead him to the car. He helped her into the SUV and quickly rounded the front of the vehicle to climb in beside her.

"Where to?" he asked, starting the engine.

Gemma named the seafood restaurant they passed on their way onto the island. Ben followed her directions, and they were pulling into the parking lot in minutes. He held open the door to the restaurant and followed her inside. Loud music greeted them from the live band playing on the stage in the far corner. Immediately, he scanned the room for threats, noting that the dance floor was full, as were many of the tables.

"Relax, would you?" Gemma said, threading an arm through his. "You made sure no one followed us here. We're safe. *I'm* safe."

He forced the tension from his shoulders he hadn't realized he'd been feeling. Instinct put him on alert the moment they walked inside. But she was right. He had doubled checked the car for tracking devices and taken multiple nonsensical turns on their way out of town before he was certain that they weren't being followed. Any threats they faced inside this restaurant wouldn't come from the psycho back home.

Ben gave his name to the hostess, then led Gemma to the bar while they waited on a table. Determined to relax and make the most of the trip, he ordered a beer. Gemma asked for a strawberry margarita.

"I haven't been here in years. And it didn't look like this then," she commented, settling next to him at the bar as they waited for their drinks.

He bent close so he could hear her over the music and crowd noise. "You've been here before?"

She nodded. "I was a teenager. A *young* teenager. My family came here for vacation the summer before Tristan left for college, and we ate here several times. I've been back to Charleston multiple times, but I haven't been back out here since then."

The bartender handed them their drinks, and Ben watched Gemma take a long pull on hers. "You planning on getting drunk on me, Mabley?"

She grinned wickedly and took another drink. "Maybe. You want me to?"

Ben's blood heated at the look in her eyes. It promised to set him on fire later, alcohol or not.

"I think you're dangerous whether you've been drinking or not," he said, voice dropping. He leaned closer. Her eyes turned to midnight as her desire flared. She sucked her bottom lip between her teeth, a blush stealing over her cheeks.

His groin swelled behind his fly, and suddenly, he wasn't very hungry anymore. He'd been fighting his reaction to her since he stepped onto the balcony to find her dressed in a low-cut, flowy top and a pair of Bermuda shorts. The heeled sandals she had donned made her legs look a mile long. She was the sexiest woman he'd ever laid eyes on.

Seriously debating whether to just grab her and head back to the condo, Ben snapped out of the trance Gemma had put him in when someone jostled him from behind. He looked away and took a long pull on his beer, trying to cool his overheated body.

Damn, she was potent.

Taking another swig, he tried to tune into the band. Regardless of what his body wanted with Gemma, they still needed to talk more about where this was going and what each of them expected from the other. He still wasn't sure he had it in him to make this work, but he wanted Gemma to know unequivocally that he was going to try.

So, here he sat. In a crowded restaurant, half aroused.

He could have circumvented this scenario if they had talked on the drive down here, but by some unspoken agreement, they had avoided the topic on the five-hour drive. Instead, he asked her about some of the crazier stories Tristan had told him about her.

Ben smiled at the memory. As much trouble as she was now, he was glad he wasn't dealing with the teenage Gemma. She had been a wildcat. And accident prone.

She leaned into him as someone pushed past her to get to the bar. Her soft curves brushed against him, threatening to send his already overheated body into a full conflagration.

Yep. Dinner was going to be torture.

Night had fallen by the time Ben parked the car in front of their condo. Dinner was delicious, but Gemma barely remembered what she'd eaten. She spent the entire time trying not to think about where they were going to end up later. She was astonished she hadn't come across as sounding like a blubbering idiot.

Covertly, she swiped her damp palms on her shorts as Ben hurried around the front of the vehicle to open her door for her. She took his proffered hand and slid out of her seat.

She didn't know why she was so nervous. They'd already slept together once. But for some reason, this time felt different. Maybe it was because it was deliberate. Last time had been an impulse. But, tonight? Tonight, they were making a conscious decision to start something. It would be more than just a roll in the hay.

She stared at the building as Ben closed the door and locked the car. She inhaled deeply, trying to draw on the peace of the island night. Her heart thudded in her ears as he tugged her hand to lead her inside.

Rather than stopping once through the door, though, he surprised her when he pulled her through the living room and outside. He led her down the steps to the boardwalk. They walked until the light from the buildings faded to nearly nothing.

Ben sat on the edge of the walk, legs dangling, and pulled her down beside him. He wrapped an arm around her and she cuddled into his side. The moon cast a silvery glow over everything and shimmered off the water. As her eyes adjusted to the low light, the stars began to pop against the black velvet of the night sky.

"I haven't seen a sky like this since Afghanistan," Ben said quietly.

Gemma frowned. "Does it bother you? Do you want to go in?"

In the dim light, she just made out the nearly imperceptible shake of his head. "No. It brought me a sense of peace then, just like it is now."

He turned his head to look at her. Moonlight glittered off his eyes. "It reminded me I'm but a speck in the universe and that God has a plan for me. That I'm exactly where I'm supposed to be, no matter the outcome."

Gemma swallowed around the lump in her throat. "Ben—"

He pressed a finger to her lips. "Let me finish or I'll never get it all out."

She nodded.

His hand drifted to rest on her shoulder, his thumb caressing her cheek. "You terrify me. I've spent my life protecting others. Doing the right thing to keep others from getting hurt. For the first time, I don't know how to do that. I don't want to hurt you, but I don't know how to love you the way you should be loved. I never had the example you had in your parents. I've had three stepmothers and two stepfathers. My brother has been married and divorced. Even my sister, who swore up one side and down the other she wasn't going to follow in our parents' footsteps, is in the process of getting divorced." He paused, gathering his thoughts. "I don't want to start something with you and hurt you in the end. I don't know if I can do forever, and that's the kind of woman you are."

Gemma's heart swelled and tears threatened. She reached out to hold his face in her hands. His eyes gleamed like steel pools in the low light. "Ben, the fact you're worried about it tells me you'll never hurt me. Your very nature won't let you. I haven't known you long, but I know you don't do *anything* half-assed. Why would you go into a relationship with a different attitude? You wouldn't. Relationships aren't easy. You have to give them everything you have every single day. I've watched my parents struggle with that at times, but they always remember what's necessary and persevere. It's when you don't give all of yourself that they end. And if you do give all of yourself and it still doesn't work, then it wasn't meant to be. As long as you give me everything and I give you the same, how could I be hurt if it ends?"

His hand slid into her hair, his fingers massaging her scalp. "I've never been tempted to try for more than just a casual relationship with a woman before. Not until you. I'm still terrified I'll fail, but you're right—it's not in my nature to quit."

She smiled up at him. "I promise not to let you quit. We both know how persistent I can be."

Ben threw back his head and laughed. "Very true."

He stood and helped her to her feet. "Come on. Let's go inside."

Gemma followed, anticipation coursing through her veins, making her senses hum. They moved quickly back up the boardwalk.

As soon as he shut the balcony door behind them, he drew her body against his. Shadows darkened the planes of his face as he stared down at her in the soft glow from the small light they left on above the kitchen sink.

She held his gaze, unable to look away from the fire that burned there.

Twining her fingers in his short hair, she leaned into him. His hands dropped to cup her hips, and he pulled her up against him. His hard angles molded perfectly to her softer curves.

Lips hovering millimeters from hers, his warm breath fanned over her face. Gemma held back the whimper of need that threatened to undo her. He was so close, and she needed him to kiss her. Now.

Ready to growl in frustration, he finally closed the distance and slanted his mouth over hers.

Sensations immediately bombarded her. So many places where Ben's big body touched hers demanded her attention that she felt like one giant tingle. His hands ghosted down the backs of her thighs to grasp her legs and lift her. She wrapped her legs around his waist, his hands firm underneath her. Instinctively, she rocked her hips, eliciting a deep-throated growl from him. The sound skated along her nerve endings, sending delectable shivers through her. She was in heaven and it was a fiery, delicious place.

Without wasting any time, he headed for the bedroom, Gemma still wrapped around him. She started on the buttons of his shirt as he walked, not breaking their kiss, and got it open as far as her body would allow. Her fingers fluttered over the hard muscles as she spread the material. Ben groaned, walking faster. Within moments, they were toppling onto the plush mattress and she was lost to the fire consuming her. All coherent thought fled as she gave herself over to the man in her arms and the feelings he provoked.

When Gemma woke the next morning, sunlight streamed through the bedroom window. She stretched languidly and rolled, reaching for Ben, only to come up empty. Her eyes popped open, and she sat up.

His side of the bed was rumpled, but the room was empty. The smell of coffee reached her nose. Hopping out of bed, Gemma dashed into the shower and quickly washed before pulling on a pair of jean shorts and a simple gray t-shirt. She wandered out to the main room and stopped at the edge of the hallway, awestruck. Ben stood on the balcony, shirtless, his jeans riding low on his hips. He held a steaming cup of coffee in his hand while he watched the waves.

Sunlight glistened off his tan torso, his tattoos intensely black against the gold of his skin. Chains coiled his right bicep and wrapped his shoulder. She knew that if he were to turn around, she would see them wrapped around the Army Ranger insignia inked on his chest. A cross adorned his left shoulder blade while the words to a biblical quote wrapped his left bicep and went up over his shoulder to surround the cross.

Heat coiled in her belly. The man was beautiful.

And he was all hers.

Getting control of her raging hormones, Gemma walked over to him and slid her arms around his waist. She pressed a kiss between his shoulder blades. "Good morning."

He turned in her arms and slid his free hand around her to hold her close. Gemma lifted her face as he bent to kiss her. She opened to him as he deepened the kiss, tasting coffee and something uniquely Ben. Her hands slid up his sculpted torso to clutch his shoulders as he took his time exploring her mouth. Gemma felt her bones liquefy and let her body melt into his.

Ben gentled the fire and pulled back. "As much as I'd like to continue this, we have plans."

She frowned as his words sank in. She pulled away slightly, so she could see his face more clearly. "Plans?"

He nodded. "I got to thinking about things we can do while we're here and googled activities. There's an equestrian place on the island. I called and booked us on the tour that starts at ten."

Gemma perked up. "Riding?" She smiled. "That sounds great. I haven't been on a horse since the accident."

Ben smiled down at her. "I thought you'd think so." He released her and swatted her on the butt. "Go eat something and we'll go."

Gemma scurried off with one last hard kiss to do just that. She found a protein bar in the small bag of groceries they'd brought along and scarfed it down, then hurried into the bedroom to change into a pair of jeans and tennis shoes.

She wished she had her boots, but they were still in her closet at home, so sneakers would have to do.

"I'm ready," she announced, poking her head out the balcony door.

Ben glanced back from where he stood on the boardwalk, watching the waves. He turned and headed her way.

The drive to the resort's stables was short. Inside, they filled out the required waivers, then waited as their guide gave a safety briefing to the group before they followed her to the corral.

Gemma studied the group of saddled horses. "This is weird," she muttered to Ben.

He dipped his head closer. "How so?"

"I'm not used to someone saddling my horse for me."

He grinned. "Isn't vacation great? All the fun without all the work."

She giggled. "I guess so."

The guide pointed them toward their horses, and Gemma swung into her saddle. It was a little wide for her taste, but it fit the horse well. And a wider saddle was better than one that was too tight for her, in her opinion. Nothing like a narrow saddle to bruise her butt.

Once they were all mounted, the guide lined them up, and they set off down the trail. It didn't take long for Gemma's focus to shift from their surroundings to Ben, who rode in front of her. She was thankful that riding a horse was almost as natural as breathing for her. The functioning, conscious part of her brain was so distracted by the sight of him on his horse, she could do nothing more than hold the reins on her mount and let it play follow-the-leader as they rode across the dunes. The man was a sight to behold atop the gray gelding the resort paired him with. He was already the epitome of masculinity, with his tall stature, wide shoulders, and beautifully sculpted muscles. Put him on the back of a horse and he looked like a god come down from the heavens. He made her mouth water without even trying.

Gemma jerked as her mount picked up the pace. She clenched her thighs so she wouldn't topple off and mentally shook herself. She really needed to pay attention. They had reached the beach and the trail guide had quickened the pace, letting the horses frolic in the surf. Gemma rolled her hips with her horse as they cantered through the sand, salty spray hitting her face as the horses splashed through the waves rolling onto the beach. She lifted her face to the sky, basking in the warm sun, happy beyond measure. If only they could catch the psycho threatening her, her life would be damn near perfect.

Ben looked back at Gemma just in time to see the euphoric grin split her face as they dashed down the sandy beach. God, she was beautiful. He was hard-pressed to remember why he'd been so reluctant to start something with her. After last night, he was all-in. The sex was fantastic, but that wasn't all that washed away the last of his doubts. She touched something in him no one else ever had, and it brought a warm light to all the dark, cynical corners of his soul. He wanted this woman in his life any way she'd have him.

He slowed his horse slightly so he could fall back to her side.

"Having fun?" he asked, grinning.

She nodded, her smile still in full force. "This is great! It's been a long time since I've ridden on a beach. Thank you for taking me."

They slowed as they reached the trail at the end of the beach. Ben extended an arm to take her hand. "You're welcome."

They continued hand-in-hand down the trail until it narrowed to the point they had to pass through single-file. Ben watched Gemma ride in front of him, her hips rolling gently with her mount. As much as he hated to admit he'd been wrong, she was right to force the issue and get them alone together, away from the chaos. They'd been walking on eggshells since they met. He hadn't realized how tense he'd been, both from their dance around each other and from the case. He still couldn't completely relax, because he knew they would have to return to reality in a few days, but it was nice to drop his guard a fraction and think about something else besides the madman terrorizing the Smokies.

The rest of the ride flew by as they wound their way down the resort's trails before ending up back at the stables. After dismounting and handing over his horse to the stable attendant, he wrapped an arm around Gemma and led her out of the barn.

Warmth unfurled in his chest as she sighed deeply and wrapped her arm around his waist. "I love the beach," she said. "The warm sea air and the salty spray. The fresh ocean smell."

His arm tightened around her, a vision of them here in the future, unfolding before him. "Maybe we'll have to make this an annual trip. And stay longer than a long weekend."

She beamed up at him. "I'd like that."

Heart lighter than it had ever been, he led her away from the barn.

Twenty-Six

"Sailing? You can't be serious. I don't know anything about sailing." Gemma stared at the small boat in trepidation. When she woke up this morning and he told her he had a surprise for her, this was *not* what she had imagined. "When you pulled into the marina, I thought we were going on like a tour boat or something. Not this."

He threw the backpack he brought with them over the stern and put one foot on the boat railing, extending a hand to her. "Come on. It'll be fun. I know what I'm doing, and the weather is perfect for a nice, easy ride today."

Hesitating a moment longer, she finally put her hand in his and let him help her into the boat.

Both feet firmly planted on the deck, Gemma looked around. Wooden benches lined both sides of the deck, blue and white-striped cushions adorning their tops. Dark blue canopies fluttered in the breeze over the benches, offering some shade from the relentless Carolina sun. Still unsure about all this, she hovered by the bench while he untied the boat from the dock.

Once the boat was free of its moorings, Ben jumped

onboard and headed for the helm, which sat mid-ship. He peered down at the controls, inserting a key into the control panel. With the flip of a switch and a turn of the key, the boat's engine rumbled to life.

He looked back at her, smiling. "Come up here."

Enticed by the excited, almost boyish smile on his face, Gemma closed the few feet of space between them to join him at the helm. Hands firm and sure on the large stainless-steel steering wheel, he guided them out of the marina into the harbor.

"So, when do we hoist the sail, Captain?" She quirked an eyebrow at him, grinning.

He gave a quick laugh. "Soon. This is a busy harbor, and while I know what I'm doing, I don't know the currents here. With so many other boats around, it's easier to steer without the sails up. We get out on open water and we'll shut the engine down and see where the wind takes us."

She looked at him, horrified. "You aren't really going to leave us at the mercy of the wind, are you? God, I hope there's a map down below. I don't think our phones are going to be able to pull up Google Maps out at sea." Worriedly, she cast a glance at the hatch. Maybe she should go have a look just in case.

Ben's laughter had her gaze snapping back to him. "Honey, unless Google Maps has some hidden nautical charts I've never heard of, it's not going to help us, even if we can get a signal." He wrapped an arm around her waist and pulled her close. "Relax, would you? I'm not going to get us lost. My dad taught me to sail when I was just a kid. It's been a favorite hobby of mine my entire life. I know what I'm doing."

"You're sure?" She frowned up at him fiercely.

"Yes. Now, here." He stepped back and pushed her forward. "You take the wheel while I go unfurl the sails."

He placed her hands on the cool steel. Gemma gulped nervously. She had never driven a boat like this one before.

"Is there anything I need to know?"

"Not really. Just keep the nose pointed that way." He pointed toward the open water at the mouth of the harbor. "And don't hit anyone."

She nodded, her eyes fixing on an imaginary point in front of them.

It took her several seconds to realize he hadn't moved away to tend to the sails, but instead stood watching her.

She spared him a glance. "What?" His sunglasses covered his eyes, preventing her from deciphering his expression.

"Are you okay?" A furrow dug between his brows as he frowned at her in concern.

Taking a deep breath, Gemma forced herself to relax a bit. She was being a little uptight. "Yeah. I'm just a little leery of the ocean. I love it, but I know how intense it can get and how quickly. When I was a kid, Mom and Dad would take us to some seaside town every summer. One year, Tristan and I were on the beach when the weather suddenly turned. I was playing near the waterline and a giant wave kicked up by the wind from the approaching storm, washed in and swept me off my feet. If Tristan hadn't been there, I would have been pulled out to sea. He ran in after me and got me back to shore." She shrugged. "I just have a healthy respect for its power, I guess."

Ben's hand curled around her shoulder and gave a gentle squeeze. "I'm glad you told me. I'll make sure to tell you before I do anything, so you know what's going on. And, if you have any concerns—no matter what they are—say something. We'll be safe. I promise."

Feeling reassured and touched by his concern, she reached up and gave him a quick kiss. "I know. Now, go get us some wind power."

With a quick grin, he hopped up the two steps to stand on

top of the forward deck. By the time the boat's engine motored them past the tiny island in the harbor that was home to Fort Sumter, he had both sails untied and was running them up the boom.

As soon as the sail reached the top and Ben tied it off, Gemma felt the craft respond to the push of the wind.

"Try to keep us headed straight for now," Ben yelled down. "There's a compass in front of you. Just stay on the same heading."

Gemma looked down at the control panel in front of her, her eyes immediately landing on the compass. Keeping one eye on the compass and the other on the boat traffic around them, she maneuvered them out into open water past the harbor. Once they were well away from the other craft around the mouth of the harbor, Ben hopped back down and took the wheel from her, turning off the engine.

"So, where are we going?" she asked, leaning against a rail.

Ben shrugged. "I don't care. We can either go south and cruise past the island where we're staying, or we can go north and see what's up that way."

"I vote north. We haven't been up that way yet."

"North it is." He turned the wheel and the sails snapped, sending them cruising north.

Deciding to try to relax and take in the view, Gemma retreated to one of the benches and stretched out along the railing. The landscape rolled past as they sailed down the shoreline. The warm breeze fluttered through her hair, lulling her into a languid state. Foggy Mountain and the serial killer seemed a lifetime away.

Once they were cruising along at a steady pace and away from other boat traffic, Ben joined her on the bench.

She looked at him in alarm. "Is it safe for you to be away from the wheelhouse?"

He nodded. "The wind is steady, and I locked the wheel to

keep us on the correct heading. I can't wander down below deck for more than a few minutes, but I can sit here with you and keep an eye on things."

Not one to look a gift horse in the mouth, Gemma threw her legs over his lap and her arms around his neck. Her grin was pure devilment as she pulled him down for a scorching kiss.

~

It was near dusk before they finally began to head back to Charleston Harbor. They had spent the day sailing up and down the coast, taking in the sun and scenery. Ben had packed a picnic lunch, which they ate on the forward deck, the salty sea air a nice compliment to their meal.

Still several miles out to sea, Gemma steered the boat while Ben adjusted the sails. She tossed her head to get the hair out of eyes and noticed something in the distance.

Eyes straining in the waning light, she struggled to make it out. It looked like a boat, but it didn't look right. Rummaging in the cabinet beneath the control panel, she found a pair of binoculars.

Adjusting the focus, she aimed them at the object. What she saw turned her blood to ice. "Oh my God! Ben!" She pulled the glasses away and pointed. "There's a boat capsizing!"

Immediately, he tensed and looked at where she pointed. Without hesitating, he began turning the boom, putting it fully into the wind. "Turn!" he yelled. "And start the engine!"

She quickly did as he asked. Within moments, they were sailing as fast as man and nature combined would allow in the direction of the sinking vessel.

"Can you see anyone on it or in the water?" Ben shouted over the rush of the wind.

She took a good look through the binoculars. It was difficult to make anything out because they were moving so fast, but she finally made out a figure in the ocean.

"There's someone in the water."

"Alive?"

"Looks like it, yes."

It took them several minutes to make their way to the listing vessel, but as they did, it became apparent it was a man in his thirties in the water, holding on to his rapidly sinking boat. He waved his arms as they approached.

Ben took over steering and pulled them up beside the disabled vessel. Gemma found the life preserver and tossed it to the man, who quickly shoved it out of the way.

"No! My mother! She's trapped inside!" He scrabbled back toward the boat and tried to pull himself back onboard, but didn't have the strength or coordination. Blood flowed freely from a gash on his forehead, and his movements were jerky.

Ben and Gemma shared a quick look before he was kicking off his shoes and shedding his shirt. He quickly radioed the Coast Guard, giving their position and status.

He situated her in front of the wheel. "Keep us right here."

"Be careful," she managed around the lump in her throat as he moved to the rail.

He locked eyes with her and nodded once before diving over the side.

~

Quickly reaching the floundering man, Ben shoved the life preserver under his arms. "Hold this."

"No! My mom!" The man tried to push the ring away again.

Ben held it firm. "I'll get her. You hold this."

Reluctantly, the man took it. "Please. She went down to get the dog, so we could get in the raft, when the boat shifted suddenly. I fell overboard. She hasn't come out, and she's not answering when I call her."

"Okay. What's her name?"

"Sarah."

"Get on my boat. I'll find her." Ben didn't wait for the man to comply. He swam the few strokes to the listing craft and pulled himself onboard. He could feel the heaviness in the small sailboat as it sat dangerously low in the water.

Making his way to the cabin door, he wrenched it open. The passageway was blocked by fallen shelves and the odds and ends they'd contained.

"Sarah!" he yelled into the darkness.

A large dog barked frantically. Water splashed at the back of the cabin.

Ben started clearing a path. "Sarah! My name's Ben. If you can hear me, make a noise." He listened intently, but only heard the dog.

The boat groaned ominously.

He froze momentarily. When the boat stayed stable, he began moving again. He had to hurry.

Wishing for a flashlight, he moved the debris aside to reach the back of the cabin. The dog's barking got more furious the closer he got. In the dim light, he could just make out a large, dark shape right before it launched itself at him. Ben held out an arm to keep the large animal from dunking him underwater. Finding its collar, he managed to get the dog under control.

"It's okay, bud. Where's Sarah? Where is she?" The dog whined and turned, barking and whining furiously. More debris floated around them, but he didn't see the woman.

The dog pulled him toward a back corner of the boat as the water continued to rise. He only had about eighteen inches of headroom back here now.

"Sarah, make noise if you can hear me."

Ears straining, the only noise he heard was the dog's soft whine and the water lapping against the walls and the outside hull.

Another ominous groan echoed through the cabin, prompting him to move. Reaching through the water, he pushed aside a myriad of floating items, searching for the woman.

"Come on, come on, come on. You have to be here." Suddenly, his hand hit flesh. He grasped onto it and pulled. From behind the floating cushions, he pulled a body from the water. Dread settled low in his stomach, and adrenaline shot through his veins. She didn't appear to be breathing.

Curling an arm around her torso, he fought his way back through the water to the stairs, stopping several times to shove the heavier items out of his path. Finally, after a long minute, he reached the door. Hanging on to a handful of the woman's shirt, he kept her face above the water while he pushed the dog through the door. It ran out onto the deck, barking wildly.

Ben backed his way out of the cabin, pulling the woman through by her arms until she was laid out on the deck. The boat now listed sharply and less than half of it was still visible above the water. He only had a few moments before it was going to sink completely beneath the waves.

"Gemma, radio the Coast Guard!" he yelled. "Tell them we have a medical emergency. Mister, call the dog. The boat's going to sink any second."

The man immediately called for the dog, an all-black Belgian Malinois, whose name was Maverick.

Ben positioned the unconscious woman precariously just over the edge of the boat, then jumped overboard. Reaching up, he pulled her over the side and into his arms. Maverick still barked from the deck. Ben whistled sharply as he swam toward his boat with the woman, calling the dog. Finally, realizing all the humans were leaving him, the animal leaped into the water.

"Take her." He handed the woman to her son, who still tread water next to the sailboat, looking more fatigued than he had just a few minutes ago. Ben needed to get mother *and* son out of the water.

Grabbing the rail, he pulled himself out of the ocean in one swift movement. Leaning over, he reached for the woman. "Hand me her arms." Doing as he asked, her son held them up as high as he could get them. Ben grasped the woman's wrists and hoisted her out of the sea, quickly handing her off to Gemma.

Leaning over the rail again, Ben thanked his lucky stars he hadn't rented a bigger boat. This would be a nearly impossible task if the hull were any deeper.

Hands nearly reaching to the water, he pointed at the Malinois, paddling next to his master. "Help me get your dog up here."

Struggling mightily now, the man tapped into whatever reserves he had left and lifted the sopping wet animal high enough that Ben could get his arms around him and pull him up. Muscles straining, he hoisted the dog over the rail. It landed on the deck in an ungraceful heap.

Hurrying back to the rail, he leaned over a final time to pull up the man, who clung weakly to the life preserver, his face ashen.

The sinking sailboat burbled. The vessel groaned mightily as it finally gave up the fight and sank beneath the waves.

Eyes wide at the speed with which the ocean claimed the boat, Ben reached for the man. That had been too close.

"Give me your hand."

The man reached up weakly, allowing Ben to clasp his wrist. Planting his feet, Ben used his height to his advantage, pulling him up and over the side. They both crumpled to the deck, chests heaving from exertion.

"She's still not breathing, Ben," Gemma stated breathlessly.

He looked over at her. She had the woman lying flat on the deck, performing CPR. Sweat dripped down her face as she worked. The older woman was ominously still, even as her body shook from the force of the compressions.

Moving quickly, he went to Gemma's side and edged her out of the way so he could take over. "Go call the Coast Guard back and tell them to step on it."

She scrambled off to do as he asked. Ben kept a steady pace, trying to bring the woman back.

"Mom?" On his hands and knees, the woman's son crawled over as Ben continued CPR. "Oh my God. Mom?" The dog sat down next to his master, nudging the man's hand with his nose and whining softly.

Gemma soon reappeared, the first aid kit clutched in her hands. She sat next to the man and pressed a gauze pad to his head. He winced at the pressure on his wound, but didn't pull away.

"The Coast Guard is about five minutes away, Ben."

He nodded as he continued compressions. Suddenly, the woman sputtered and water spurted from her mouth. Immediately, he rolled her onto her side as she began to cough up seawater.

"Mom!" The man moved closer, reaching out to the older woman.

Ben placed a gentle hand on the man's chest. "Give her some space."

Nodding in understanding, he cupped her shoulder softly. "It's okay, Mom. I'm here."

She moaned and her eyelids fluttered, but she never fully opened her eyes. Watching the woman's labored breathing, Ben wished the sailboat came equipped with oxygen. He willed the Coast Guard to get here quickly.

The man turned to Ben, teary-eyed. "Thank you."

Ben nodded, glad that at least for now, the older woman was alive. "What happened?"

The man shrugged. "I'm not quite sure. We were getting ready to head back to the harbor. I turned on the engine and there was a small explosion. Smoke started billowing, and we began taking on water. I didn't even get a chance to radio for help. The boat lurched as it took on water, and I went flying." He touched the cut on his head, now covered in gauze. "I hit my head on the boat on my way into the water. If you hadn't come along—" His voice trailed off and he inhaled shakily. "Anyway, thank you for saving us. My name is Carter, by the way. Carter Townsend. That's my mother, Sarah. We were out here for her birthday. She had always wanted to go sailing, so I took some classes and rented that boat to surprise her. We had such a good day until the engine died." The dog, sensing his master's distress, snuggled close and licked the man's chin. He rubbed the dog's head and hugged him.

"We're just glad we were here," Ben said. "I'm Ben Davidson. This is my girlfriend, Gemma Mabley."

"It's nice to meet you both." Carter's eyes dropped to his mother, who remained semi-conscious on the deck. "I can't believe this happened."

Ben laid a hand on Carter's shoulder. "We got her back. Hopefully, with a little time, she'll make a full recovery."

Barely holding it together, Carter nodded.

The roar of a boat engine caught Ben's attention. He stood to see a Coast Guard cutter bearing down on them, to his immense relief. Within moments, the larger boat was pulling up alongside them.

Three crew members from the cutter jumped on board, medical bags in hand. Ben quickly filled them in on what had happened.

One Coastie quickly put oxygen on Sarah, while another assessed her vitals. The third man evaluated and wrapped Carter's wound. Ben was impressed when they had both patients assessed and ready to transfer to the Coast Guard cutter in under five minutes.

"Can you take the dog with you?" one of the Coasties asked. "They both need to go to the hospital." He motioned to mother and son.

Ben didn't hesitate. "Of course." He looked Carter in the eye. "We'll take good care of him and make sure he gets back to you."

Carter nodded, giving the dog a final scratch before following the Coasties onto their cutter.

From the deck of the Coast Guard ship, its captain motioned to Ben. "Follow us back to shore. We need statements from the two of you."

Ben nodded and helped the Coasties transfer Sarah Townsend to the cutter. Once she was safely on board the Coast Guard vessel, he readied the little sailboat to head back to the harbor. Gemma found a length of rope and tied it to Maverick's collar. The dog glued itself to her side. She wrapped a towel around the animal and started to rub him dry.

Putting the boat in gear, they followed the cutter back to

Charleston, the return trip much faster than planned. Even with the throttle open all the way and the sail into the wind, they still fell behind the cutter, its bigger engine pulling the boat through the water at a rapid pace.

Gemma came up beside him, Maverick on her heels, and snuggled into his side. Ben wrapped an arm around her and kissed the top of her head.

"Do you think she'll be all right?"

The memory of the woman's lifeless body in his arms had doubt weighing down his shoulders. "I hope so," he finally replied. "I don't know how long she was underwater before I found her."

"So much for our peaceful break from the chaos."

"We did make it several days, though, before the mayhem caught up to us."

He could feel her smile against his shoulder. Ben kissed her hair gently. He hoped this was as bad as it got—here and at home. He had a feeling, though, that the foe waiting for them back in North Carolina was going to be much tougher to defeat than a sinking sailboat.

Night had fallen by the time they made it to the hospital. Unwilling to leave the dog alone in the car after what he had been through, even if the temperature had cooled down, they stopped and bought a leash. Then Ben fibbed and told the hospital staff that Maverick was a working dog. Coupled with Ben's badge and the dog's well-behaved nature, the staff didn't question it.

They found Carter in an E.R. cubicle, lying on the cot, his eyes closed. He still looked awful, Gemma thought. His blond hair stuck out oddly from the new, stark white bandage that covered the gash on his head. The nurses had cleaned the blood off his face, which only made it glaringly apparent how pale he was beneath his tan.

Maverick whined, alerting Carter to their presence. His gray-green eyes snapped open, and he sat up. Still unsteady from his head injury, he wobbled on the bed. Ben's hand shot out to help steady the younger man.

"Whoa, there."

Carter's balance stabilized, and he offered them a tired smile. "Hi."

Maverick put his front paws up on the bed and demanded attention. Carter dutifully scratched the dog's ears and neck.

"How's your mom?" Gemma asked.

"Alive, thanks to you two. She still hasn't regained complete consciousness, but she's breathing on her own. She's on oxygen, though, because she inhaled a lot of seawater. The doctor said it will help her body process whatever water is left in her lungs."

"And what about you?" Ben asked. "You took quite a knock to the head."

Carter fingered the bandage at his temple. "Yeah. I have a concussion, and I lost enough blood to make me a bit weak. They want to keep me overnight, but I need to take care of this mutt." He looked down at the dog briefly. "My mom lives alone and I'm only visiting."

"We'll take him." The words were out of Gemma's mouth before she could stop them. Their condo reservation didn't include pets, but Gemma figured they could be sneaky for one night. There had been an option for pets on the reservation form, so she knew the owners didn't mind.

"I can't ask you to do that. I'll be fine at my mom's with Maverick."

"You didn't ask," Ben stated. "If the doctors think you should stay, you should stay. Gemma and I can look after Maverick for the night."

Carter looked back and forth between the two of them, obviously debating whether to take them up on their offer or not.

Finally, he nodded. "If you're sure you don't mind, that would be great. I'm not sure I need to stay, but I do know it'll be nice to get a full night's rest without having to worry about taking care of Maverick."

"Of course we're sure," Gemma said. She laid a hand on the dog's head. Maverick looked up at her and wagged his tail. "He's a great dog."

Carter stroked the dog's ears. "That he is. I'm amazed he's taken to you so well, though. He's usually only so relaxed with me. How did you get him in here, anyway? He doesn't have his vest on. It's at my mom's."

Gemma shared a frown with Ben.

"Vest?" Ben asked.

Carter nodded. "He's a police dog. I'm a cop in Fort Carrington, south of Asheville, North Carolina. Maverick is my partner."

Gemma's eyes about bugged out of her head. Talk about a small world.

Ben smiled ruefully and pulled his badge from the pocket of his shorts. He showed it to Carter. "I'm an FBI agent. We told the hospital staff he was a working dog. Guess I wasn't lying after all."

Carter grinned. "Guess not. You're the agent in charge of that serial killer investigation, aren't you?"

Ben nodded.

"I thought I recognized your name earlier. I just didn't put two and two together until now."

The door to the cubicle swished open and a nurse entered. "All right, Mr. Townsend. We've got a room ready for you upstairs. Are you going to take it, or are you still determined to leave us?"

"I'll take it. My friends here are going to take Maverick for the night." He gestured to the dog, whose tongue lolled happily out of his mouth as Carter continued to scratch his ears.

The nurse frowned. "How did you get him in here? There aren't any pets allowed. You're going to have to take him outside."

Ben held up a hand. "He's a police dog, ma'am. He just doesn't have his vest on."

The woman crossed her arms and arched an eyebrow at him, challenging his statement.

"He really is," Carter interjected. "I'm a cop. He doesn't have his vest because we were just out on a pleasure cruise. I'd offer you my credentials, but they went down with my sailboat. Along with my driver's license and insurance card you keep asking about."

Gemma bit her tongue to keep the smile off her face at his obviously annoyed tone.

His outburst seemed to mollify the nurse, though, and she moved into the room to the computer. She typed a few things into the system before turning her attention to him. "There will be an orderly coming soon to take you upstairs. I suggest you say your goodbyes now." She gestured to the dog. "You don't want to create a ruckus where people are trying to rest."

Carter offered her a blinding smile, dimples flashing in his handsome face. "No, ma'am."

Mirth bubbled up in Gemma's throat as the nurse turned fiery red. She pressed her lips together tightly to keep it in. The man was a charmer.

Nodding once and trying to act unaffected by her handsome charge, the nurse walked out, closing the door behind her.

Unable to contain it any longer, Gemma's giggles slipped free. "I don't think she was very happy with you."

Carter shrugged. "I don't appreciate bossy people, and she was most definitely bossy."

Ben grinned. "It's not a bad thing if it's the right kind of bossy." He looked down at Gemma, devilment making his eyes twinkle.

She whacked him on the arm in faux outrage. Looking at Carter, she rolled her eyes. "Ignore him." She picked up Maverick's leash. "We're going to go now so you can rest. Ben, leave him your cell number so he can call us when he's ready to leave tomorrow."

Carter laughed as Ben just sighed and picked up a pen and a sticky note from the desk in the corner.

An hour later, Gemma released Maverick from his leash as they walked into the condo. The dog immediately ran off to sniff every nook and cranny. She filled bowls with food and water for him while Ben laid out the takeout they brought back with them on the patio table. They were both starving after the evening's events.

Grabbing the bottle of wine and two glasses, Gemma joined Ben outside. The pensive expression on his face as he stared out over the darkened dunes made her frown. He had grown increasingly quiet after they left the hospital.

She poured them each a glass of wine and handed him one. "You going to tell me what's put that pinched expression on your face?"

He took a sip of his wine before looking at her. "Carter."

Gemma's frown deepened. "Carter? What about him?" She found the man to be nice and extremely charming.

"It's just a little too coincidental that he lives in North Carolina—very near to us—works in a profession that wears a uniform easily confused with a ranger, and he just happens to be here the same weekend we are. Not to mention he fits Caleb's description of Ranger Jack to a T. Right down to his eyes."

She took a sip of her own wine, thoughtfully. It was all very suspicious, but there were still some things that didn't fit. "What about his mom? It's a bit of a stretch that she would just happen to live here."

Ben shrugged. "We don't know that she does. Or that the woman we rescued was even actually his mother. We never got to talk to her because she wasn't conscious enough. Maybe he hijacked the boat and the woman was collateral damage."

Gemma's eyes widened. It had never occurred to her that someone could be so devious. That was why Ben was the FBI agent and she was just a therapist.

Maverick padded out onto the balcony with them, licking his chops. He wagged his tail softly and nudged Gemma's hand.

She stroked a hand over his glossy fur. "I don't know, Ben. I find it hard to believe that a man who is so gentle with an animal, who has obviously gained its trust, can be a stone-cold serial killer. I mean, don't most of them take out their initial urges to kill on animals?"

"Some do, but not all." He sighed. "All I'm saying is we should be cautious until we get more information." He pulled out his phone.

"What are you doing?"

"Putting my mind at ease." He typed a text as he talked. "I'm asking Tristan to run a full background check on him. I'm not putting your safety at risk because he's played to our sympathies. It may all be false."

Disturbed at the implications, she leaned back in her seat and took another sip of wine. She didn't like all this cloak and dagger stuff. Being distrustful of others was not her default, and it bugged her that she had to be suspicious of everyone she met.

Absently, she picked up one of her fish tacos and took a bite. It was good, but she barely tasted it, her mind on Carter and their serial killer. The two men just didn't jive in her mind.

"I still don't think he's involved," she finally said.

"We'll know soon enough," Ben replied, putting his phone back in his pocket. "I hope he's not either. He seems nice."

Tristan needed to hurry with the background information. Gemma's gut screamed Carter was innocent, but she would rest easier knowing for sure.

Twenty-Seven

The next day, gray skies and a cool breeze whipped through the trees as Ben parked the car in the hospital parking lot. Carter had called an hour earlier to say he was being discharged.

Leaving the windows cracked, they left Maverick in the car and headed inside. Upstairs, Gemma breezed down the hallway, her sundress fluttering around her knees as she walked into Carter's room. He smiled at them both from where he stood near the window.

"Well, you look better today," she remarked, returning his smile. And he did. The color was back in his face and while he still looked tired, the fatigue didn't seem to weigh on him like it did yesterday.

"Thanks. I feel better."

"Good. How's your mom doing?"

"Much better. She's awake and aware. They think she'll be able to go home in a couple of days."

"Do you want to go see her before we leave?" Ben asked. Gemma looked at him askance. She knew what he was doing. They hadn't heard back from Tristan yet about

Carter's identity. Her handsome FBI agent was still very suspicious.

"I actually just came from there, but she would like to see you two. I told her what happened and how you saved her. She wants to thank you."

"All right. I think Gemma and I would both like to see for ourselves how well she's doing."

Gemma nodded in agreement. "Definitely." She might not be as suspicious about Carter as Ben was, but she would definitely like to see the woman who had been clinically dead on the deck of their sailboat yesterday evening.

"Are you ready to go?" she asked.

Nodding, he picked up a plastic patient bag next to the bed and a small stack of papers off of the tray, then slid his feet into a pair of rubber flip-flops.

Gemma couldn't help but laugh at his look. "I think you're going to start a new fashion trend. Scrubs and flip-flops."

He held up the patient bag. "My shirt bit the dust from all the blood and my shorts are crusty with salt from the ocean. My shoes—" He looked down at his feet. "Well, they went down with the sailboat. The hospital hooked me up." He held his arms out. "I think I look pretty good, all things considered."

Gemma concurred. He looked like death warmed over yesterday. Today, he looked like a normal human, albeit a little banged up.

"Come on." She motioned him toward the door. "Let's go meet your mom."

The three of them headed down the hall and took the elevator to Sarah Townsend's floor. Turning into her room, the low murmur of the TV playing greeted them. The older woman sat on the bed, watching the screen when they entered. An oxygen cannula snaked under her nose and around her ears beneath a fall of silvery blond hair. Dark circles rimmed her eyes, but there was a rosy tinge to her cheeks.

She looked over as they stepped inside and smiled warmly. "Hi, honey."

"Hi Mom. I have some people for you to meet. This is the couple I told you about. Ben Davidson and Gemma Mabley." Carter motioned them forward.

Sarah smiled brightly and sat forward. She stretched a hand out to Gemma, who was closest. "Oh, it's so nice to meet you. I don't know how to thank you for what you did. Words just don't seem adequate."

Gemma took the woman's hand. "No thanks are necessary. We're just glad you're all right."

"Me too," Sarah replied, her voice low with emotion.

"Same here," Carter said. "We're both extremely grateful you came to our rescue." His eyes took on a moist sheen. "To think what would have happened if you hadn't seen us—" He shrugged and blinked away the moisture in his eyes. "Just, thank you. And if there is ever anything I can do for you, please don't hesitate to ask."

"We'll keep that in mind," Ben said graciously.

"Have you been discharged, dear?" Sarah motioned to the bag and papers Carter carried.

He nodded. "Yep. Thankfully, the car and house keys were in my pocket and not my backpack, so I won't have to call a locksmith to get into your house."

"Oh." Her eyes widened in surprise. "I hadn't even thought about that. My purse was on the boat."

"So was my wallet." He patted his mother's hand. "All of it can be replaced, though, Mom. We're okay, and that's all that matters."

She turned her hand over in his and smiled up at him. "I guess you're right." She placed her other hand over their clasped ones. "We'll get it all straightened out. You go on home now and rest."

"I will. I'll be back tomorrow, but if you need me before then, call the house. The seawater killed my phone."

She nodded.

Gemma stood back with Ben while mother and son said goodbye. "Are you satisfied he's on the up and up now?" she whispered.

Ben crossed his arms. "Not completely, but it's a start. I'll feel better once we hear back from Tristan." He looked down at her. "But yes, I'm starting to believe he's not involved in our case."

With a final kiss to his mom's forehead, Carter stepped away from the bed. Ben and Gemma both wished Sarah Townsend a speedy recovery, and they headed out.

After a very enthusiastic welcome from Maverick, the three of them climbed into the SUV. Ben looked back at Carter, who had the dog practically in his lap. Maverick had his head tilted and one paw wrapped around Carter's arm, holding his master in place. The animal had clearly missed his owner.

"Where to?"

"The marina. My car is there still."

Ben frowned. "You can't drive. You could barely stay afloat yesterday because of your head wound."

Gemma held up a hand. "If you don't mind, I can drive your car back to your mom's house."

"That's fine. I just don't want it to sit there any longer than necessary. The police said the marina agreed to let it stay parked there, but the longer it stays there, the more of a target for thieves it becomes."

"Works for me." Ben plugged his phone into the holder on the dash and typed in the name of the marina. As the map loaded, he put the SUV into gear and backed out of the parking space.

Traffic was light, and they quickly made their way through downtown from the hospital to the marina district. Carter directed Ben to the parking lot where he parked his car yesterday. It wasn't far from where they had parked their own before their excursion.

Pulling up next to a dark blue pickup, Gemma took the keys Carter offered her and hopped out of the SUV. Carter moved to the front seat to help Ben navigate while Gemma climbed into Carter's truck. After a few quick adjustments to the seat and mirrors, they were on their way.

Ben studied his passenger from the corner of his eye as he drove to Sarah Townsend's condo. Carter appeared relaxed as he looked out the window at the passing surroundings. Ben's phone had remained silent throughout the day, so he still didn't know any more about the man than what Carter had told him.

Impatient and worried about Gemma's safety, Ben decided a few questions wouldn't be out of order.

"So, how long have you been a cop?"

"Seventeen years."

"Really? Same department the whole time?" he asked.

"No. I was a military police officer, then a dog handler in the Marines for almost twelve years. I moved to Fort Carrington after I left the Marines."

"Why did you leave, if you don't mind me asking? Twelve years is a long time to stay and then up and leave. You were more than halfway to retirement."

Carter's expression grew pinched. "My last tour—it didn't

end well. People died who shouldn't have. Let's just leave it at that. I'm sure you can understand." He looked at Ben knowingly.

"You saw my tattoo, I take it?"

Carter nodded.

Ben could definitely relate to not wanting to talk about what he had experienced. There were some things that were just too painful to discuss or, at times to even think about.

The phone trilled on the dash and Tristan's name popped up on the screen. Ben cursed silently. He had terrible timing.

Afraid that Tristan would text him the info—which would come up with a preview on the phone screen—Ben grabbed the phone from its holder and answered it, thumbing down the volume until he could barely hear the voice coming over the line.

"Hey, Tris. You got something for me?"

"Yeah. Your vic is who he says he is. Carter James Townsend, thirty-five. Originally from Charleston. Enlisted in the Marines right after high school. Was military police and eventually selected to be a dog handler. Did four tours in Iraq before he separated from the military. Ended up in Fort Carrington, North Carolina a little over five years ago, taking a job as a K-9 officer. Never married, no kids. Mother, Sarah Ann Townsend, still lives in Charleston and his dad, James Robert Townsend, passed away two years ago. I ran his credit cards and bank account activity for the last month. Nothing suspicious. He's been in and around Fort Carrington and Charleston. I hate to say it, but I think it really is just a coincidence he's there at the same time you and Gemma are."

Ben had pretty much reached the same conclusion just by spending time with Carter, but it put his mind at ease to have that confirmed. "Okay. I appreciate the info."

"Anytime. How's my sister? She relaxing any? For that matter, are you?"

A corner of Ben's mouth tilted as memories of just how *relaxed* they had been the last few days floated through his mind. He didn't think Tristan would want to know about that, though. "She's doing fine. Definitely more relaxed than I am, but she's naturally more carefree."

Tristan laughed. "That's a good word to describe Gemma most days. Stuff just rolls right off of her."

"That it does." Ben shared Tristan's amusement. Gemma's carefree nature was something that attracted him to her. She brought a lightness to his life that was sorely lacking. "Hey, listen, I'm driving right now and my phone's my map, so I need to go. Thanks for getting back to me so quickly, though."

"Of course. I want this bastard as badly as you do. There is one more thing, though, before we hang up."

Tristan's brief pause had the hair on the back of Ben's neck standing on end. "What?"

"Gemma's plan is working. Our guy is pissed. I got a very, um, creative letter this morning. You need to watch your back when you get back to town, and Gemma goes absolutely nowhere alone."

Ben frowned fiercely. "What did it say?"

"You can read it when you get back, but basically he just detailed exactly what he wanted to do to her," Tristan explained, his voice growing hard. "After he sends us both to hell."

Knuckles turning white, Ben gripped the steering wheel and barely managed to keep from crushing his phone. "The bastard won't get close enough to do any of it." Taking a deep breath, he forced himself to relax. "Did you get anything off the letter this time?"

"Nope."

"Of course not. Okay. Keep me posted. I'll let you know when we're headed home."

"Will do. Keep my sister safe, Ben."

"Always."

Ben hung up and barely resisted the urge to fling the phone across the car. Very deliberately, he opened the map app again and put the phone back in the holder on the dash.

"I know it's none of my business, but is everything okay?" Carter asked.

Sparing the man a quick glance, Ben sucked in a breath through his nose, still trying to calm his anger. "I need to tell you something, and it's going to sound bad, but I need you to look past that because I have questions I'm hoping you might have some answers for."

Carter frowned, turning toward Ben in his seat. "Questions for me? About what?"

"You know what I do for a living. That I'm the lead investigator on the serial killer case in North Carolina. Have you seen the description of the man we're looking for?"

"In passing. It was way north of us, so we were just briefed on the killings. I think I saw the BOLO once."

"Blonde hair. Six feet or so. Gray eyes. Possibly a park ranger," Ben told him matter-of-factly.

Ben could tell the moment it hit Carter that he matched that description. His eyes widened almost comically.

"You think *I'm* the guy killing those women? What the hell?"

"I thought it was possible, but not anymore."

"Why not? Wait. The phone call. You had me investigated?"

The man was quick, Ben would give him that. He shrugged, unapologetic. "You matched the description, you're from the Asheville area, and you work in a job that could very easily be confused with a park ranger. I'm sorry if that offends you, but I'm not going to let a potential killer go free because of events designed to play on my sympathies."

"So, you thought I faked the whole boat thing to get to you?" Carter asked, incredulous. "You watched it sink!"

Ben gave Carter a long look. "The man who killed those women is a devious and cunning sociopath. He would do anything, set any trap, to lure me in and kill me, then take Gemma. So, I might have watched the boat sink, but that doesn't mean it wasn't deliberate."

"It wasn't! My mom was on that boat. I would never hurt her." Carter fired back.

"I know that—now. Look, I'm not accusing you of anything. I'm just trying to explain what's going on. Why I'm asking the questions I'm about to ask."

"Fine. Ask." He folded his arms over his chest and stared at Ben, stone-faced.

Maverick whined from the backseat, sensing the tension.

"Do you and your dog ever work outside your jurisdiction?"

"Yes."

"Search and rescue with park rangers? Or just police work?"

"Both."

"Did you ever go north of Asheville or do you stay in the southern part of the state?"

"We go wherever we're needed."

Oh, how Ben wished Gemma was here right now. She would have done a much better job explaining all this and could have gotten more than the terse answers he was getting.

"Did any of the rangers you worked with look like you?"

Carter's stony expression grew slightly less hostile as he thought about the question. "I only dealt with a handful of them anywhere I went. The ranger in charge, of course, who was usually an older man or woman. There were several rangers I worked with more closely than others, but none of them are ringing any bells. As for others that crossed my path,

I didn't pay them that much attention. I was focused on finding the missing person, not on socializing."

"What about in Tennessee? Did you ever go up there in an official capacity?"

"Once. They had a missing child case just over the border. The search area was large and the child had a medical condition, so they put out a call for any available team. I went up with Maverick as a volunteer."

"Do you remember anyone from Tennessee you later encountered working in North Carolina?"

Thinking briefly, he finally shook his head. "No, sorry, not that I recall. But again, I didn't really socialize. I was there to do a job, and that was it."

Ben tapped his fingers on the steering wheel, ticked that once again, he'd hit yet another dead end. He just wanted one break. Just one shred of evidence that would lead him to a name.

"You know something I don't understand?" Carter asked. "Why are you down here if you're working such a big case? Shouldn't you be up there? Investigating?"

He couldn't stop the laugh that bubbled up. "Have you met the woman driving your car?" Ben glanced in the rearview mirror, a soft smile still on his face. Gemma followed right behind them, jamming away to some song on the radio.

"This psycho—he's decided I'm public enemy number one and has made it no secret he's willing to do whatever is necessary to make sure I stop looking for him. He's nearly killed Gemma twice to try to get me to stop investigating. All it's done has spurred me to work harder to catch the bastard. Gemma, in an attempt to help, thought that if she disappeared for a few days, it just might unhinge the guy enough he would make a mistake and get caught. Her brother, my counterpart at the local sheriff's department, thought it would be a good idea for me to go with her."

"And you didn't?"

"I thought it would be better if I stayed and kept investigating and her brother went with her. Obviously, I got overruled. She and I had some things to work out and none of us wanted her going anywhere alone, so here I am."

Carter watched him thoughtfully. "Has it worked?"

"Tristan—Gemma's brother—seems to think so. He got a rather nasty letter from the killer today. Only time will tell us for sure. Our hope is he'll make another attempt to get to me or Gemma and we'll be there to nail him, or at the very least, he'll screw up the attempt and leave some evidence behind."

Ben rubbed the bridge of his nose, frustration at the situation still clawing at him. "We just need something that leads us to a name. This guy has left very little for us to go on."

"Which is why you investigated me," Carter concluded. "I get it now. I still don't like it, but I understand."

"Good. It was nothing personal. I just want to catch the son-of-a-bitch."

Carter nodded. "I'll keep my eyes and ears open once I get home. I talked to my boss this morning and eeked out another day of leave, but I'm the only K-9 officer in our department. They've been relying on help from the county while I've been away. One of their officers is scheduled to leave for training Tuesday, which puts a further strain on the system if I'm still gone, so I only have through Monday."

"What about your mom? She needs you."

"Her sister will be here tomorrow to help out. She's retired, so she'll be able to stay as long as she's needed."

"Good."

"What I said earlier still stands, Ben. If there's ever anything I can do for you, just call. I owe you for saving my mom's life."

"You don't owe me anything. I'm just glad I could be there

to help." And he was. Knowing that Sarah Townsend was going to be okay was thanks enough.

After dropping Carter off, Ben and Gemma headed back to their own condo. There was more they could see and do in the city, but talking about the case just made Ben want to shut out the world. It would all come roaring back when they went home tomorrow. Right now, all he wanted was to spend time with Gemma and forget everything else. He planned to do just that for the next twenty-four hours.

The silence closed around Gemma like a wet cloak when Ben shut the engine off after he pulled into the garage at her house. Her bubble had officially popped, and they were back in the thick of things. Oh, how she wished they could have stayed in South Carolina.

But she wanted her life back, and she wanted that life to include Ben. Until they caught the psycho murdering young mothers and trying to kill her, that would never happen.

So, pull up your big girl panties and get back into it! Gemma sucked in a breath, silently cursing that voice in her head, and pulled on the door handle. Ben followed her out of the SUV and into the house.

More silence greeted them inside. They put off coming back as long as they dared, lingering in the city and even stopping a couple of times on the way home for extended periods, reluctant to return to Foggy Mountain. Now, it was nearly midnight, and the house was eerily silent. Figuring Tristan had turned in for the night already, Gemma crept quietly through the kitchen toward her bedroom.

"Christ, what'd you guys do? Take a detour to Florida? It's fricking midnight!"

Gemma shrieked and braced herself against the living room doorway as light flooded the room and Tristan's large frame rose from the couch. Ben wrapped an arm around her to steady her.

"Tristan! You scared ten years off my life!" She sank into Ben's chest and willed her heart rate to slow.

"Sorry. Next time, don't come home so late." His tone made it clear he wasn't sorry in the least. In fact, he sounded rather ticked to Gemma.

"Give her a break, Tristan. She didn't want to come back here. Neither of us did," Ben said quietly.

"I keep telling her to disappear. You still can, Sis. I can have you squirreled away in a safe house far, far away from here in no time." His voice implored her to take him up on his offer.

"No. I'm still not running, Tristan." She heard Ben groan, but she ignored him as he sighed. She looked up at her brother beseechingly. "I just can't. We'll never stop him if I'm not around. He wants me and he's not going to stay here if I leave. He's going to come looking for me, and he'll probably kill someone else in an attempt to draw me out. I'm not sentencing someone else to die, and I'm not spending my foreseeable future on the run."

Tristan spun away and started pacing. "You didn't read that letter he sent, Gemma. Didn't hear the vehemence of what he wanted to do to you leaping off the page with every damn word."

"I can't leave," she said softly.

"Why do you have to be so righteous? So considerate? God, do you have any idea how much I wish you were a selfish bitch right now?"

His eyes swung to Ben. "And you know what I don't understand? How you're not handcuffing her little fanny to the chicken bar in your SUV and hauling ass for anywhere but here?"

Ben stared hard at the younger man. "For exactly the reasons she wants to stay. We can't sentence another woman to death by hiding Gemma away. I'm also not a hundred percent certain this bastard won't follow us wherever we go. This guy is meticulous, and I'll bet dollars to donuts he's got a law enforcement background. It's the only reason I can see that we've found so little forensic evidence and for why he's *always* one step ahead. It'd only be a matter of time before he would track us down. Then I'd be alone with little backup. I'm not willing to risk Gemma's life on those kinds of odds."

Tristan muttered several epithets and scrubbed his hands down his face. "So, what do we do?" he finally asked.

Ben smiled for the first time since they walked in the door. "We go ahead with our plan. With the right planning, and enough people in the right places, she'll be safe and we can catch the guy."

Gemma stepped forward, clasping a hand around Tristan's arm. "Let's end this."

Tristan's shoulders straightened in resolve, and he nodded. "All right. Let's get this bastard."

Twenty-Eight

Gemma wrung her hands for what had to be the thousandth time that day. Today was the day. They were going to set the killer up and take him down. With her as bait. Ben and Tristan had spent several days devising their plan. SWAT was on standby and would be hiding a few blocks over. Tonight, when she left work, she and Ben were going to stage a huge fight in the parking lot, and he was going to leave her alone at the therapy center to wait on a different ride.

She was both utterly dreading it and highly anticipating it. If all went according to plan, and she really was being watched like they thought, the killer should take the bait and try to get into the center to kidnap her. Inside, there would be two armed men—men who had snuck in overnight and had been hiding out in her office all day—waiting to take him down. If something went wrong, however—well, she preferred not to think about that.

Gemma nearly jumped out of her skin as her cell phone buzzed in her pocket. She pulled it out and frowned as the number for Sally Coleman, the head of an equine rescue league of which Gemma was a part, appeared. Frowning, she answered the call.

"Hello?"

"Hi Gemma. I'm sorry to bother you at work, but we've got a situation outside of Rose. I need as many bodies with trailers as I can drum up. The locals there stumbled across a farm with a dozen horses all in dire shape, and we need to get them relocated as soon as possible. I wouldn't call you during the day if it wasn't an emergency. Can you come and get a couple of the animals to board at the therapy center?"

Gemma's brain kicked into overdrive. Rose was about an hour and a half to the southwest. If she left now, she could get there and back before she was supposed to leave for the day, and they could still go ahead with the operation this evening.

"Let me talk to Mara, but I'm sure it will be fine. If you don't hear from me in the next fifteen minutes, then I'll be there. Are they going to be ready to transport when I get there? I've got something going on later I can't miss."

"Yes. They're being rounded up now and evaluated, so we can place them appropriately. By the time you arrive, we'll have a couple ready for you to take back."

"Okay, then. I should see you soon." Gemma hung up. Ben was *not* going to like this. But with a seizure that size, the therapy center needed to help out.

Gemma hurried down the hall to Mara's office and poked her head in. "Hey. Got a minute?"

Mara looked up from where she was diligently pecking away at her keyboard and smiled. "Sure. What's up?"

Gemma quickly outlined the situation.

"I don't know, Gemma. I mean, I don't have a problem housing the animals, but I'm not sure you going out there is the best idea."

"I know. But I'm going to call Ben. I won't go alone, and Sally promised it would be a quick pick up."

Mara continued to frown. "I still don't think it's wise, but if Ben agrees, then it's fine. We've definitely got the space."

Gemma grinned. "He will. Thanks, Mara."

"Be careful!" she called as Gemma hurried down the hall toward the stables to get the trailer ready. She could call Ben while she worked.

Ben looked up from the reports on the canvasses of the area around the therapy center when his phone buzzed across his desk. Gemma's beautiful face smiling from beneath the floppy brimmed hat she had donned at The City Market in Charleston greeted him. Despite the happiness in the picture, worry punched him in the gut. She didn't usually call him until her lunch break, and that was over an hour away.

He slid his finger across the screen and answered. "Hey, baby. What's up?"

"I need to go out for a bit," she said by way of greeting. "I'm part of an equine rescue league and the head of it just called, asking if I could come pick up a couple horses to bring back to the therapy center. Some locals stumbled across a farm with a dozen horses in urgent need of medical care and rehoming. I know you don't really want me going anywhere, but with a seizure of this size, there aren't many options to put all those animals. I need to go, Ben." The story came out in a rush and Ben could feel his brain rush to catch up to the flow of words.

He blew out a breath, remembering what happened the last time she went out at the last minute. "No. I know it's important, but it's just too risky. This guy has proven he can get to you anytime he wants. Remember Biltmore?"

He heard her sigh and the sound of something heavy hitting metal.

"What are you doing?" he asked.

She grunted and something else heavy dropped. "Unloading all of Jasper's crap from the second stall of the trailer."

Ben stood and grabbed his keys, frustration making him snap at her as he hurried from the station. "Gemma, I said no. It's too dangerous."

The line suddenly got very quiet. Ben pulled the phone away from his ear to see if she had hung up. It was still active. "Gemma?"

"Ben, I know you're trying to keep me safe and that you're worried about me, so I'll let that tone slide, but I'm telling you that I am going." The banging resumed. "With that many animals, Sally has probably pulled every string she has to get people to take them. If we don't take them in here, they'll likely have to euthanize the two weakest. I can't sit by and watch two horses die, knowing I could have given them a chance. If that puts my life in danger, so be it."

Ben cursed silently. This was one quality in her he both loved and hated. She had a weak spot for animals—people too —who were in need, and there wasn't much she wouldn't do to help, even if it meant putting herself in harm's way. "I get that, darlin', I do. But why do you have to be the one to go? Can't Mara go or one of the other therapists?"

"Mara's got a quarterly review due tomorrow, so she's swamped. And Liz and Stacy both have full sessions this afternoon. I don't." The banging ceased again.

"Dammit, woman. You're killing me, you know that, right? I'm on my way. Do *not* leave until I get there or I swear to God I will handcuff your pretty little ass to the bed frame for the foreseeable future."

Gemma giggled. "Sounds kinky."

Ben couldn't stop the frustrated growl that escaped. "It's not funny, Gems. I'm serious. Stay put." He disconnected the call and threw the phone onto the passenger seat as he peeled out of the station parking lot. His knuckles shone white on the steering wheel as he drove as fast as he dared. He had to force his jaw to unclench, fearing he'd break a molar. He couldn't remember the last time he was so furious. She insisted on putting herself in danger, and it was starting to wear on his nerves. They may not have to fake that fight this afternoon.

He slammed his fist into the steering wheel and sucked in a breath, knowing he was partly to blame for the danger. He should have listened to Tristan and squirreled her away in protective custody until he caught the killer, but he'd let her emotions and the threat of putting some faceless woman in harm's way sway him. He had wanted to spare her the heartache of having to deal with someone else's death because she had chosen to live.

He wouldn't have blamed her if she had hidden away—most people would have—but he admired the guts it took to stay in the line of fire when she didn't have to. And she had been right. Putting her up as bait was the most effective and efficient way to catch the killer. It didn't mean he liked it, though.

"Dammit!" He slammed the wheel again. He was terrified everything was going to blow up in their faces and the killer would not only get away, but that he'd take Gemma with him. He couldn't lose her.

~

The arena door slammed open, banging against the wall, making Gemma jump. She looked over to see Ben stride through looking for all the world like a pissed off Greek god. If there had been obstacles in his path to get to her, they would have withered and sunk into the ground.

Man, he's pissed.

Gemma straightened her spine. Let him be mad. She had a lifetime of dealing with Tristan's temper. She could handle Ben's too.

He came to a stop a few feet away and glowered down at her. Gemma stared back. If he was hoping to break her and get her to cave by intimidating her, he had another think coming. She had a stubborn streak a mile wide, which she'd honed on her brother over the years.

"You're not going to back down on this, are you?" he finally said, his low voice rolling over her.

She simply shook her head.

His jaw worked, and he glanced away before turning his gaze back to her. This time, the steely determination was replaced by something far softer as well as a healthy dose of fear. "I know you probably think I'm being heavy-handed, but I can't help it when it comes to you. I don't like feeling like this. This isn't me. I never lose it, but the thought of something happening to you is enough to tear off all my armor and leave the nerves exposed."

Gemma's heart squeezed painfully. She threw herself at him and felt tears slip down her cheeks. "I'm sorry, Ben. I'm not trying to worry you," she whispered against his neck. "I just have to do this. I couldn't live with myself if something happened to those animals because of me." She pulled back so she could look up at him. "This is part of who I am. I have to help when and where I'm able. And I can promise you that this won't be the only time I run off to do something like this. I wish there was someone else who could go today, but I'm the only one free at the moment. If there were any other way, I'd have jumped on it. I don't like putting myself in danger, but in this instance, if I don't, it might keep me safe, but I'll never be the same." Her voice caught on a sob and she choked it down. "I'll have to live with the guilt that I could have done something and didn't." She framed his face in her hands, imploring him to understand.

"I know, darlin'. It's part of what makes you, you. That generous spirit is part of what draws me to you." One hand slid up her back to twist around her ponytail. He tugged until her head tipped back slightly. "Do you mind if I come along? I'll feel better if I'm the one who's looking out for you."

"I was hoping you'd say that." She let her hands slide around his head to link behind his neck as he bent to kiss her. "And for the record—" She slid a hand between them to cover his lips briefly before he could kiss her. "I was never going to go by myself. I was going to take Jake with me."

Ben frowned at the name. "Who the hell is Jake?"

Gemma smiled. "Deputy Maxwell. His name is Jake. He's on guard duty out front, and since he and I have a track record with horses, I figured I'd take him along for this one too. I mean, lightning can't strike twice, right?"

Ben couldn't stop the smile that spread across his face. "Baby, I'm beginning to think that with you, lightning will strike wherever and whenever it wants."

He silenced her giggle with a fierce kiss.

TWENTY-NINE

Gemma pulled up on the scene and gaped at the number of trucks with trailers there. She'd never been on a rescue like this before. She parked in the long line of other vehicles and climbed out. Ben came around to stand next to her.

"Is it always like this?" he asked, staring at the people running to and fro.

Gemma shook her head, searching the crowd. "It's usually much quieter with about a fourth of the people. But then there's not normally so many horses to rehome." She looked up at him. "This is the largest seizure I've ever been to. Before this, my record was eight." She scanned the yard again. Several horses stood stoically inside the corral. Each one was severely underweight. They all looked like they could drop at any moment. "This is awful," Gemma said softly, starting toward the fence.

"Gemma!"

She whirled to the left at the sound of her name. Smiling, she recognized her friend, Sally. She had her long blonde hair drawn up into a ponytail and her clothes were streaked with straw-caked mud.

"I'm glad you made it. This is turning into a real circus." She gestured to the chaos around them. "I'd give you a hug, but I don't think you want what I've got on me all over you."

Gemma chuckled and embraced her friend anyway. "I've been covered in it before. It washes away." She pulled back and gestured to Ben. "Sally, this is my boyfriend, Ben Davidson. Ben, Sally Coleman."

He shook her hand. "Nice to meet you, ma'am."

"You too." Her grip on Ben's hand lingered as she looked at Gemma. She arched an eyebrow in appreciation and smiled. "Boyfriend, huh? Does Tristan know about this one?"

Gemma and Ben both laughed.

"He does. And he actually approves. Albeit, grudgingly," Gemma told her.

Sally turned back to Ben as she released his hand. "Well, you must be something, then."

Ben smiled down at her. "No. He just doesn't scare me. I'm bigger. And he isn't the only one with a badge."

Sally laughed. "I like this one, Gems."

Gemma hooked her arm through Ben's and glanced up at him. He grinned down at her. "Me too," she said happily.

"Well, good. I'm happy for you." She turned to look at the crowd. "You ready for this?"

Gemma nodded. "Do you need my trailer closer, or can the horses walk that far?"

Sally started off toward the corral. "The two I want you to take can walk there. The worst ones are going to the ASPCA barn or to a couple of local vets. Yours just need some extra feed and hoof care." She unlatched the gate, and Gemma and Ben followed her into the pen. "I'm guessing he only acquired these two in the last few months. They aren't as bad off as some of the others."

Sally stopped at the line of horses tied to the corral fence. She walked down the line to the last two and started untying their ropes. She had just handed one rope to Gemma when a pickup roared into the yard. People scattered as it made a beeline for the corral. Gemma felt the steel band of Ben's arm wrap around her waist as he prepared to pull them from the danger.

Just as Ben started to pull her back toward the barn, the truck came to a halt inches from the fence. A red-faced man rocketed out of the truck and practically tore the gate from its hinges, a shotgun clutched in his hands.

"Who's in charge here? You can't take my animals! You got no right coming onto my property. I told you people on the phone what would happen if I caught you out here again." He cocked the shotgun. People cowered behind any cover they could find.

"Shit," Ben muttered.

Gemma mentally echoed the sentiment.

"You are a friggin' trouble-magnet, Gemma," he said softly in her ear.

That was no lie. Bad stuff seemed to be following her everywhere.

Suddenly, the man fired the gun and buckshot peppered the side of the barn. The horses skittered and whinnied, pulling at their ropes, trying to break free. The one she held reared, and Gemma broke free from Ben's hold to calm the terrified animal. The gun swung her direction as she moved.

"You! Let go of my horse!"

Gemma registered the sound of the gun cocking again, but couldn't let go of the terrified animal for fear he would trample someone.

"I said, let him go!"

She spared a quick glance at the man. "I can't. You've scared him to death, and if I let go, he's going to hurt someone." She saw Ben creep toward the fence. With the man's attention on her, he didn't notice Ben slide through the corral rails and slink behind the horses so he could circle around the crazed man. Hope lit in Gemma's chest. If anyone could resolve this, it was Ben.

Keeping the man's focus on her so he could get into position, she faced the man squarely. "Why don't you quit waving that gun around? You're not helping your situation by threatening us."

"I'll do as I please, lady. This is *my* land." He motioned with the gun. "Now get over here with that animal."

"If you'll let me calm him, I can tie him up again and move away. I don't want any trouble."

~

Ben followed the fence rail. He could hear Gemma trying to talk the man down from the frenzy he was in.

Good girl.

While he was terrified to see the shotgun pointed at her, she was keeping the man's attention trained on her, so he could end this.

He glanced around the yard and saw the sheriff's deputies who were already on site, advancing toward the corral. Making sure the irate owner couldn't see him, he flashed his badge at the deputies and waved them back. They took cover, and Ben turned his attention back to the man and Gemma.

He peered around the last horse and stifled a curse. There was at least twenty feet of open territory before he could get behind the man. With the angle, he'd never make it without being seen. He saw Gemma's eyes dart toward him, and it gave him an idea. The man needed to turn toward the barn so he could get behind him. He motioned to Gemma to get her attention.

Quickly and quietly, he gestured with his hands that he wanted her to shift so the man would turn away. By now, she had calmed the horse enough to hold his rope with one hand. She let one hand drop to her side, where she made a quick okay sign.

"He's calm now, so let him go." The man advanced on Gemma several steps. Ben gripped the fence rail to stop himself from running out there. He'd had enough of people threatening his woman. With the mood he was in, this jackass was going to feel the brunt of Ben's frustration when he took him down.

Come on, baby, Ben pleaded silently. *Get the bastard to turn so I can ambush him.*

"Okay. Please don't shoot again. I'm just going to walk him over here to the barn and tie him to the post. I don't want him to get scared again and take off. He could hurt someone."

That's it, baby. Ben watched Gemma slowly move toward the barn. The man turned with her, his rifle still pointed at her.

Ben didn't hesitate. He ran out from his hiding place, stepping lightly, and snuck through the still open gate. He motioned for the deputies to be ready. Drawing on every ounce of his special forces training, Ben crept toward the man, thankful Gemma was milking the task of tying up the horse for all it was worth.

He made it within a few feet of the man when the guy got irritated with Gemma's slow progress.

"God almighty, lady. How long does it take to tie up a horse?" He took several steps in her direction. Ben froze to see what he would do next. Gemma pulled the rope tight around the post and lifted her hands.

"I'm done. He's secure," she said.

"Good. Now who's in charge? You?"

Gemma shook her head. "No. I'm just one of the trailer drivers. I haven't seen the person in charge yet. I got here right before you showed up," she said, stalling for time and obviously not willing to give Sally up.

When the guy started to move toward Gemma again, Ben knew he couldn't wait. If he got close enough to grab her and Ben missed his chance to disarm the guy, Gemma was going to be in a lot more danger.

He slipped forward with two long, quick strides. Using his larger size to his advantage, he reached around the man and grabbed his wrist from behind, jerking the gun up. It spun the man around, and Ben landed a solid left hook to the guy's face. The gun pulled free from the man's grasp as he landed in a heap on the ground. Ben quickly spun it around to aim at the man.

"FBI. You're under arrest," Ben said, his voice deadly calm.

The man looked up at him incredulously, a hand pressed to his bleeding nose. "The feds? How the hell are my horses a federal matter?"

"They're not, you jackass, but that's my woman you just held a gun on. We were just here to help remove the animals from your property," Ben stated matter-of-factly. "Now, get up."

The man rose, cursing a blue streak, still clutching his nose with blood dripping from between his fingers. One of the sheriff's deputies took his free hand and twisted it around, leading him to a squad car. Ben lowered the shotgun and handed it to another deputy before turning to Gemma, who still stood near the horse.

He was at her side in two long strides and wrapped his arms around her. "Are you okay?"

She nodded against his chest. "Yeah." She chuckled. "I really do have the worst luck," she said, looking up at him.

He grinned. "You really do." Pushing the hair back from her face, his grin slipped. "Are you sure you're all right?"

She nodded and smiled up at him softly. "Yes, I'm sure. It'll probably hit me later, but right now, I'm fine. You ended it before he could get *really* irate."

Ben kissed her hard, some of the adrenaline leaving his system. He pulled back to look down at her. "You have no idea how happy I am you're one smart woman. You did exactly what I needed you to do, and I didn't have to say a word."

"That's because I know you," she said. "You were telegraphing loud and clear what you intended to do." She shot him a sly look. "And for the record, that whole grab and punch thing you did was *really* sexy."

Ben lifted an eyebrow. "Is that so?"

Her arms rose to encircle his neck. "Yep." She rubbed against him like a cat, and Ben had to bite back a groan.

"You need to stop that. There are people everywhere, and I imagine one or two of them are going to be over her any minute to take our statements," he said through gritted teeth. Gemma's curves glided along his torso, lighting a fire in his blood.

She giggled and moved against him one more time before kissing him hard and stepping back. Ben made a grab for her and brought her back against him, just as someone called her name.

They both turned to see Sally walking up to them with a sheriff's deputy in tow.

"I'd ask if you're all right, but I can see you came through just fine," Sally said to Gemma.

Gemma nodded. "I'll admit to a little fear at having a loaded weapon pointed at me, but I trusted him to take care of it," she told her friend while gesturing to Ben.

"I'm very glad you were here, Agent, is it?" Sally said. "I

guess you really do have a badge, and a pretty nice one at that. I can see now why Tristan doesn't intimidate you."

Ben grinned at the comment. "I'm glad I tagged along too. Trouble seems to be following Gemma around lately."

The deputy spoke up then. "I'll need to get statements from the two of you."

"Give us a couple minutes, and we'll come find you, deputy," Ben said.

The man nodded and walked away, Sally following to give him her own statement.

Ben turned to Gemma. "I need to call Sheriff Raymond. I don't think we're going to make it back in time to execute our plan tonight."

Gemma's shoulders slumped. "I'm sorry, Ben. I really thought we'd be out of here by now and on our way home."

Ben rubbed a hand down her back, soothing her. "It's all right, Gems. We'll just have to set it for another day."

He pulled out his phone and dialed.

THIRTY

Several days had come and gone since the horse rescue and their aborted bait and trap mission. Ben walked into the station house after dropping Gemma off at work, only to be immediately hailed by one of the deputies.

"Mail, Agent Davidson." The deputy held out a manila envelope addressed to him. He looked at the postmark on the envelope. It was from Asheville again, just like all the other letters.

Adrenaline shot through his veins. It seemed the killer had more to say. Ben just hoped it wasn't that there was another body hiding somewhere. "Find Detective Mabley and send him to my desk," Ben told the deputy.

The deputy scurried away as Ben made his way to his desk, holding the envelope by the corner. He donned gloves and slit the top of the envelope.

"Please tell me that's not what I think it is," Tristan said, stopping several feet away.

Ben reached inside and carefully pulled out the contents. This time it was pictures. Of him and Gemma last week at the horse rescue. Of Gemma calming the riled horse. Of her facing off with the madman. Of him holding the owner at gunpoint, Gemma looking on. Of them kissing. Each one had an "X" drawn over Gemma's face. A lone sheet of paper on the bottom of the stack contained a simple typed note: *It would have been so easy.*

The rage coursing through his body at the images quickly gave way to shock. "Tristan." Ben flipped through the photographs again, stopping on the first image of Gemma calming the horse. "Tristan, look at this." He showed him the picture.

Tristan frowned. "What about it?"

"We'd only been there a few minutes at that point. I didn't notice anyone following us on the way there, so that means whoever took this picture—"

"Was already there!" Tristan finished for him.

Ben stabbed the photo with his finger. "Exactly! Our perp messed up. We're looking for someone affiliated with Gemma's equine rescue league."

Tristan whipped out his phone. "I'll call Sally Coleman and get a list of all the people she called in and the helpers she had with her. You get a hold of the county sheriff's department that was there helping out and find out what deputies were dispatched to the scene."

For the first time since they discovered Diana Lowell's body, Ben felt hope that they could finally catch this killer.

Within hours, lists of names flooded into the office from the various organizations and individuals who were involved in the horse seizure. The number of people involved was staggering. Sally had called in four different teams to rehome the horses, and each team had arrived with at least two people. The two larger teams had four people and Sally had brought a handful of her own helpers with her to the seizure. With the local law enforcement there, Ben and Tristan were looking at nearly thirty individuals. They had quickly crossed off the women, but were still left with seventeen men whose alibis they needed to check.

And three of them were rangers—rangers Ben had already run background checks on.

He shuffled through the papers in front of him again, looking for the original background checks.

There had to be something they missed.

Gemma jolted awake at the sound of ringing near her head. Still groggy, she turned toward the sound and realized it was her cell phone. She had placed it on the coffee table after Ben called to tell her they had a lead in the case and that he didn't know when either he or Tristan would be home. She must have fallen asleep on the couch waiting for them if the sun streaming in through the windows was any indication.

She sat up and picked up the phone, frowning at the unfamiliar number.

"Hello?"

"Hello, Ms. Mabley."

Terror slammed through Gemma at the malice running through the man's voice on the other end of the phone.

"Who is this?" she asked, hating that her voice shook, but powerless to stop it. Dread filled her, telling her she already knew who it was.

"I think you can take a guess as to whom you're speaking. It's time we ended this little game we've been playing, don't you think?"

Fury replaced the terror at his words. She shot to her feet. "*We* were never playing a game, you sick jerk. That was all you."

A cold laugh came through the line. "So fiery is Davidson's little lady. I'm going to enjoy you."

"You have to get me first, and that will never happen. Ben will never let you take me." Gemma told him fiercely.

"Now, see, that's where you're wrong, because he won't have to stop me. You're going to come to me of your own free will."

"You really are insane." Gemma couldn't believe how cocky the psycho was. He seemed so sure of himself.

"No, Ms. Mabley. I'm just very, very smart."

Before she could make a retort, another voice came over the line. Small and scared.

"I want to go home."

Gemma felt her heart slam against her ribs. She sank back down to the couch as her knees gave out at the sound of Caleb Lowell's voice.

"Caleb?" Gemma swallowed hard past the lump in her throat. "Hang in there, sweetie. I'll make sure you get home soon."

"The boy is fine right now, Ms. Mabley, but he won't stay that way if you don't cooperate."

"You sick bastard! He's just a child!" She was going to strangle this man with her bare hands for frightening Caleb.

"And he will be fine, so long as you do what I say."

Gemma inhaled a deep breath through her nose, trying to calm her nerves. "What do you want me to do?" she asked, knowing she may very well be signing her own death warrant, but unwilling to let any harm come to Caleb.

"I want you to meet me. In the forest." He gave her directions, which Gemma repeated to herself, so she wouldn't forget.

"How am I supposed to get there? There are two cops sitting outside my house, and I don't have a car because you made Stacy drive it into a tree," Gemma argued. Her only hope right now was to lure him closer to town so she would have a better chance of escaping. Of having help close by.

The man laughed. "Yes, that is unfortunate, but it is of your own making. If you hadn't loaned that poor girl your car in the first place, this whole thing would already be over. Although," he said thoughtfully, "I guess I should thank you. I've thoroughly enjoyed toying with Agent Davidson these last few of weeks. Watching him run around in circles trying to find me has been quite satisfying. But you are quite right. Getting here will be difficult. I do think, though, that you would do anything to save this little boy. I suggest you get busy. You have ninety minutes. When you get to the parking area, follow the trail into the forest, then I'll find you. Oh, and I don't think I need to tell you not to warn your boyfriend about all this, do I?"

The sound of him hanging up cut off anything she would have said. Gemma dropped the phone next to her and thought furiously. She knew she could get out of the house without being seen, but getting to her dad's truck and to the forest in that amount of time was going to be difficult. She glanced out the window at the officer sitting in an unmarked car, a plan forming.

～

"What do you mean, she's gone?" Tristan's voice rang out in the quiet conference room as he answered his phone. Ben's head shot up, the documents in front of him forgotten. He rose and leaned his fists on the table, waiting for information.

Tristan looked up, the phone still to his ear, his face pale.

"What?" Ben asked.

"Gemma's gone. She lured the officers inside, then ran out and took one of the cruisers while they were distracted."

Ben let the curses fly. He should have seen something like this coming. The woman was too damned smart. "Do they know why?"

Tristan repeated Ben's question to the person on the other end of the line. Ben watched as his face got even whiter.

"She went after Caleb Lowell."

Dread filled Ben. There was only one reason she would take off secretly after the boy and that was if the killer had him and was demanding Gemma in exchange. He knew she would do anything to save the boy. He also knew she was too smart to think the killer was just going to let Caleb go once he had her.

Ben's mind whirled as he threw open the conference room door and raced toward the sheriff's office. Gemma had a plan, and he was betting she'd left bread crumbs for him to follow. That thought alone was what kept him sane. He couldn't dwell on the fact she was driving into the hands of a ruthless killer.

He burst through John Raymond's door, startling the man as he stared at his computer screen.

"Gemma's gone. We think she got a phone call from the killer. He has Caleb Lowell, and she went after him."

Raymond cursed.

"Can you send a unit to Marcie Trent's house? She might be hurt."

Raymond nodded and picked up the phone to call dispatch just as Tristan stepped into the room behind Ben.

"I'm going to call our tech department too," Tristan said. "She took one of the cruisers, and they all have a GPS locator in them. We'll be able to track her."

Ben nodded. "We have to hang back and not stop her, so tell all the officers in the field to just report in if they see the car. As much as I hate it, I think she's our only chance of getting Caleb back and bringing this killer in."

Tristan nodded reluctantly in agreement.

Ben struggled not to pace the floor like a madman as Tristan called tech and got a trace on the cruiser. When they put him on hold while they traced it, Ben growled in frustration.

Tristan put a hand on his shoulder. "Gemma knew what she was doing, Ben. As much as I may act otherwise, I know my sister is smart. She took that cruiser because she knew we could track it. That bastard likely told her not to contact us, but if he's anything like most men, he sees a pretty face and her bubbly personality, and he underestimates her intelligence. She'll guide us to her. We'll get her back."

Ben nodded. Logically, he knew all that. But right now, he was ruled by his heart, which was still stuttering in fear that he would never see her again.

Forcing the emotions back, Ben turned his brain to the case. He ran back to his desk to grab the folders on the three rangers who had been at the horse seizure. Their killer *had* to be one of those three. He had read and reread the information they compiled on the men several times, but a new sense of urgency had him wanting to take a closer look.

When he reached his desk, a new fax sat on top of his stack of folders. Ben glanced at the header and felt his heart speed up. It was from his office in Richmond. His partner had been running deeper background checks on the three rangers associated with the equine rescue league and had found something.

Ben skimmed the fax, eyes widening. "Holy shit!" he breathed. One of the three had been adopted as a toddler, along with his infant brother, and his adoptive parents had changed his name from *Jackson* to Derek. Derek—or Jackson—had also been a seasonal ranger in all three districts at the time of the murders.

He definitely had his killer.

Now he just had to find him before it was too late.

Thirty-One

Staring off into the trees through the windshield of the cruiser, Gemma tried to gather her courage around her like a cloak. She had parked the car off the side of the road where the bastard holding Caleb had told her to, and now she had to walk into the woods. Alone. She prayed fervently the officers she tricked into coming inside the house had found her note and relayed the info to Ben and Tristan.

She also prayed the officers wouldn't hold it against her that she locked them in her bedroom. Truthfully, telling them she thought she heard something at the back of the house and then locking them in her room when they had humored her and checked out the "noise" had been the only thing she could think of to get them to leave their cars and get them temporarily out of the way without bodily harm. She'd told them it sounded like it came from her bedroom. Once they were inside, she'd quietly closed the door behind her, then looped a leather cord around the knob and tied it to the room next door. To be honest, though, she was more afraid of Ben and Tristan's reactions. They were going to blow a gasket.

Inhaling a deep breath, she pushed open the car door. If

she could get Caleb away from the killer, any amount of yelling and fury they threw at her would be worth it. And she'd be damned if she was going down without a fight. She wasn't an idiot, and she hadn't come unprepared. Before she called the officers into the house, she'd packed a back pack with her hiking boots and a couple knives as well as a map and compass.

Once she got up into the mountains, Gemma had pulled off onto a rarely traveled road and changed her shoes and duct-taped a folding pocket knife to the very top of the inside of her thigh and tucked one of Tristan's longer fixed blade tactical knives into her boot. If she had a small caliber pistol, it would be hiding in the other. Unfortunately, she never thought she'd have a reason to have one. That was going to get rectified as soon as she was safe and sound at home.

Using the map and compass, Gemma set off into the woods to the wildlife area the man specified. She moved as fast as she dared. It had taken her nearly an hour to set up and execute her plan and get here. Now she had to hike a mile through the dense Appalachian forest and only had about thirty minutes to do it.

"The techs got the tracker location on the cruiser. She's north of here, near the state line. The car's in the middle of the woods and not moving," Tristan said, rushing up to Ben's desk.

Ben held up a finger, listening intently to the person on the other end of the line. He ran over to the murder board and drew circles on the map they'd put up of the locations where they'd found the victims. "Which of these did he frequent the most?"

More rings went around two of the locations. Tristan frowned and picked up another marker. He put an "X" on the map not far from one of the heavily ringed areas Ben drew.

Ben mumbled a thanks into the phone and hung up. "That was the ranger in charge of scheduling for one Derek Sutton, formerly known as Jackson Halliday. These spots"— Ben gestured to the circles on the map—"are where Sutton was sent out on patrol." Ben pointed at the two more heavily rimmed areas. "These are the two he was sent to most often."

"It looks like that's our killing zone, then." Tristan gestured to an area near the Tennessee border. "That's where the cruiser is." He pointed at the "X" he marked on the map. One of the more frequented patrol areas and the site where Diana Lowell's body was found weren't far away. "How sure are you that Sutton's our guy?"

"Pretty damn sure. I had my partner do some digging on the three rangers on Ms. Coleman's list. Of them, Derek Sutton was adopted as a toddler. My partner managed to track down a living relative of the adoptive family and found out that his new parents changed his name from Jackson. Sutton had a baby brother too. Lucas. Their adoptive parents were into alternative medicine and very rarely took the children to a western doctor. Lucas died at the age of fifteen from a staph infection. Derek was seventeen. The family member said his parents tried to treat the infection with holistic medicine. Sutton's definitely our guy."

Ben stared at the map. The "X" marking where the cruiser Gemma took now sat stared back at him, tauntingly. She was so close, but that was a vast area of dense wilderness they had to search. "Okay, so this guy's smart and he's got to know we're keeping close tabs on Gemma, which means he knows he doesn't have much time. There aren't any service roads here, so any transportation he has is from an ATV."

"Right, but he's not going to be able to control both

Gemma and Caleb and drive the ATV, which means Gemma probably has to hike to wherever Sutton is," Tristan said.

"And, I'd bet that hike isn't going to be more than a mile to a mile and a half, tops, because he knows he's on a time crunch. He knows he has to end this and get out of the area before we figure out where he is. "But we have an edge, because of the cruiser's GPS tracking bug." He uncapped his marker and drew lines out from where the cruiser was, representing a mile and a half, then connected them into a circle. "That's our search zone."

"Ben, look." Tristan pointed to a spot about a mile south of the car. "Didn't Caleb's grandmother say that Diana and Caleb liked to go birdwatching at a wildlife preserve near Hot Springs?"

Ben stared hard at the map, hope lighting in his chest. "That's got to be it."

Hang on, baby. We're coming.

Thirty-Two

After Gemma was sure she was a mile into the forest, she stopped and looked around. She could hear water close by and wandered to the stream running through the trees. The forest was still dense even here, and she had no idea how the bastard was going to find her. Eager to get Caleb out of the madman's clutches, Gemma decided to help him along. She lifted her face to the trees. "All right, you bastard! I'm here! Now come out and let Caleb go!" she yelled at the top of her lungs.

Rustling from behind made her whirl around. A figure stepped from the trees about ten yards away, a hand fisted in the back of Caleb's t-shirt. Gemma was shocked to recognize the man as a member of her equine rescue league. Derek Sutton. She'd had encounters with him, before and he had always been friendly. She never would have suspected him of the murders.

Shoving aside her shock, Gemma ran toward the boy. "Caleb!"

Sutton lifted a pistol and aimed it at the boy. "That's far enough, Gemma."

Gemma skidded to a halt and swallowed down her fear. "Caleb, are you okay?"

"Wanna go home, wanna go home, wanna go home," he muttered rapidly in a small voice.

Her heart broke for the little boy. Any normal child would be scared out of his mind in a situation like this. Caleb, with his inability to cope with change, had to be utterly terrified. He was holding up remarkably well, though, for an autistic child. Rather than becoming hysterical in the face of stress, his brain had simply shut down. Gemma was grateful. If he had reacted violently, she doubted Sutton would have bothered to keep him alive. At the very least, he'd be unconscious.

"I'm here now, Derek. You need to let him go. Let him loose, call the authorities and tell them where he is. You can take me wherever you want so long as he's safe."

Derek scoffed. "And let the police track us from here? I don't think so. I'll turn him loose when you're dead and I'm long gone from here." He gestured for her to come closer. "We're going to go for a short walk to where I have some things stored for you."

Gemma walked closer.

"You go in front, so I can keep an eye on you," Derek said, watching her every move.

She did as he asked. She needed to find the right opportunity to try to take Caleb and run, so she intended to cooperate until the time was right. Following the river, she walked deeper in to the trees.

"Turn left," Derek directed.

Gemma did, crossing the stream. A hundred yards in she saw a tiny clearing where an ATV sat parked next to a tree, a duffel bag tied to the back.

"Sit down against that tree," Derek commanded. Gemma complied and pulled Caleb down with her. Derek walked over to the bag and pulled out a length of rope.

He threw it at Caleb's feet. "Tie her up, kid."

Caleb didn't respond. He simply sat next to Gemma and rocked, muttering that he wanted to go home.

Derek kicked the boy's feet. "Do it, kid!"

Caleb whimpered and buried his head in his knees.

"Stop! Stop!" Gemma yelled. "He's autistic. He's not going to respond to you. He's locked inside his mind now because you've scared him to death by kidnapping him."

Derek growled. "Fine." He knelt down and grabbed the rope, laying the gun aside.

Gemma's heart thudded in her chest. Now was her chance.

Quick as lightning, Gemma pulled the knife from her boot and lunged. He saw her and moved at the last second, so her aim wasn't true. She aimed for his neck, but the knife glanced off of his shoulder. He bellowed and fell back.

Quickly, Gemma rose, pulling Caleb up with her. She turned to run, but the sound of the hammer on the gun cocking stopped her.

"I should shoot you now, you bitch," Derek growled.

She froze, slowly turning around to see him aiming the gun at her chest, blood trickling down one arm. Staring at him defiantly, she silently dared him to shoot her, knowing he wouldn't. It would ruin his grand plan.

His aim shifted until he pointed the gun at Caleb. "How about I just shoot him instead?"

"No!" She stepped in front of the boy. "No. I'll behave. Just please, leave him alone."

Derek's lip curled in a snarl, but he lowered the weapon. "You try anything again, I will shoot him and leave him to die miserably. Now, take off your shirt."

Her eyes widened. "What?"

"Your shirt. I want to make sure you didn't tuck a knife or some other weapon into your bra."

She crossed her arms. "I didn't."

He smirked. "Take it off."

Glaring, and vowing to make him pay for this when she finally got the best of him, she whipped her t-shirt over her head, thankful that she had the forethought to tape the smaller knife to her thigh. So long as he didn't make her take off her shorts, he would never find it.

Completely exposed down to her lacy scrap of a bra, she arched an eyebrow at him. "You want to come look in my bra?" If he came close enough, she was going to deck him, using the moves Tristan showed her years ago.

His eyes darkened at her suggestion, but she could tell he knew what she was thinking. "How about you just take it off, too?"

Vehemently, she shook her head. "Not a chance. I think we can both agree that the outline of a weapon would show. Can I put my shirt back on?"

"No." He tossed the rope at her. "Tie yourself up. Use your teeth if you have too."

Gemma turned the length of rope over in her hands several times, contemplating how she could get out of using it. Or using it in a way he didn't want her to.

Derek trained the gun on Caleb again. "Do it."

Deciding it was best not to test him too much, Gemma tied up her hands. It was awkward and didn't look very pretty, but she wasn't going anywhere.

Finished, she held up her now bound hands. "Satisfied?"

Instead of answering her, he stepped closer and grabbed Caleb by the arm. The boy immediately shrank back and screamed.

"No!" Gemma yelled. "What are you doing?"

Derek pulled the boy to ATV and picked him up, depositing him on the vehicle. He climbed on behind the crying child. "Throw the end of your rope to me."

She did as he asked. He caught it and quickly looped it around the steering column, tying it off.

The grin he tossed her way was positively evil. "I hope you've been keeping up on your exercise routine, Gemma. You're going to need it."

Dread pooled in her stomach as he twisted the key to start the ATV's engine. The rope pulled taut as he squeezed the throttle, making the four-wheeler leap forward. Gemma's arms nearly jerked out of their sockets. It took all of her strength to remain on her feet as he took off through the trees.

Legs pumping, she ran behind the ATV as he drove. Within a few minutes, her lungs burned from the pace, but she knew she couldn't slow down. He wouldn't stop if she fell, and she would end up being dragged through the forest to their destination.

Praying they weren't going too far, she put all her focus into staying upright.

~

Screeching to a halt, Ben pulled in behind the abandoned sheriff's cruiser in the parking lot at the wildlife preserve. The other vehicles that followed his breakneck pace up the mountain pulled in behind him. Doors slammed as everyone piled out of their cars to amass near his SUV.

He prayed they weren't too late. Gemma had done a bang-up job of trapping the officers in her room. The two men spent several minutes trying to break through the door before they turned to the window. To their consternation, they discovered that she jammed the lock on it, forcing them to break the glass so they could shimmy out. Once through the window, it took them several more moments to untangle themselves from the climbing rose bushes in the flower bed below. Scratched and bleeding, their clothes torn, they finally made their way to the patrol car behind the house to relay her escape.

Ben was just thankful the officers had thought to go back inside the house to look for clues as to why she duped them and fled. Because of their actions, they now had a place to start their search.

He whistled sharply to get everyone's attention. "Everyone fan out. Standard search distance. Stay alert. Sutton is likely armed and won't hesitate to shoot. Remember, he has a child captive, so be very careful about engaging our suspect." He clapped his hands once. "Let's go."

The group dispersed through the trees, eyes and ears peeled for any sign of Gemma, Caleb, and their suspect. The dense foliage made it difficult to see further than a few yards, and the rustle of the leaves in the wind masked the noise of anyone walking. It was tiring and frustrating. If time hadn't been of the essence, Ben would have called in search dogs from around the state to help. He might still, if their search didn't yield something quickly.

After forty-five minutes of walking through the forest, they reached a stream. Footprints dotted the area, sending his heart soaring. He quickly radioed Tristan, who was roughly fifty yards to his right. The footprints were headed his way.

The radio crackled to life. "Ben, you need to get over here. Follow the footprints and cross the stream."

Tamping down his rapidly building anxiety, Ben took off in a sprint as fast as his damaged leg would allow. Dashing along the bank, he ran until the footprints disappeared into the stream. Splashing across, he charged up the embankment and into the trees, running until he broke into a small clearing. Tristan stood on the far side, a piece of cloth clutched in his hand.

"What is that?" he asked as he got close.

Tristan held it up. "Gemma's shirt." He pointed to the ground. "I found it there, along with tire tracks from a four-wheeler."

Ben's stomach plummeted to his toes. They were too late. Gemma could be miles away by now.

"We're going to need more help, Ben."

THIRTY-THREE

The woof of a dog caught Ben's attention as he perused the map for their new search grid. After they discovered the tire tracks, Ben had called in as many K-9 units as he could get to help track down Gemma and their suspect. It sounded like the first of them had just arrived.

He looked up to see Carter Townsend and Maverick bearing down on him. A butterfly bandage still covered the stitches on Carter's forehead and a colorful bruise decorated the top left side of his face, but his expression told Ben he was feeling fine and ready to get to work.

"Thanks for coming, Carter." Ben shook the man's hand and gave Maverick a good scratch on the ears.

"I told you all you had to do was call. I'm glad I was back and able to get here so quickly. I just wish it wasn't Gemma we were looking for."

Ben echoed that sentiment wholeheartedly.

"Where do you want us?" Carter asked, patting Maverick on the side as the dog pranced around, eager to get to work.

"Over here." He led Carter and Maverick over near where they found Gemma's shirt. That area was roped off to preserve any scent trail. Tristan stood there with the sheriff. They had a map open like Ben's and were showing two deputies where to search.

"Tristan."

He looked up as Ben and Carter approached.

"This is Carter Townsend and his dog Maverick. Carter, this is Gemma's brother, Detective Tristan Mabley, and the sheriff, John Raymond."

The three men shook hands and exchanged pleasantries.

Tristan handed Carter the ziploc bag containing Gemma's shirt. "We found this here on the ground next to the four-wheeler tracks. I don't know how much good it'll do you since they had the vehicle, but we figured it wouldn't hurt."

"Maverick might be able to air scent from it." He opened the bag and held it in front of his dog's nose. "Seek, Mav."

Maverick immediately put his nose to the ground. In seconds, his body went taut, and he quickly reached the end of his leash. He looked back at Carter and whined.

"He's got the scent."

"I'm going with you," Ben said immediately.

"So am I." Tristan passed the bag to the sheriff.

Raymond nodded. "Go. I'll hold down the fort. Make sure your GPS locators are on and radio in every ten minutes."

Ben and Tristan both flipped switches on their radios to enable the GPS function. Giving Carter a nod, they took off into the woods.

～

The cabin materialized out of the forest like a specter. One minute, there was nothing but trees, and the next, a dilapidated, ancient shack that looked like something straight out of a horror movie emerged from shadows.

Still, she was happy to see it because it meant she could stop running. Her lungs felt like someone took a torch to them and her bruised ribs ached with a renewed vigor.

She sank to her knees when they finally stopped in front of the cabin's porch.

Derek climbed off the ATV, pulling Caleb with him.

"Get up," he told her when he saw her on the ground.

"I just—need a second," she panted.

He flung Caleb at her. She barely caught him awkwardly as he crashed into her.

"I said, get up!"

Caleb sobbed against her as she struggled to stand. Her legs were Jell-O.

Derek untied the rope from the ATV and yanked. "Into the cabin."

Shuffling forward as best she could on her wobbly legs while holding up Caleb, she walked over the threshold and into the tiny cabin.

It was as horrifying on the inside as the outside, except the inside boasted a bed with clean sheets and a table free of dust. Apparently, Derek had prepared this place for her arrival.

As much as she wanted to sit down, she refused to go anywhere near that bed.

The barrel of Derek's pistol poking her between the shoulder blades prompted her to move forward. He followed her in and closed the door, shutting out a good deal of the light. The cabin only had two windows, and both were covered in years of grime.

"Tell the boy to sit on the bed."

Gemma murmured the request to Caleb and gently urged him over to the bed. He sat down, immediately drawing his knees up, hugging them. His face quickly disappeared into the well he created.

Her heart broke at the sight. She was going to make Derek

pay for all he'd done to the child. The man had no idea what was coming.

She whirled around, glaring. "He's sitting. What now?"

Derek motioned to the corner at the foot of the bed. "Put the end of the rope through the eyelet and pull it down."

Glancing over, she saw the eyelet bolt he was talking about. It was anchored into the wall nearly two feet above her head. For the first time, fear for herself pushed its way forward. She gulped nervously, but did as he asked, knowing he would hurt Caleb if she didn't.

Once the rope was through the bolt, she stood there defiantly as he moved close enough to grab the end of the rope. He pulled it tight, stretching her arms above her head until she was standing on her tiptoes, then strung it across the room to tie it off on another eyelet on the other side of the cabin.

Rope secured, he put the gun on the table and walked back to her, pulling the knife she used on him from his belt. He touched the tip of the cold steel to her chest and ran it lightly down between her breasts.

The hard steel scratched her skin, not enough to bleed, but enough to leave an angry red line down her middle.

Her jaw ached as she clenched her teeth together in an effort not to lash out and kick him for all she was worth. She needed time to think and Caleb needed to calm down before she could make any kind of move to get them out of here.

"I can understand why Agent Davidson fancies you, Gemma. You are a beautiful woman. I've always thought so." He touched the knife tip to her cheek. "It's a shame to destroy such beauty, but Davidson brought this on himself. He should have just left me alone."

Gemma held his gaze, refusing to show him her fear. "You've got me. Let Caleb go. He has nothing to do with any of this. I thought you were all about protecting children, yet here you are hurting one."

His eyes went hard half a second before he backhanded her.

"Don't you lecture me on protecting children! You put them up on a horse and pretend it makes them all better. That's not therapy. It's playtime. They need real counseling and therapy."

Biting her tongue to keep back the fiery retort, she just stood there, her face throbbing from the blow.

"Why are you doing this? Why kill all those women? They were just trying to do what was best for their children. The last woman you killed kicked a drug habit for her kid. She didn't deserve to die."

"She should have left that baby in foster care. At least then she would have had access to better food and medical care. I watched that girl beg her mother for chicken at the grocery store. Do you know what the bitch said? That it was full of antibiotics that were bad for her. Antibiotics aren't a bad thing!" He flung his arms out, irate. "If my brother had gotten antibiotics when he needed them, he would still be alive. These women I've killed aren't protecting their children. They're killing them! *I'm* saving them. Those women deserved to die for what they did. Just like my mother." He said the last word like it was dirty.

"What exactly did your mother do?" she asked hesitantly. Even though she was afraid she would set him off and he would hurt her, she had to know. Had to know what drove him to do such despicable things.

"She let my brother die," he spat. "From a simple cut. She didn't think he needed a doctor, but he did. He died in my arms, his leg black and rotting because she refused to get him the antibiotics he needed."

Bile rose in her throat at the picture he painted. What a horrible, painful way to die. Still, it didn't justify killing women because they chose alternative medicine.

"I'm sorry that happened to him. But not all alternative therapies are bad, Derek. Many can do a lot of good."

He spun away angrily. "No. And anyone who subjects a child to such foolishness needs to be punished." He picked up a rag and a roll of tape from the short counter near the sink and returned to her side. Holding her jaw in one hand, he squeezed brutally until she opened her mouth. He stuffed the foul-tasting rag inside and slapped a piece of the duct tape over her lips before she could spit it out.

Panic set in as the filthy cotton threatened to choke her. She struggled mightily against the rope. A scream built in her throat, but she was unable to voice it.

Derek's evil laughter penetrated her panicked brain. Slowly, she came back to herself. Taking a deep breath through her nose, she tried to quash the panic.

He patted her on the cheek as she glared at him before moving over to Caleb. Without giving the boy any warning, he scooped the child off the bed. Gemma renewed her struggles. She couldn't let him hurt Caleb.

"I'll be right back. You stay put now." He tossed a wicked smile over his shoulder as he carried a screeching Caleb from the cabin.

Her muffled sobs were the only sound besides the rumble of the ATV as it drove away. She could only pray that Derek would let Caleb go and not kill him.

~

"Shh!" Carter held up a fist. The three men had been jogging through the forest for nearly an hour, following a strong trail, when a noise brought them up short.

"That sounds like an ATV," Tristan whispered.

"We're getting close," Ben replied. "Be ready."

All three of them drew their weapons and Tristan radioed

in their position, requesting backup. Maverick, nose still to the ground, continued to follow the trail. Carter had said he thought the killer made Gemma walk or run beside the ATV. Maverick was too locked in for it to be anything else.

Ben's heart thundered in his ears as the adrenaline surged. Calling on every ounce of special forces training he had, he forced his heart rate to slow. He needed to be calm and focused.

Cautiously, they walked deeper into the woods.

The door banged open, and Gemma jerked at the sound. Derek strode inside, closing and bolting the door behind him. Immediately, he walked over to her and yanked the tape off her face. She spit out the rag and ran her tongue around her mouth, trying to work up some saliva to relieve the dryness.

"Where's Caleb?" she finally managed.

Derek shrugged. "Not here."

Trepidation tingled down her spine. "Did you kill him?"

"No. I just let him go. I hope your boyfriend brought dogs, because they'll never find him without one."

"No," she whispered brokenly. This was bad. Very, very bad. That sweet child was out there in the wilderness all alone, and God only knew how long it would be before someone went looking for him.

She started struggling against her bonds again. "You bastard! Forget Ben, I'm going to kill you myself!"

He just laughed, angering her further. "You can go ahead and try." He glanced at the rope binding her hands, then stepped closer. "Face it, Gemma. You're at my mercy." He lifted the knife and held it against her cheek. "I'm going to do to you what I did to those other women. Then I'm going to leave your body on display for our dear Agent Davidson to find."

Rage surpassed the fear coursing through her. With a fury born from her concern for Caleb and a desire to see this bastard pay, she acted.

Whipping her head forward, she head-butted him in a move worthy of a superstar soccer player.

He bellowed at the contact and covered his face, backing away. Bright red blood spurted from between his fingers out of his nose.

Gemma got a perverse sense of satisfaction watching him drip blood all over the floor. Even if he killed her, they had his DNA now. There was no way he would ever it get it all out of the cracked and weathered floor boards.

Her triumph was short-lived as he came at her with renewed vigor. Using the knife, he sliced through the rope and threw her onto the bed.

Squirming, she fought for all she was worth as he landed on her. She tried to buck and bite, but her bound hands handicapped her movements. A searing pain lancing across her mid-section brought her fighting to a halt.

Derek straddled her, a crazed, maniacal look in his gray eyes. "Stop struggling or I will gut you like a fish."

"You're going to kill me anyway, so what's the difference?" she ground out through clenched teeth.

He bent close, blood from his broken nose dripping onto her collarbone and hair. "The difference is that after I rape and torture you, I will cut you open from stem to stern, then take you out into the woods and let the bears finish you off. You will be alive when they start to eat you. If you behave, I'll make sure you're dead first."

She stared at him stonily, but stayed still.

"Good girl." He sat back and turned his focus to her half-naked body.

Her entire body was rigid as he ran a hand down her torso over her lace-covered breasts. Bile rose in her throat as his hand moved to the fly of her shorts.

"It'll be such a triumph for me to know I brought Agent Davidson to his knees by torturing and killing you. You deserve to die for your part in setting all those children back in their recovery, and he deserves every ounce of agony this causes him for refusing to back off his investigation. One day, he will end up just like you will. Battered and broken, strung from a tree for all to see your sins."

Tears leaked from her eyes as she realized just how unhinged he was. He was never going to stop, never going to let her go, no matter what she said or did.

Praying fervently for a way out of this, she steeled herself against his touch.

The material of her shorts pulled as he tried to undo the closure, but it didn't come free. She quickly realized he was having trouble unbuttoning the button-fly with one hand.

When he laid the knife on the bed, Gemma took full advantage of the opportunity. She surged upward, slamming her bound hands into his already broken nose. As he tumbled away, she grabbed the knife and rolled off of the bed.

He made a grab for her foot as she tried to stand, but she kicked his hand away, then delivered a second kick to his face with her booted foot.

Dazed from the blows, he floundered on the floor. Gemma didn't wait to see if he got up. She sprinted for the door, throwing the bolt and wrenching it open.

Hoping to slow him down, she slammed the door shut, then wedged the knife in the crack.

Heart pounding, she took off into the forest. She needed to find Caleb.

Once out of sight of the cabin, she stopped to free herself.

Tearing the pocket knife free of the tape on her thigh, she used it to awkwardly saw through the rope binding her hands.

"Gemma! You can't hide forever!"

Her head snapped up at the sound of Derek's voice. She attacked the rope with renewed energy. It hadn't taken him as long as she hoped to come around and break free of the cabin.

Glancing back at the sound of his voice bellowing through the trees again, she sawed harder at the rope until it finally frayed enough she could slip free. The growl of the ATV sent a surge of adrenaline through her veins, spurring her into action. She took off deeper into the woods, running as fast as her tired legs would carry her.

Noise from her left drew her attention. Hoping and praying it was Caleb, she turned toward the sound.

The bark alerted her just as a large black dog appeared.

Maverick!

She dropped to her knees as the dog reached her, Carter on his heels. She had never been so glad to see anyone in her entire life. Maverick leaned into her, licking her face and whining. She hugged the dog for all she was worth, his soft fur reassuring her that he was real.

"Maverick, heel." The dog immediately backed off, but stayed glued to her side.

"My God, Gemma!" Carter knelt next to her, placing a hand on her shoulder. "Are you all right?"

She nodded, choking back a sob of relief. "I'm fine," she managed to whisper.

"Gemma!" Ben raced to her side, landing next to her, Tristan right beside him. She threw her arms around Ben's neck, and the dam broke. Crocodile tears poured down her cheeks as she sobbed into his chest.

He stroked her hair, murmuring softly. Tristan's hand settled on her back and she could feel it shaking in relief.

Aware of the danger still lurking, as well as the need to find

Caleb, Gemma quickly pulled herself together. Leaning back, she looked up into Ben's handsome face. "I'm so glad to see you."

"Same here, baby. Are you all right? You're bleeding." He touched her abdomen near the long cut crisscrossing her midsection.

"I'm fine," she reassured him. "It's superficial. But Caleb—he's out here somewhere all alone. Derek—the man behind the killings—took him out here and just left him. I don't know where. He left me tied up in the cabin back there when he did it." She hooked a thumb over her shoulder. "We have to find him. He's all by himself and terrified."

Ben looked sharply at Carter, who immediately nodded in understanding.

Stripping off his vest, Ben unbuttoned his shirt and took it off, holding it out to her. "Here, put this on." She took it from him and shrugged her arms into it. It was enormous on her, but it covered her mostly naked state.

"There are more units coming to help aid in the search," he told her as he put his body armor back on over his undershirt. "Tristan and I are going to go after Sutton. You and Carter start looking for Caleb. Okay?"

She nodded. "You know who's behind this?"

"We do," Tristan replied. "Ben's partner in Richmond did a deep dive on the three rangers from Sally's list. Derek Sutton was once Jackson Halliday. He was adopted as a toddler. Apparently, he had a brother who died when they were teens."

"He told me," she said, pushing to her feet. "I don't care why he did it, though. Just go stop him."

"We will, Sis." He laid a hand on her arm. "You find Caleb."

She laid her hand over his and squeezed. "Be careful," she said to both him and Tristan. "Derek's completely off his rocker."

"We've got this, don't worry."

That was easier said than done. They hadn't heard the things Derek said or seen the crazed look in his eyes.

Ben kissed her quickly, but with so much feeling, Gemma nearly broke into tears again. His relief that she was safe was palpable.

When he pulled back, he turned to Carter. "Keep in touch and watch your back. On that four-wheeler, Sutton will be able to move quickly. He might double back and stumble upon you before we can catch up."

Carter nodded. "I will. Go. I've got her. We'll find the boy."

With one last lingering look, Ben and Tristan hurried off toward the sound of the ATV prowling through the trees.

~

Running quickly through the dense forest, Ben's leg protested loudly. He was going to look like an old man, hobbling around tomorrow, but for now, he pushed the pain to the back of his mind. Sutton wasn't going to get away because his leg couldn't hack it.

Tristan radioed their position to the other officers combing the forest and discovered that several of them were close.

Because Sutton was on an ATV, he was easy to track. Even with the echo, they were able to pinpoint his location. It also helped that he kept bellowing for Gemma to come out.

Following the man's progress through the woods, Ben tamped down the restless energy that threatened to make him do something rash. Jumping the gun and acting before they had the net in place would only lead to Sutton slipping through their fingers.

Tristan called for a final check-in of everyone's position. The other two teams quickly called in that they were in place.

"On my mark," Ben said softly into the mic.

Sutton drove into view, right between two of the officers.

"Now!"

En masse, Ben, Tristan, and the four other deputies moved from their hiding places to surround Sutton on his ATV.

"Sutton! Turn off the four-wheeler and put your hands up!" Ben aimed his weapon at the man's chest.

If the situation hadn't been so serious, Ben would have laughed at the expression that crossed Sutton's face. Surprise didn't even begin to cover it.

He quickly recovered from the shock, though. Sitting back on the ATV—as it continued to run—he grinned darkly. "Agent Davidson. So, you figured it out. I have to say, I'm surprised. It was my car, wasn't it? I ditched it, but not soon enough, apparently."

"Actually, no. It was the last set of pictures you sent. I know Gemma and I weren't followed to that farm, which meant you had to have already been there. It wasn't hard to get a list of everyone involved that day. So, thank you for narrowing our suspect pool."

Anger turned Sutton's eyes to steel.

"Seems you let your arrogance overrule your common sense. Now turn off the ATV and step down. You're under arrest."

Eyes darting around from deputy to deputy, a crazed expression came over Sutton's face moments before he pulled a gun from his waistband.

Ben fired without hesitation, as did the others. Several bullets struck the man. Sutton got off one wild shot before shock rendered him immobile. His eyes went wide, then rolled up, and he toppled off the ATV.

Hurrying forward, weapon still drawn, Ben kicked the gun

away from Sutton when he reached him. Kneeling, he felt for a pulse. Sightless eyes stared back at him. Derek Sutton was dead.

"Agent Davidson!"

The urgency in the deputy's voice had Ben whirling. His blood turned to ice at what he saw. Tristan lay on the ground on his side, blood covering his left shoulder and chest.

"Detective Mabley's been hit!"

THIRTY-FOUR

When Ben reached Tristan's side, he could immediately see the wound was bad. Blood flowed freely from Tristan's neck around his fingers where he covered the injury. It was quickly pooling on the ground beneath him.

"Shit!" Ben ripped off his vest again and pulled off his remaining shirt, pressing it against Tristan's neck.

"Radio for a chopper and tell them to hurry," he told the deputy next to him. "Tris, hang in there. Help is on the way."

Stark fear shone brightly in Tristan's eyes. He knew as well as Ben that the injury was grave. Blood soaked the shirt where Ben pressed it over the wound. He pressed harder, making Tristan wince.

"I'm sorry. Just hang in there."

Tristan's eyelids began to flutter. He was growing weak from blood loss.

"Tristan! You stay awake. You are not going to die on me, do you hear? Your sister will have my ass if I let you die. I want her to marry me, not hate me for the rest of her life."

A ghost of a smile passed over Tristan's lips. "She's lucky —to have found you." He grasped Ben's arm with a bloody hand. "You take care of her. Tell her I love her. And that I'm sorry for always being such an ass."

Emotion clogged Ben's throat. He swallowed hard. "You can tell her yourself."

A pat on his arm was Tristan's only answer as his eyelids fluttered again.

"Where's that chopper?" Ben demanded.

"On its way," the deputy replied. "It was already in the air to assist with the search. They're picking up a paramedic and heading our way. The sheriff said there's a clearing on the rangers' map about a hundred yards due south of us. It's going to land there."

"Get the ATV," he ordered.

Ben peeled off Tristan's vest, then removed both their belts, looping them like a sling around Tristan's shoulder and neck and tightening them as much as possible to hold pressure on the wound. What he wouldn't give for some QuikClot right about now, but this was the best he could do with what he had on hand. It had to be enough until the chopper arrived.

The deputy drove up on the ATV. Ben picked Tristan up in a fireman's carry and stood, his leg screaming at the strain. His balance wobbled as it threatened to give out, but he managed to plant his feet and stay upright.

Realizing there wouldn't be enough room for all three of them, the deputy jumped off. Ben straddled the machine, holding Tristan across his shoulders with one hand. Twisting the throttle, he headed south. Two of the deputies ran behind him, while the other two stayed with Derek Sutton's body.

The steady thwomp-thwomp of the chopper's rotors echoed through the forest. Ben pressed harder on the accelerator, praying the helicopter would be landing when they reached the clearing. He could feel the blood seeping through the makeshift bandage to trickle over him.

After what felt like an eternity, they broke through the tree line into a large clearing. The helicopter roared overhead, circling as it attempted to land. As it made a slow descent, the deputies who had run with him caught up and helped him climb off of the ATV and carry a now unconscious Tristan to the waiting chopper.

The door on the bird swung open as they approached, and one of the tiniest women Ben had ever seen jumped down.

"Lay him flat across the seats," she yelled over the noise of the rotors.

One of the deputies hopped into the cabin of the chopper while Ben and the other deputy lifted Tristan's two hundred twenty-pound frame through the door. As soon as he was settled, the paramedic climbed inside into the small area between the pilot's seat and the rear bench. She ripped off the makeshift bandage and slapped a QuikClot gauze pad over the wound. She pulled several rolls of gauze from a medical bag next to her and started wrapping his neck and shoulder tightly, much the way Ben had with the belts.

Once the bandage was secure, she tapped the panel next to her head. "Let's go!" she yelled at the pilot.

She turned her gaze to Ben briefly as the pilot prepared to take off. "I'll take good care of him."

With a final long look at his friend and hoping it wasn't the last time he saw him alive, Ben stepped back, closing the door. Almost immediately, the chopper rose into the air, performing a perfect one-eighty before screaming over the treetops toward the trauma center in Asheville.

~

Two hours after she heard gunshots in the woods, Gemma arrived at the emergency room. She had wanted to come right away when Carter relayed that Tristan had been shot, but he and Ben convinced her she needed to stay and find Caleb. Once her panic at the thought of losing her brother subsided, she'd realized they were right. If anyone was going to be able to find the boy and get him to come peacefully, it was her.

It had taken them nearly an hour after the shooting to find the child, who had found a crevice in a rock formation and squeezed himself inside. If it wasn't for Maverick and his amazing nose, they would have walked right past him and never known he was there.

After coaxing the boy out of the crack, Gemma convinced Caleb to let Carter give him a piggyback ride back down the mountain. By the time they reached the parking lot and the waiting ambulance, Caleb's tears had dried, and while he wasn't smiling, he wasn't frowning either.

He also refused to let Maverick out of his sight. The boy had latched onto the dog like a lifeline. She couldn't blame him. The animal had a way about him that set people at ease. She'd noticed that in Charleston.

In an effort to preserve Caleb's calm state and make it a smooth ride to the hospital, Gemma managed to convince the paramedics it was in everyone's best interest to let Carter and Maverick ride with him in the ambulance. She followed right behind in a separate ambulance.

Now, anxious to find out Tristan's status, she grilled the first nurse to cross her path.

"My brother, Tristan, was brought in by air a couple of hours ago. He was shot. Can you tell me how he's doing?"

"I don't know off the top of my head," the woman replied. "He went straight to surgery. Let's get you situated and I'll find out."

Gemma nodded. "And the little boy who came in with the K-9 unit—that dog needs to stay with him. Caleb is autistic, and Maverick is the only thing keeping him calm right now. Make sure the staff know that."

The nurse smiled reassuringly. "I will. You sit tight. I'll go find out about your brother."

Thanking the nurse, she sat back and closed her eyes, releasing a long breath as they rolled her into an exam cubicle. The adrenaline that had kept her going for the last several hours was ebbing, and she was feeling the effects. Everything hurt now. Her legs ached from running, and her stomach felt like it was on fire. Every breath she took reminded her that her ribs were still healing. She would gladly let a doctor examine her just so she could get some painkillers.

Her eyes snapped open at the swish of the cubicle door. The nurse she snagged in the corridor was back and accompanied by a doctor.

"Your brother is still in surgery," the nurse immediately stated. "That's all I can tell you right now. I'm still working to learn more. As soon as I find out anything else, I will let you know."

Disappointed there wasn't more news on his condition, Gemma slumped against the bed. Worry ate at her, and she wished Ben was there to offer her some support. She didn't know what she would do if she lost Tristan.

The doctor was quick with his exam, recommending an over-the-counter antibiotic cream for the cut on her abdomen, and ordering her a painkiller. When he was done, Gemma asked the nurse if she could go to Caleb's cubicle. She agreed and pointed Gemma in the right direction.

Gingerly, Gemma climbed off the bed and made her way to the neighboring exam room. Inside, Carter rested against the wall while Caleb laid in the bed sound asleep, Maverick pressed to his side. In the chair next to the bed, his grandmother, Marcie, worried the strap of her purse between her fingers. A bruise colored the left side of her jaw, and her eyes were red and puffy. Red marks marred her wrists.

The second Marcie saw Gemma, she jumped up, rushing to hug her. "Oh, Gemma! I'm so glad you're okay."

Gemma returned the hug, studying Marcie's face when she pulled back. "I see now how he got Caleb. I'm so sorry. I should have known it was him."

Marcie waved away her concern. "How could you?"

"I knew him. Not well, but well enough that I should have noticed he was a bit insane."

"He fooled a lot of people, Gemma. People who knew him better. This is not your fault. I'm just glad you and Caleb are okay. I am sorry to hear about your brother, though. Officer Townsend told me what happened. Is there any news?"

Blinking back tears, Gemma shook her head. "No. He's still in surgery."

Marcie hugged her again. "I'm sure he'll be fine. If he's anything like you, he will pull through this with flying colors."

Swallowing hard, Gemma only managed to nod.

"So, where's that handsome agent friend of yours? You two looked close."

She sniffed, wiping the wetness from her cheeks. "He's still at the crime scene. He had to wait until the CSI unit got there and took over the scene."

Her gaze landed on Caleb's sleeping form. "How is he?"

Marcie looked over at her grandson. "Okay. Physically, at least. Mentally—well, that is to be determined. I'm sure there will be lots of nightmares and bad days, but we'll get through it. We have to." She turned back to Gemma. "I think I may have to figure out how to get the Fort Carrington Police Department to give up their dog, though. I'm not sure either of them are willing to part with the other."

"Hmm. Maybe we can convince Officer Townsend he's needed here." She glanced at Carter, a half-smile on her face.

"It's definitely more interesting here," Carter replied.

The door to the cubicle opened and a fiftyish, dark-haired man in surgical garb entered. "Ms. Mabley?"

Instantly, Gemma's hands began to shake. "Yes?"

"I'm Dr. Luoni. First, let me say that Tristan is alive. The bullet nicked his external jugular vein. I was able to repair the damage, but he lost a large amount of blood. Once he leaves post-op, he'll be transferred to the ICU. With time, though, I am happy to say he should make a full recovery."

Relief turned Gemma's bones to liquid. She took two steps to her right and sank onto the end of Caleb's bed and buried her face in her hands, happy tears coursing down her cheeks.

The doctor stepped closer and placed a hand on her shoulder in support. "Your brother is a very, very lucky man. It was only because of the phenomenal job done on scene to stop the bleeding that got him here. And if that bullet had been another few millimeters to the right, it wouldn't have mattered what they did."

Eternally grateful things turned out the way they did, Gemma dried her tears and inhaled deeply, trying to steady herself. "Can I see him?"

"Soon. I'll have one of the nurses take you up to the ICU once he's been transferred up there."

Gemma thanked the doctor, and he left.

Marcie hugged her again. "See. I told you he'd be okay."

"You did." She sniffed and stood. "I need to try to call Ben and let him know." She reached for her purse, only to realize she didn't have it with her.

Marcie noticed immediately and handed Gemma her cell. "Here, use mine."

Murmuring her thanks, Gemma stepped out to make the call.

~

The aseptic smell present in every hospital everywhere assaulted Ben's nose as he entered the main doors. Heading straight for the bank of elevators, he got on and pushed the button for the ICU, tapping his foot impatiently as he waited for the elevator to take him to Tristan's floor. It had taken longer than he hoped to get the two crime scenes secured. They'd had to bring in ATVs to haul in Dr. Tate, his staff, the forensics team, and all their equipment.

Ben stepped off the elevator and strode down the hall to the nurses' station. "Excuse me. I'm looking for Tristan Mabley."

Before she could reply, Gemma spoke from behind him. "Ben!"

Turning, he saw her in the doorway to a room ten feet away. She still wore his shirt, but she had washed the blood off her face and hands.

In three long strides, he was at her side and had her in his arms. He buried his face in her hair and breathed deeply, letting her scent wash over him like a balm. She curled her fingers into the clean t-shirt Sheriff Raymond gave him, clinging tightly.

He closed his eyes and savored the contact. Holding her and knowing she was safe, chased away the haunting images of that cabin with the rope hanging from the wall and the tools they found under the bed.

With a light kiss on the top of her head, he pulled back to look into her face. "How is he?"

"As well as expected." She looked back over her shoulder at the figure sleeping on the bed. "He woke up briefly when I got here, but they just gave him more pain medication, so he's going to be down for the count for a while."

"Rest is probably the best thing for him right now."

Gemma nodded. "The staff said he lost a third of his blood

volume before he even got here. He lost even more during the surgery to repair the vein. They gave him seven pints of blood total."

Ben stared at Tristan. He was still pale even after the transfusions. "I thought we were going to lose him before we could get him into the chopper. The blood just poured out." He blinked quickly, clearing his eyes. Gemma kissed his jaw softly and hugged him tight.

"He's alive. Thanks to you and that paramedic."

"Yeah." Inhaling deeply to regain control of his emotions, he pulled back to look at her again. "Have you eaten?"

She shrugged. "I had a candy bar earlier."

"That doesn't count. Come on. Let's go grab something. You need a change of clothes too."

She laughed softly. "I need a shower before I change into anything else. I can't believe you even want to stand next to me right now. I smell so bad."

He tucked her under his arm. "You're not so bad. Not any worse than me, at least."

She giggled softly. "We make quite the pair, don't we?"

"We do," he said, smiling down at her.

Slowly, his smile faded, his expression turning serious. He brought one hand up to cup the side of her face, tracing her cheekbone with his thumb. His heart lodged in his throat and he had to swallow hard to speak. "I love you. I should have said that before now, I know. You are my light in the darkness. A balm for my jaded soul. I want forever with you. If you'll have me?"

Gemma's smile was blinding. All traces of fatigue vanished from her pretty face as she lit up like the sun. She looped her arms around his neck. "Forever sounds good. I love you too." Standing on tiptoe, she kissed him.

Ben couldn't help but think that forever did indeed sound good. Very, very good.

Thank you for reading Smoky Mountain Murder! I hope you enjoyed it. Please consider leaving a rating or review on Amazon and/or Goodreads. It would be greatly appreciated! If you'd like a FREE romantic suspense novella just for signing up and EXCLUSIVE looks twice a month at my latest work-in-progress, you can join my mailing list at ashleyaquinn.com. You can also stay up-to-date on my newest projects by joining my Facebook readers' group, Ashley's She Shed. See you next time!

~

Keep reading for a sneak peek at Book 2 in the Foggy Mountain Intrigue series, Smoky Mountain Baby.

Smoky Mountain Baby

Foggy Mountain
Book 2

PROLOGUE

Sound reverberated all around Tristan Mabley like an echo in a long tunnel. A steady thwump-thwump vibrated through his chest, a strange accompaniment to the pain that had him in a vice grip. Pressure in his neck and shoulder pushed against the pain to the point it was almost a pain in and of itself. He tried to blink, but could only make his eyelids flutter. What was happening? Why couldn't he wake up?

Gathering every ounce of will he could muster, he forced his eyes open. The face of an angel stared down at him. Warm, cinnamon brown eyes looked back at him from a beautiful heart-shaped face. Long blonde hair scraped back into a ponytail hung over her shoulder. He tried to lift a hand to touch the silky strands, but a pain like he had never known screamed through his shoulder and neck. Bile rose in his throat, and he swallowed hard several times, trying desperately not to throw up.

The angel touched his face softly, her warm fingers sending ripples of sensation through his skin.

"Try not to move, detective. I finally got the bleeding to stop, and I don't want it to start again."

Bleeding? What the hell was she talking about?

Memories niggled the back of his mind, but he was too tired and in too much pain to focus enough to pull them forward.

"You just rest. We'll be at the hospital soon."

Hospital? Why were they going to the hospital?

Must have something to do with the pain he felt. He still couldn't muster up the energy to figure it out, though.

Deciding to take her advice, Tristan let the darkness crowding his mind take over, and he sank into oblivion.

ONE

"Why the hell are you hiding out in a corner?"

Tristan looked over to see his new brother-in-law, Ben Davidson, approaching, two glasses of champagne in his hands. He reached Tristan's side and held out one of the flutes.

"Thanks." Tristan accepted the glass and took a sip. The cool bite of the tangy liquid was refreshing. "And, I'm not hiding."

Ben just arched an eyebrow.

"All right. Maybe I am. A little. But that woman—Jamie—won't leave me alone. I had to use the 'I need to use the restroom' card to get away. And then she tried to follow me. Said she'd wait in the hall." Tristan shook his head, still in disbelief. He glanced behind Ben, looking for the telltale red hair of the woman who had been following him around for most of the evening. "Why the hell did you invite her?"

"I didn't. She's your sister's friend from college."

"Gemma needs less crazy friends," he mumbled, taking another sip of his champagne.

"You know, if you'd brought a date, you wouldn't have this problem."

Tristan shrugged. "Bringing a date to my sister's wedding seemed like kind of a big deal. There isn't anyone in my life who warrants being my companion to an event like that."

"Not even her?" Ben pointed at the tiny blonde woman talking to Tristan's mother. Her long hair, hanging loose, fell in a shiny curtain down her back. The lavender lace dress she wore highlighted every curve she possessed, of which she had plenty. The woman was a blonde bombshell wrapped in a teeny tiny package.

His jaw worked while his emotions warred with each other as he watched her interact with his mom. "No." His feelings for Laurel Hunt—the paramedic who saved his life half a year ago—were complicated.

Ben tilted his head, looking at him questioningly. "Why not?"

Tristan just pursed his lips and refused to answer. He didn't have an answer. At least not one he wanted to admit—to Ben or to himself.

"You know," Ben started, swirling the champagne in his glass. "Someone once told me not to run from a good thing." He drained his glass. "It was good advice. I'm going to go find my wife. You should go dance."

With a brilliant smile, Ben walked off, leaving Tristan to contemplate what he said. Leave it to Ben to throw his words back at him.

Inhaling deeply, he stared out at the room from his secluded spot, free to observe in the shadows. The party was in full swing. People were talking and laughing and dancing. Everyone was having a great time. As they should. It was a wedding, after all, and his sister's happiness permeated the entire room. From the brilliant violet orchids to the gauzy fabric and fairy lights draped from the rafters of the converted barn, Gemma's vibrant personality was everywhere.

He seemed to be the only one not enjoying all this reception had to offer.

The truth was, he was feeling a bit melancholic. He never thought he would see Gemma married before him. He was six years older than she was, and he didn't even have a prospect for a wife.

Unconsciously, his eyes sought out the blonde bombshell still talking with his mom. Maybe Ben was right to throw his own words back at him. Maybe he was letting something good slip through his fingers. But he didn't know what to say to her or how to approach her. Heaven knows he had tried. He'd asked her to dinner after he was released from the hospital as thanks for saving him, but she shot him down, then proceeded to avoid him at every turn. Every time he saw her in the field on a call, she barely looked at him. She wasn't rude, but she didn't go out of her way to be friendly, either.

It was exasperating. He didn't know why he couldn't get her out of his mind when she obviously never spared him a second thought. Even when he slept, images of her warm, cinnamon-colored eyes invaded his dreams.

He wanted to get to know her better, but he didn't know how without making her uncomfortable. He'd never had so much trouble with a woman before—either getting a date or getting her out of his mind. She had him firmly between a rock and a hard place, and he had no idea how to get out of it.

Slamming back the remaining champagne in his glass, he decided he was being ridiculous by continuing to hide in the shadows. Stepping out from behind the floral spray that kept him concealed, Laurel's laughter immediately drew his attention like a beacon in the night. The tinkling sound was like fairy music.

He meandered past the bar and handed his empty glass to

the bartender. Laurel laughed again, sending his pulse skittering.

This was absurd.

Spinning around, he made a beeline for the two women. A dance wasn't a date. And this was a party. She wouldn't turn him down for a dance at a party.

At least he hoped she wouldn't.

He just knew he would kick himself later if he didn't ask.

As he walked up, both women erupted into giggles. They sounded like schoolgirls.

"Hi, Mom." He bestowed a smile on the older woman before his eyes dropped to the diminutive woman in front of him. She really was very, very small. The top of her head barely cleared his chest. He felt like he could pick her up and lift her like a dumbbell with just one hand. "Laurel. It's nice you could come. You seem to be enjoying yourself."

He watched, completely mystified, as her entire demeanor changed. Where she had been relaxed and open, laughing with his mom, now that he was standing there, she'd grown stiff and wary. The pretty smile that had graced her face was missing as well, along with the sparkle in her warm brown eyes.

"Hello, detective. Yes, I'm having a nice time, thank you."

Tristan frowned. "You're at my sister's wedding. I think you can call me Tristan."

She rolled her lips inward nervously, but nodded.

Eyeing her speculatively, he held out a hand. "Dance with me?"

If he hadn't been watching her so closely, he likely would have missed the miniscule widening of her eyes and the accompanying flash of apprehension. It was there and gone so fast he could almost believe it was a coincidence. Almost. Her abrupt attitude shift told him otherwise, though.

"Oh, I don't really dance. Your mother, though, would make a nice partner." She pointed to his mom, Caroline.

Caroline waved her off. "You go, dear. I'm going to go get off my feet for a bit. These shoes—while gorgeous—aren't the most comfortable things." She gestured to the silver heels on her feet. "I never understood how women could wear these things all day, every day."

Tristan arched an eyebrow at Laurel. "She shot me down. What do you say?" He held his hand out again.

He watched her wage a war with herself as she stared at his hand. Her eyes held both a desire to dance as well as a healthy dose of fear.

Vowing to get to the bottom of that last emotion, he breathed a mental sigh of relief when her desire to dance with him finally won out and she took his hand.

The band had just switched to a slow song as he led her onto the dance floor. Wrapping an arm around her waist, he pulled her close. She held herself stiffly in his arms, touching him only where she had to.

"Relax," he whispered in her ear. "I won't bite unless you want me to," he said, a hint of a teasing smile in his voice.

Laurel stiffened at his words until she resembled a board before she forced herself to unwind a little. She was being ridiculous. Tristan Mabley was not a threat. He was a cop, for heaven's sake. And a nice man. Not all men were scumbags.

She closed her eyes and inhaled a deep breath through her nose.

Bad idea.

The scent of Tristan's cologne flooded her senses. He smelled so *good*. She stared at the knot of his tie, trying to ignore the flare of heat his nearness induced.

Gemma did a good job picking out clothes for the wedding party. Laurel fought a grimace at the absent thought as she stared hard at the wide male chest in front of her and the purple and gray tie he wore. The wedding and reception were both understated and elegant.

Unable to help herself, her eyes wandered over his broad shoulders and up the column of his strong neck, pausing on the long, jagged scar on the left side. It was a stark reminder he nearly died in her care several months ago. "Your scar looks good." Instantly, her face flushed bright red. What an idiotic thing to say.

He pulled back enough to look down at her. "Thanks."

She glanced up at him and got caught in his brilliant blue gaze. Quickly, she looked away, now even more flustered.

"Laurel."

God, she loved the way he said her name. It just rolled off his tongue like music. Her gaze darted upward again, skittering away as she saw he was still looking down at her.

"Hey, is there a reason you seem to be afraid of me? Did I do something in the helicopter? If I did, I'm sorry. I remember very little from that day after the actual shooting."

Startled, she looked up at him, her timidity forgotten. "No, you didn't do anything. You were only semi-conscious and then only for a few brief moments." She could still remember how the blood had poured out of the hole in his neck when she took off the t-shirt bandage Ben strapped on him to stem the bleeding. It had immediately flowed over his shoulder to pool on the leather seat. She'd thought she was going to lose him. If it wasn't for the QuikClot dressings that had become a standard part of her kit, and her ability to tie a really tight bandage, she would have.

"Then why are you acting like I'm about to attack you at any second?"

She shifted uncomfortably. That was a topic she didn't really discuss. With anyone.

Instead of giving him a truthful answer, she just shrugged and skirted the truth. "I'm just shy." That wasn't a lie. She was shy. But that wasn't the only reason he made her nervous.

He stared down at her until she felt like a bug under a microscope. She had a feeling he could tell there was more to the story.

To his credit, though, he didn't push. Just tightened his arms around her and kept dancing.

Laurel felt herself relaxing for real as they danced. His scent, the warmth of his body, and the rhythm of the music all combined to help her forget she didn't like being around men, especially big men.

When the song ended, Laurel was shocked to realize she wanted to keep dancing. As Tristan tried to step back, she tightened her grip on him. Nervously, she looked up into his sapphire eyes. "I'd like to keep dancing. That is, if you want to?"

His smile was soft and charming. "I'd like that too."

Smiling shyly, she settled back into his arms. This time, she laid her head on his chest and closed her eyes, soaking in the feeling of being held tenderly by a handsome man. She'd never had this before and was going to enjoy it while it lasted.

Through several more slow songs, they danced, unhurriedly moving around the dance floor, lost in their own little world. When the music finally switched to something more upbeat, Laurel felt the loss of his arms acutely.

He seemed reluctant to have her leave his side too. Twining their fingers, he tugged her off the floor. "Come on. I'll buy you a drink."

Heart thudding, she followed him to the bar, where she ordered a glass of white wine. Anything stronger and he would have to peel her off the floor. She was not a drinker. He ordered a scotch, neat, then led her to a table on the outskirts of the room.

She perched on the edge of the seat and took a sip of her wine. The cool, crisp liquid helped wet her parched throat and give her an ounce of courage, something which had waned now that they were no longer dancing.

"So how is work going? Did you have any problems with flashbacks when you returned to the field?" She had read studies on the instance of PTSD among police officers returning to work after a shooting. The numbers were staggering. Almost half had symptoms three months after an incident, while ten percent still had severe reactions. Five percent still had severe reactions after a year. Laurel fervently hoped that Tristan fell into the category of those who had fully recovered.

He swirled the amber liquid in his glass. "The first time I had to draw my gun was hard, but otherwise, it hasn't been too bad. A few sleepless nights."

"Nightmares?" She knew all about those.

He nodded. "Yeah. But I haven't had one in a few weeks, so here's hoping they're finally gone." He lifted his glass in a salute before taking a sip.

Laurel took another sip of her wine, looking away awkwardly. God, she hated being shy. She never knew what to say or how to carry a conversation. This was the reason she hid out in her little house and avoided people. She hadn't been able to say no to Gemma, though, when the woman personally invited her to the wedding. Laurel had a feeling not many people could say no to Gemma. Including the man in front of her. She was extremely persuasive. And tenacious.

"So, Laurel, tell me a bit about yourself. I know you work for Northridge Fire Rescue and that you know how to apply a hell of a tourniquet on an awkward wound, but not much else. Are you from Northridge?"

"No. I'm actually from West Virginia. I moved down here about nine years ago."

"What brought you down here?"

He didn't know it, but that was a loaded question. One she didn't want to get into too deeply. "Family stuff. I needed to get away. I saw an ad for a paramedic's course at a technical school in Asheville, so I applied and got accepted. I worked as a housekeeper at a hotel until I finished school and got hired on in Northridge."

He gave her that look again that said he knew there was more to the story. Trying to appear as nonchalant as possible, she willed him not to pry.

"Do you have a big family?"

"Three older brothers and one younger."

"That must have been tough, being the only girl."

Oh, if he only knew. "It had its moments, yes."

Again, that look. She needed to work on her poker face.

"There you are!"

Startled, Laurel looked over as a woman with flaming red hair approached their table, her eyes fixed on Tristan. She heard him groan softly under his breath.

"Jamie. Hi."

"I've been looking all over for you." She took his hand and tried to tug him from his seat. "Come on. I want to dance."

Tristan didn't budge. The woman frowned down at him. Laurel just sat and stared, unsure as to what exactly was going on.

"Jamie, this is Laurel Hunt. Laurel, this is Jamie Sutercliffe. She's a friend of Gemma's from college."

Laurel smiled and waved. "Hi."

Jamie didn't return her smile. She frowned at her instead, seeming to have just noticed her, before turning back to Tristan. "I thought you didn't have a date. Gemma said you came by yourself."

"I came late," Laurel heard herself reply. "I had to work." *What the hell was she doing?* She hoped Tristan didn't mind that she was pretending to be his girlfriend. Considering the look of distress on his face when the woman approached, she didn't think he would.

If possible, Jamie's frown intensified. "She said you were single."

"She's been a little preoccupied with the wedding. Laurel and I have been seeing each other for a few months now. I'm sorry if you had the wrong impression."

"Me too." Disappointment colored her voice. "I guess I'll see you around."

He nodded and Jamie walked off much more slowly than she had arrived.

"Thank you," Tristan said as soon as Jamie was out of ear shot. "She's been following me around all evening."

Laurel smiled, feeling strangely delighted that he would rather be seen with her than the red-haired dynamo who just walked away. "You're welcome."

He finished his drink and stood, holding out his hand. "How about we get some air?"

Laurel tipped up her glass, draining it, and took his hand. "Air sounds good." Maybe it would help her deal with her sudden attraction to this man.

He led her across the room to a set of double doors that led to a deck that ran the length of the barn. The whole structure had been built into a hill, so the deck they stepped out onto was twenty feet off the ground and overlooked a large pond.

Laurel's breath caught at the beautiful scenery. It had snowed a couple of days ago, so the landscape was completely white, and it gleamed in the light from the full moon overhead. Fairy lights wrapped the trees on the path to the pond, ending in a large gazebo at the water's edge. It was like a post-card come to life.

"Wow," she breathed. "This is beautiful."

"Yes, it is."

She looked up at him and found him looking at her, not the view. Blushing, she looked back out over the grounds. The wind kicked up, sending a swirl of snow around them. Even with the heaters on the deck going full-blast, Laurel felt the chill and shivered. She'd left her wrap inside.

Tristan noticed and shrugged out of his suit coat. "Here. I didn't think about the cold when I suggested we come out here." He draped the heavy fabric over her shoulders. The jacket engulfed her in warmth and the scent of his cologne. His hands lingered on her shoulders. Laurel could feel the firm, comforting weight of them through his coat.

Tipping her head, she looked back at him. "Thanks," she said softly.

"You're welcome," he murmured.

Caught in his azure gaze, Laurel slowly turned until she faced him. His hands slid down her arms as she turned, coming to rest on her waist. She laid one palm against his chest, feeling the contours of muscle beneath his dress shirt.

He stared down at her, his eyes turning to midnight pools in the moonlight.

"Laurel." He cupped the side of her face in one large hand, a questioning look in his eyes.

Understanding what he was asking, she nodded. She was tired of being scared. She wanted to feel something other than fear. Her reaction to Tristan when they danced promised that a kiss would lay waste to any negative emotion her brain tried to feel.

Shuffling his feet, he moved closer, his arm wrapping around her waist to pull her flush against his body. Tingles broke out all over her as he bent his head until he was within a hairsbreadth of kissing her.

Standing on tiptoe, she grasped his head and pulled him down, closing the gap. Fireworks exploded behind her eyelids the second their mouths touched. Her entire body went on instant alert, screaming for more. Instinctively, she pressed against him, seeking closer contact.

He didn't disappoint her. Bending at the knee, he tightened his arm around her and lifted her off her feet, his other hand sliding into her hair to hold her head steady. She wound her arms around his neck, his jacket falling heedlessly to the ground.

Never in her entire life had she been kissed like this. It was exciting and mind-boggling.

Earth-shattering.

Suddenly, down to the marrow of her bones, she knew this was how it was supposed to be. That this was what all the books and movies were about. She'd never had that before. Hadn't really believed such passion existed outside of fiction.

But it was real, and it was happening to her right here in Tristan Mabley's arms.

Breathing hard, he pulled back, his eyes glittering like blue diamonds. He stared at her hard for several seconds, his thumb brushing her cheek. "This is insane."

"Agreed. But it's nice." She laid a hand on his jaw. "Do it again?"

The words were barely out of her mouth before he swooped in to kiss her hard. The intensity of the pleasure racing through her made her dizzy. She swayed into him, clinging tight.

With a groan, he pulled back abruptly. "We need to stop."

Chest heaving, she frowned. "Why?"

His eyes widened. "You know where this is leading if we don't, right?"

She nodded. "Yes. And I'm okay with that."

She was? Her mind raced as she mulled over the words that had popped free before she could stop them. Would it be so bad to let this play out? She had never just jumped into bed with a man before. But the heat Tristan evoked was completely foreign to her. She'd never had that with any other man.

Laurel knew she was throwing caution to the wind, but dammit, she was tired of being a wallflower. She had worked hard to make something of herself. She needed to stop letting her shyness and fear hold her back from the things she wanted. Avoiding Tristan the last several months had been a mistake, but she hadn't been able to overcome those two emotions to take a chance on something that could be life-changing.

Well, no more. Spine stiffening in resolve, she held Tristan's gaze as he stared down at her incredulously.

"An hour ago, you acted like I was going to attack you. What changed?"

"I realized I was being an idiot. That I can't keep letting fear get in the way of my life."

"Whoa." He lowered her to her feet, her words putting an effective kibosh on his ardor. "You're going to have to explain that."

Laurel sighed. She was making such a mess of this. There was a reason she avoided relationships. People in general, really. They were not her forte. "Just that my experiences with men haven't really been positive. What you make me feel— well, it's the opposite of that. I want to know that I *can* have something positive with a man."

He continued to scrutinize her. Laurel was sure he was going to call a halt to things. She had been too honest and scared him off. Dammit! If she had just kept her mouth shut and given some generic answer, they would be on their way back to his room at the lodge and she wouldn't be worrying about how to politely excuse herself.

Just as she was about to mutter something and walk away, he framed her face in his hands and bent down to her level.

"Someday soon, you're going to tell me all about those experiences. But not tonight." He kissed her quick and hard. "Let's go say goodbye to the bride and groom." Tugging on her hand, he led her back inside. They made quick work of finding Gemma and Ben. She prayed her face wasn't flaming red as they said goodbye. Thankfully, they were distracted by other guests and barely acknowledged their farewell.

Formalities out of the way, they left the barn. The wedding venue was part of an inn, and the bridal party all had rooms. Nerves fluttered in Laurel's belly as they navigated the path to the main building and went inside. Tristan paused in front of a door on the second floor and unlocked it. She still wanted to go through with this, but it had been a long time since she was with a man, and her previous experiences hadn't been the best.

Standing in the middle of the room, she clasped her hands in front of herself and tried not to fidget. Tristan walked up and stood in front of her, larger than life.

God, he was so big.

But he's nice, she reminded herself. Big didn't always mean bad.

"Nervous?"

She nodded shakily. "A little."

He reached out with one finger and traced her cheekbone. "We don't have to do anything. I will take you down to your car right now and kiss you goodnight."

It was that simple offer that made her relax. He was leaving this entire thing up to her, giving her control, and she appreciated it.

Sliding her hands up his chest, she linked them behind his neck. "I don't want to go home, Tristan."

He stared at her hard for several moments, assessing the

truthfulness of her statement, before he swooped down and took her mouth in a fierce kiss.

Laurel's entire being responded. She was instantly flush with heat. Arousal pooled low in her belly, making her ache. Oh, how she wanted this man. Her need pushed away any remaining doubts she had about what she was doing or why. All that mattered was Tristan and the way he made her feel.

He felt the need too. They didn't stand there long before he pulled her close and lifted her off her feet, carrying her to the bed. He laid her down and settled next to her. Continuing to kiss her, he ran one hand up and down her torso, leaving a trail of fire wherever he touched. Wrapping a hand around his tie, she pulled him closer and kissed him back for all she was worth, getting a groan in response.

His hand slid beneath her and found the zipper on her dress, pulling it down. Cool air whispered over her skin as he skimmed the material down her arms. The fabric pooled around her waist, baring her to his view with only her lacy bra still covering her.

He sat back to look down at her and trailed a hand lightly over the skin he had exposed. Her nipples peaked beneath her bra, rubbing tantalizingly against the fabric. Laurel bit her bottom lip to hold back the loud moan that wanted to break free. He had barely touched her and she was ready to pop like a champagne cork.

Hooking a finger in her bra, he pulled the cup down, completely exposing the rosy tip. He bent and sucked it into his mouth. This time, she couldn't hold back the moan. It just felt too good.

She felt him smile against her chest. "Feel good?"

Unable to speak, she gave a jerky nod.

Reaching beneath her again, he unfastened her bra and pulled it off. He filled his hands with her generous breasts, kneading her flesh with his strong fingers.

"God, you're beautiful," he murmured softly.

She had never really felt pretty. Her whole life, she had been told that she was plain. Too many freckles on her face to be pretty. Too short. But looking at Tristan and seeing the look in his eyes and the way his body responded to her, she believed that she was beautiful. A man like him wouldn't look at a woman with such need and desire if he didn't believe it was true.

Ready for more, she attacked the knot in his tie, quickly freeing it from his collar. He helped her with the buttons on his shirt and it quickly joined her bra on the floor, exposing his muscular torso.

She looked her fill. The man was beautiful. All hard planes and golden skin. Tattoos covered his upper arms. A military patch of some kind on one and an intricate map and compass design on the other. She wondered at the story behind them briefly before his mouth on her breasts short-circuited her brain. When he slowly ran his hands down her sides to grasp her dress, she lifted her hips so that he could pull it off, then kicked off her heels, leaving her in her lace panties and garter belt.

Tristan froze, his eyes raking down her legs. "God almighty. Do you have any idea how sexy a garter and stockings are? I am a firm believer that pantyhose should be outlawed and only stockings should ever be worn."

She didn't, but was glad that she opted for the stocking set instead of the pantyhose she normally wore for special occasions. She would never buy another pair of pantyhose ever again.

He drew his fingers up her leg, trailing fire in his wake, until they met the tabs at the tops of the stockings. With a flick of his fingers, he had the first fastener open, freeing the stocking. In moments, he had them all undone and was pulling the silky material off her legs. She felt very naked compared to him.

Sitting up, she picked at his belt buckle. Her hand brushed the hard ridge behind his fly.

A strangled groan got caught in his throat. "Christ, woman." He brushed her hands out of the way and quickly unfastened his pants himself. She helped him pull them down over his hips, taking his black boxer briefs with them. He kicked free of the material and knelt next to her on the bed, his hard body aroused and ready.

Laurel gulped nervously. He was big everywhere, and she was not.

"Your turn." He put two fingers in the waistband of her panties and garter and tugged, pulling the lacy material down. The fabric barely cleared her feet before he was moving between her legs, his shoulders spreading them wide.

"Tristan?" Was he doing what she thought he was? She'd never had a man do that before.

He glanced up at her, his blue eyes glittering. A lock of his chestnut hair fell over his forehead. He looked like he could be Prince Charming's doppelgänger. Except tattooed. "I am fully aware of how tiny you are compared to me. I want to make sure I don't hurt you."

Before she could do more than nod, he swiped his tongue through her folds, sending her hips rocketing off the bed and startling a cry from her.

Holy crap, that felt good.

He slid one finger inside her channel, slowly moving it in and out. Fire spread out from her center to make her limbs hot and languid. Coils of heat tightened in her belly. He added a second finger and then a third, stretching her. Just when she didn't think she could take anymore, the dam broke, and she came with a whimpering cry. Wave after wave of pleasure rolled over her until she was limp and boneless. Her legs fell open as she lost all muscle tone.

Breathing hard, she laid there savoring the languorous feeling of the aftermath. She didn't think it could get any better than that. It had certainly never been anywhere close to that before.

The bed dipped as Tristan moved, and the sound of crinkling reached her ears. She opened her eyes to see him rolling a condom on over his erection.

He crawled over her, the tip of him poised at her entrance. "I think you're ready now."

She grinned up at him lazily. "Ready? I'm a boneless pile of mush."

"Good. That's what I was aiming for." Slowly, he started to push inside. Her muscles were still melty, but his sheer size compared to her tiny frame made for a tight fit. She tensed slightly at the intrusion and he withdrew partially before pushing back in. Bit by bit, her body relaxed until he was seated fully within her. Flames spread outward from their intimate contact to engulf her, threatening to send her rocketing back over the precipice before they had even really gotten started.

He buried his face in the crook of her neck, lines of tension evident in every inch of his muscular frame as he held himself still above her.

"Are you good?" He nipped at her ear.

Shivering at all the delicious sensations flowing through her, she nodded.

"Thank God." Withdrawing, he pushed back inside in one fluid motion. They both groaned.

She clutched at his head and shoulders as he moved, the pleasure so incredibly intense. Never had it been like this. So electrifying. So powerful.

He increased the pace until she was panting in his arms,

her entire body strung tight as a bowstring. When the thread finally broke, she tumbled into the abyss headfirst. Tristan was right beside her as they fell through the sea of pleasure. Slowly, they reached the bottom where they settled, limbs tangled and bodies sated.

Trying to control her breathing, Laurel let her body melt into the mattress. She had been wrong. It could get better.

About the Author

Ashley started writing in her teens and never stopped. Her first novel, Smoky Mountain Murder, came out in 2016, and she has since published two more series and has plans for more. When not writing, you can find her with her nose stuck in a book or watching some terrible disaster movie on SyFy. An avid baseball fan, she also enjoys crafting and cooking. She lives in Ohio with her husband, two kids, three cats, and one very wild shepherd mix.

Website: https://ashleyaquinn.com

goodreads.com/ashleyaquinn

amazon.com/Ashley-A-Quinn/e/B07HCT4QST

ALSO BY ASHLEY A QUINN

Foggy Mountain Intrigue

Smoky Mountain Murder

Smoky Mountain Baby

Smoky Mountain Stalker

The Broken Bow

A Beautiful End

Wildfire

In Plain Sight

Close Quarters

Scorched

Light of Dawn

Pine Ridge

Sweetness

Loner

Shark

Katydid

Homespun